TRUTH

Carys Shannon is originally from north Gower, Swansea, and now divides her time between Wales and the Spanish Pyrenees. She has had short stories published by Honno Press, Parthian, and *Mslexia Magazine*, as well as broadcast on BBC Radio 4. When not writing, Carys is happiest enjoying slow time in big nature.

TRUTH LIKE WATER

Carys Shannon

Parthian, Cardigan SA43 1ED
www.parthianbooks.com
© Carys Shannon 2025
ISBN: 978-1-917140-54-6
Editor: Carly Holmes
Proofreader: Sarah Harvey
Cover Designer: Matt Needle
Typesetter: Elaine Sharples
Printer: 4Edge Ltd, England
Published with the financial support of the Books Council of Wales
British Library Cataloguing in Publication Data
A cataloguing record for this book is available from the British Library.
Printed on FSC accredited paper

TRUTH LIKE WATER

1

The first dead body I ever saw was my mother's. She looked mythical, lying like a mermaid in the shallow estuary water; her skin the lightest shade of blue, an ebbing tide pulling at her dark curls making them stream out like black algae. Her hands were loosely clutching a bunch of wildflowers, their heads heavy and soaked in water.

I stand now on the same estuary that took her away. Look at the ditch I found her in – empty.

What did I expect? To see her again? This time spluttering water and turning to me with a smile that says, *Catrin, I'm fine.* At twenty years old, I still haven't grown out of the childish fantasy that one day she might just come back.

My mother was the one who taught me to notice the tiniest of details out here. That's how I can find this exact spot every year, with nothing to mark it out as extraordinary; nothing so sentimental as plastic flowers, or as permanent as a stone cross. Only the dips and shadows of an ever-moving landscape.

Today is October 6th nineteen ninety-two – the third anniversary of her death. A date with nothing to celebrate. The day everything I knew was carried away on the tide that filled her lungs. Nothing has made sense since then.

No answers.

No truth.

I pick up a long piece of driftwood and jab at the ditch.

The letter arrived this morning. I scooped it up and shoved it in my jacket so my father wouldn't see. It sits there now in my breast pocket taunting me, willing me to make a choice.

I slam the stick deeper, pushing all of my rage into the sucking mud. The wood is drawn down further as if the estuary is greedy for life, these treacherous sands that trap animals and cars, even people.

If I knew *why* it happened – my mother's so-called accident – this heavy pain might go away.

Above me the wide estuary sky is thick with the swelling promise of afternoon rain. It presses me from all sides, cradled like a baby. These flats. The channels and ruts of mud and sand that change with every tide.

My mother knew all about the treacherous waters and sucking sands of local stories. Both true and exaggerated. She taught me how to be careful and listen for the tiniest trickle of water, the first sign of a boisterous tide about to sneak up on you.

Was it an accident?

The same question every year, yet nothing changes.

They said it was a tragedy. Caught out by the tide. Foolish. A fool and her art. But the doubts have always needled at me like razor shells, for all the good it does. She knew the tides and would never have risked getting caught out. And her camera was always in her hands or hanging heavy on her hip, sometimes slung over her shoulder when she was called upon to be a mother or a wife.

The wind whips around my shoulders.

She's gone and I'm still here.

Swift stirs next to me and I run my hand through the

warmth of her black and white coat. The breeze is an easterly, carrying the scent of rancid cockles baking in the last of the autumn sun. My father will be glad of the rain when it comes.

I drop my hands to my knees, take in a deep breath and scream, emptying myself until my stomach aches with the effort. Another ritual. My throat stings raw. I want an answer. But this year, just like the last, the ditch stays as silent as everyone else in our village.

I drag my gaze upwards. The morning light spreads across the horizon, a crow arcs overhead. The tide is up, a sliver of grey on a silver horizon.

I take out my sketchpad, always in my left pocket. The pencil, newly sharpened this morning, pricks at my fingers.

Then, nib moves across paper. Greys come, blacker here, lighter there. The shape of the crow spreads across the page, midflight.

This was the only place she was happy. My mother made an enemy of my father, the farm, of everything else about this place that she claimed was keeping us stuck.

I slap the pad closed, satisfied at the light and shade captured on the pages. As I slip it into my pocket, I finger the letter again. Part of me wants to tell her. To say, *you were wrong*, but that would mean signing it and sending it back. And I can't do that.

'Come on, girl.' I ruffle Swift's fur and zip up my father's old wax jacket, another hand-me-down in my life of wearing other people's clothes. Sometimes it feels that nothing here is mine – except my drawings.

Swift barks and scampers away. I'll take the long way to the village over the back of the mudflats. I can't face seeing anyone else – not today.

*

Along the flats, a weak morning sun lights up yellowing reeds and browning hummocks. I pick my way over and around the ditches without having to look. A herd of four marsh ponies amble past nodding their heads in warning at Swift. Two have bulging bellies, unusual for October. The result of Dai's stallion getting out at the end of last summer.

He'll be none too happy about wasting his prize cob on lowly marsh stock, not when they all end up at the knacker's yard anyway. They'll be foaling soon, and he won't be out to claim them.

I reach out and brush the backs of their coarse fur as they strut past. They've got no one to look out for them. Stuck in their routine of waiting the tide in and out. Dust flies off my hand. I'll keep an eye on how they go. A cormorant soars overhead stretching out its dark wings. I follow the curve of its flight back down to the reeds.

There's someone out there, a little further on and right in the middle of the path.

As I get closer, two people come into view, stood so they appear as one, bodies tense and voices spitting fire. I pull Swift to my side and consider turning back just as one of the heads looks up and spots me.

It's Mr Thomas.

Oh God, not him. The strange man who walks up and down the marsh road like a lost clockwork toy twice a day, stopping only to stare at me as we pass each other. His glare full of accusation as if my presence is an unwelcome trespass on his thoughts. His routine so clear, I can usually avoid him.

He takes a deliberate step backwards as he sees me. Distancing himself from the other figure – a girl dressed in a large purple jumper, bright blue jeans, and white trainers that have no place out here.

He utters one final word, the angle of his mouth giving away a hint of disgust, then marches towards me. His body moves so fast I brace myself for the impact of his anger, but when he gets close, he stops dead.

'Catrin…' His voice trails off and I wish he would look away from me. I'm not in the mood for any of this. His stare makes me squirm, and I run my hand over the top of Swift's coat again and again to steady myself. I nod curtly and try to pass him, but he catches my arm with his hand.

'I've told her it's dangerous. Silly girl.' His eyes flash with fear. He takes another look at me, examining my face, and his expression changes as if he can't find what it is he's looking for and instead discards my arm like an afterthought. 'You try.' He huffs and pulses off towards the marsh road.

I turn towards the girl, her small form swamped in the oversized jumper, eyes staring across the estuary waters. Irritation scratches at my insides. This is *my* space where I come to be alone. I didn't want to see anyone today and now I'm stuck with a conversation.

As I get closer, it's clear the girl's crying.

'Morning,' I try, then squirm. Come on, Catrin, she's obviously upset, is that the best you can do? It is though. I don't have a way with people, my mother told me that often enough. Maureen at the shop calls me surly when I refuse to join in her gossiping. What they don't understand is, I just want to be left alone, nothing more. The girl looks as if she'd like to be by herself too.

Fair enough.

I move around her. What business is it of mine anyway? It's better to keep to yourself here, give people less to talk about.

'Wait.' A shaky voice calls me back. Her blonde head turns and presents an anxious, blotchy face. 'Is it really dangerous?'

He must have got wound up warning her about the tide, although his reaction seems overstated, even to me. Not worth making someone cry.

'It comes in really fast. You have to be careful not to get stuck.'

Her eyes widen. There I've done it, scared her when I probably should have said something reassuring. I try again.

'You're okay for a few more hours though.'

'That's alright. I was waiting for someone but they're obviously not coming.'

She looks at me, seeming to take in my faded leggings and muddy boots. I touch my hand to my hair, tucking a dark curl behind my ear.

'Strange place to wait,' I say.

She shrugs.

There's an expectation that I'll offer something else to fill the silence. Ask another question.

I won't.

Staying quiet is my specialism, and I don't mind it at all. It's only other people who seem to get uncomfortable.

The girl takes a tentative step towards me. Swift rushes

forwards and the girl smiles, bending down to stroke her fur. For a second she looks younger, full of delight.

Oh, Swift.

Now we're really stuck. I shift from one foot to the other, my attention caught by a small movement in the rushes out to the west, probably a rabbit waiting for us to move so it can carry on with its day. I know the feeling.

I pat my leg and Swift jumps up and away from the girl, circling behind me. Always loyal.

The girl's face falls like an afternoon thundercloud.

'Has anyone ever lied to you?'

So much for a peaceful morning with my thoughts.

'I mean, do you know when someone is lying? How can you tell?' She presses her lips together into a petulant frown.

Her question rattles me. Doubts creep through my body like a slow rising tide. My father has never spoken about where he went the day after my mother died. And no one will tell me why she didn't notice the rushing water or didn't care.

I don't owe this girl anything.

'Why?' I demand. My tone is harder than I mean, and she takes a small step backwards, her eyes brimming over again with tears. I look away.

'Someone promised me something... but... it doesn't matter anymore. I'll work something out.' She gulps air between her sniffs as if inviting me to ask more.

That would mean I'd have to help her, listen while she pours her heart out, and that's not me. I can't even look at my own life fully, let alone someone else's. Besides, if she wants to stand out here all morning waiting for someone who's never coming, that's up to her.

No. She can answer her own questions.

I touch Swift's head lightly.

'Come on,' I whisper. Then louder, to the girl. 'He's right about the tides. If you're going to wait around. When you hear water trickling nearby, you need to get back to the road as quick as you can.'

She looks at me hopefully, as if I'll help with the rest of her problems or explain why someone wouldn't talk straight.

I can't. Today the only thing I want is answers, not other people's questions. I whistle to Swift and walk on.

2

I reach the village just as a fat drop of rain lands on my cheek, spilling its way slowly down to my chin. My face stings from the easterly wind. I wonder if my father has finished up in the fields in time. Probably. Not a drop falls that he doesn't know about.

I pass the park at the very end of the marsh road. It floods when the tide's up high, submerging the swings and leaving just the top of the roundabout posts visible. If the current is really strong you can sometimes see them turning in a ghostly circle with the force of it. There's a story about that – children who didn't come in when they were told and got swept away, except we all know that one isn't true.

Opposite is the cockle processing plant, all concrete walls and rancid smells, then up the hill to the heart of what is supposed to pass for a village; old stone houses leading to two pubs, so if you're banned from one you can still go to the other; one chapel and last of all the centre of the world, Maureen's shop.

If it was just a shop, life would be simple. Instead, it's a hotbed of gossip and grudges, not to mention home to a glut of overpriced tinned food. Still, if you live here, you have to be loyal, those are the rules.

Maureen knows everything about our lives, from the newspapers we read, to who's got a sweet tooth or not. And I have to come here every week to pay a little off last month's order. No money changes hands day to day, not if you're local. Everything is on account until Maureen reminds you it's time to pay up, granting you more or less charity depending on her mood that day.

'Wait here.' I stroke Swift's head and she sits next to the trestle table of carrots, parsnips and potatoes set under a green and white awning. I glance inside hoping someone else will be there. Maureen alone is more than I can handle today. She might just get the reaction she's always baiting me for.

Good. She's talking to someone, leaning forward with a smile, and tapping her talon like nails on the counter. Although I can't see who it is, from her rapt expression I'll bet it's a man.

I open the door and the bell trills out. The twist of her mouth as she looks up confirms I'm about to spoil her fun.

'Catrin, when are you going to run a brush through that hair of yours, girl?' She tuts theatrically and takes the opportunity to flick her own glossy black mane over her shoulder, fixing the man in front of her with what would be a charming smile if it wasn't for the sharpness of her teeth setting her mouth like a shark.

The man turns around though I should have recognised him from behind; his stout, muscled presence under a too-tight T-shirt, the poke of an anchor escaping from under the left sleeve. I see him flexing that arm often enough in the small driver's cab of our local bus. It's Mac.

'Hello stranger!' He takes his time looking me up and down much to Maureen's annoyance.

I don't say anything. Silence is the best weapon in this place, everyone will get bored of you much quicker if you give them nothing to play with, especially Maureen. I place the money for our weekly contribution on the counter with a thud. Maureen smirks. She's not going to let me get away that easily.

'Always so charming, this one.' She tilts her head towards me and bats her eyelashes at Mac.

He laughs, turning from her to me and back again as if it was important to give his public what they want.

'I'm used to Catrin, aren't I kid?' He jabs me with his elbow until my blank stare wipes the smile from his face.

Kid.

I'm twenty now and there's not much difference between us in age. A couple of years at school; he didn't used to speak to me back then, didn't bother with anyone from down this way, not when he could have his pick.

He turns to Maureen again.

'The number of times I asked this one out and she's never taken me up on it. What's wrong with me, eh?'

I could give him a long list. Starting with that New Year's Eve fumble we had last year at the local. Nothing to write home about. I was hoping for oblivion, a way to forget, and all I got was someone who wanted an ego boost. No thanks.

Maureen rolls her eyes and inches closer over the counter.

'Not worth the trouble. Always been the same – a proud little madame, just like her mother. From up town, she was. No clue about farms, wanted to keep pets and save the runts. Cried over every dead lamb like a baby. You name it, she drove us all bloody mad!' She flashes her eyes towards me to check for a reaction.

She won't get one. I clench one hand into a fist behind my back, digging the nails into the skin. She swings back to Mac.

'Anyway, I'm sure you've got them lining up, nice bloke like you.'

He pretends to bat away her compliment.

'Always getting messed around, me.'

'Maybe you should try playing hard to get?' The words are out of my mouth before I have a chance to check myself.

Maureen raises her eyebrows. Everyone is fair game here and she'd love a showdown to tell people about later. Mac shakes his head at me and chuckles to himself.

'She's going to keep on breaking my heart, this one.'

I roll my eyes and finger the five pound note I've left on the counter.

'Right. Got to go.' He waves a bottle of pop. 'The bus won't drive itself,' he exclaims, wiping his hand over his brow as if he's a doctor or a firefighter going back into the breach.

Maureen stands back, crosses her arms over her chest and watches him walk out.

'Not very friendly.' She pouts at me.

I shrug. She snatches the five pounds from under my nose and pops it into the till.

'You'd save money on bus fares at least.'

Trust Maureen to be thinking about the benefits.

'Now you've sold the car,' she continues, her words prowling around me like a cat. She hears everything. I sold the car two weeks ago to pay the electricity bill. The money I just gave Maureen is the last from the pot in the kitchen and I can't ask my father for more. It hasn't been full for a long time. The work I do at Dai's yard only just tides us over for food. He doesn't need help with the horses, but he wouldn't see us go without.

Maureen clicks her fingers at me. God, she's so annoying.

'I said, maybe your dad should take Simon up on his offer.'

'What offer?' I say, caught off guard. Simon runs the cockling plant; he'd have no business with us.

Maureen rolls her eyes as if it's obvious.

'Buying your land on the marsh road. He needs somewhere to park up the Land Rovers.'

'He's got somewhere.' My voice rises. Our marsh land is where the sheep stay in between roaming on the estuary. It's our only access and gives us grazing rights. My father would never sell that land.

'Dai sorted it for your dad. Simon's been putting pressure on a couple of people down your way to sell up. Doesn't take no for an answer, that one. Got his eye on a cockle-shaped fortune. Thought Dai would have told you.'

There it is – the little knife in the back she's always so happy to jab us with.

Dai.

If he's sorted something, it's because my father has asked him to. A familiar ball of rage burns in my stomach. I don't think it's possible to despise my father more than I already do – the silent, cold man who I share my suppers with.

Maureen shrugs then reaches under the counter. She hesitates for a second, which isn't like her.

'Look, I've been having a clear out. Just a couple of things.' Her eyes sweep over my face before she carries on. 'Too grown up for my Jade, so I thought you could have them.' She proffers the bag at me; it's bulging with nearly new clothes.

Shame burns through me. Is it that obvious? How little we've got. I back away from her. She looks hurt and cocks her head to one side.

13

'Haven't got time to take them up town to the charity shop. You'd be doing me a favour.'

'No... thanks...' I stammer, 'I'm fine.' My cheeks are burning now. What must Maureen see when she looks at me? A scraggy, scruffy girl wearing hand-me-downs? It's the pity I can't stand.

'That land is not for sale, and I'll tell Dai myself,' I exclaim, looking for something to distract us both.

I turn and rush out of the shop. Maureen calls after me.

'A good day to you too.'

3

I ignore the buzzer next to the two metal gates that mark the entrance to Dai's stud farm. Formal entry is only for visitors – the once-a-year wellington-clad crowd who grace him with their haughty presence, then spend hours poking around and inspecting his stallion to make sure he's worthy of their precious mares. Dai's been in this business for decades, refining his stock year after year. The huge, muscled bay cob is his pride and joy.

Swift wriggles under the gate, even though I hold it ajar for her. Old habit. I smile. She loves Dai almost as much as his own dogs do. They come out to meet us now, a huddle of black, circling low with throaty yaps until they recognise her scent, then the tail wagging and excited yelps begin. I bend down and greet each one of them, receiving a thrust of wet noses and wildly moving bodies in response.

Dai gave Swift to me a few months after my mum died. She'd been his best dog. Few people would know what it meant for him to give her away, but I did. He said I'd need someone to talk to and his dogs had never failed him. I'll love him forever for that.

I lean over the door to the stallion's loose box, and there's Dai, bent low talking to the cob in a soft voice as he gently lifts first one hoof then the other. The cob throws his head up with a snort and Dai looks around.

'Here comes trouble.'

A smile breaks on my face. There's no use trying to be angry with him. He's been like a second father to me when my own proved useless. He's stood by Bev too, never once spoken badly of her after their son Rhys' death even though the whole village hears her clinking back home from the shop every week, bags heavy with bottles to make the pain go away. And my mother. He always knew how to make her laugh, blowing away the gathering clouds between my parents before the storm of an argument had a chance to break.

'Glad you're here,' he says. 'Need a chat.'

A man of few words like most of them around here, more into doing than saying.

'What about?' I haven't seen him for three weeks since we've been getting the sheep in for winter. Strange he didn't phone if there was something urgent.

'I got some help in.' There's an awkward pause. 'Won't be needing you over here for a bit.'

How could he?

That money is the only thing keeping us in food. He knows that, might as well have given it directly to Maureen himself except he'd never humiliate us like that. We're more like family than not.

I study his face, waiting for him to say it's a joke. He looks away and stuffs a chunk of hay into the net.

'Doing someone a favour by having their girl here. Bev can't stand too many people about, you understand?' It's not a question but a statement. The other side of Dai, the one that doesn't baulk when a ton of horse charges at him; the one who would tell anyone to go packing if I asked him to. What I don't understand is who he would rather help than me.

A childish petulance purses my lips together. He gives me a weak smile.

'It's just for a couple of weeks. She's a young 'un, knows nothing about horses.' He shakes his head. 'She'll give up on it soon enough.'

'Why bother then?' My voice is cold.

He watches me out of the corner of his eye the same way he'll track the movements of his horses, to see if one is going to bolt or rear.

'You know you've got to get on with your life, girl. Can't keep helping us out forever.'

The letter burns in my pocket. Does he know?

'I was good enough when you needed someone for Charlie-horse.'

He sighs and shakes his head, still refusing to look at me.

'It's not for me to say...' He pauses and adjusts his collar. 'If you're not for taking on the farm with your dad, what else is it going to be?'

Has Maureen sneaked a look at the post and told them all? I can't believe even she would do that. It doesn't matter anyway. That pull, that madness my mother had for her art. I don't want it. Not if it means ending up the same way.

'That doesn't answer my question,' I tell him. 'Why?'

'I owe her mother a favour.' His tone is like a door slamming, and any more doubts I might have about the girl are quickly swallowed.

'And Charlie-horse?' Poor old Charlie with his musty smell and sticky out ribs. Dai can't bear to look at him. He keeps him at the back of the stables in an old outbuilding and I'm the only company he has.

It was Bev who wouldn't let him shoot Charlie after Rhys died, although if you believe Maureen, he came close. The striking chestnut cob he'd bred for his son, all that pride and Dai still can't forgive himself or the horse. The most he'll do is let Charlie live out his days in peace without ever having to cross his path.

Dai rubs his chin with his hand.

'She'll see to him too. Already has today if you don't feel like it.'

I falter. This is my routine: the marsh, the sheep, Swift and Charlie, a world full of animals and sky, better than having people around. He can't take that away from me. I search for something to express my anger.

Maureen's message about the land.

'We're not selling. So, you can tell Simon to leave Dad alone.'

He raises his eyebrows but doesn't say a word. There is rage circling in my stomach now, swishing around and looking for a way out. Usually I walk, march so fast, until I get rid of it out of my body and into the cool marsh air.

Not today. Dai can have it.

'Those fields give us grazing rights, you know that.'

'And you won't help your dad with the lambs; there's no money for hired help, so what's he to do?'

The question hangs between us for a moment. Dai picks up a bucket and pushes the stable door open. The stallion clunks at the ground with his front hoof.

'It's our land,' I say stubbornly.

'You need some help. So, take it.' He thumps the bucket on the ground and switches on the hose. The sound of water hitting the metal bottom fills our silence.

'We're fine as we are.'

He shakes his head, his mouth a grim line.

'That's exactly what your father would say, thought you'd have more sense. More of your mother in you.'

I open my mouth to speak but he cuts me off.

'Your dad is getting tired. He can't go on forever. You going to run that herd on your own? For fun?'

I look at my feet. The sheep are a hard point between my father and me. During the summer months they're mine. I roam the marsh with them, keeping them out of trouble and watching them eat samphire and estuary grass. But I won't have a hand in their slaughter.

I turn away from Dai and look for Swift; she comes running towards me as if she knew. I bend down and breathe in her wiry fur, the smell of farm and dried mud.

When the lambs call for their mothers it's nearly more than I can bear. That sound. The sound of wanting to live, of wanting to be together, a family. How could I, after everything I've seen, be part of that? No one understands. They think I'm soft like my mother was. She hated the business of the lambs, begging my father to think again, farm something else. Grow things rather than kill them. He thinks I'm doing it for her, and I could never explain the strangled panic I feel when I hear their bleating. I would do anything in my power to stop their anguish and place them back where they belong, next to their mothers.

Dai is silent and watching me. His eyes are kind, but I can tell he's worried about where my mind has got to.

'It's today, isn't it?' he asks.

I nod, refusing to meet his eye, turning back to Swift instead and rubbing her belly until she dives onto the floor and wriggles around on her back like a puppy. He squats down next to us.

'Doesn't get easier, does it?'

I shake my head, jaw tense, studying the burrs that have caught on the curly hair of Swift's stomach, pulling at them with my fingers.

'Knowing why it happened would make it easier,' I say with a sullen mouth.

'No, it wouldn't, Catrin. Take it from me.'

I look up now into his eyes. There it is, that pain that never goes away. Have I got it too? Can you tell just by looking at people if they've lost someone they love, if their world has split open and will never be whole again? But Dai *does* know what happened to Rhys. He was there when he fell, that's the point. All I have are questions. Fears about what I missed. About who I might become.

'It's been three years, Dai. I want to know.'

He sighs. We've had this conversation so many times before and it never ends well.

'Catrin, you were seventeen. You must know your mam had an adult life. The way you do now. She had her problems.'

'What were they?' I hold his gaze until he looks away.

There it is. Some secret that is locked away, withheld from me since the day I found her body.

I jump up.

'She knew the tides.' My voice is strong and low. The line so practised and obstinate I don't even have to think about it.

'She did,' he says, crossing his arms.

I kick at the bucket with the edge of my boot.

My mother was unpredictable, *artistic* Maureen called her, and her moods changed like the estuary light. She'd been down those last few weeks before she died, out of sorts. Something was wrong and she either couldn't or wouldn't tell me what.

I bend down and switch the hose on.

'She wasn't happy those last few weeks. Something was up.'

Dai doesn't say a word, just watches me until the bucket is full, then he switches off the tap. I grasp the full weight in my hand and open the cob's door with the other. He snorts at the sight of me. Dai follows me inside as I put the water down. I turn to him.

'Rhys could ride any horse. Why did he fall that day?'

'We'll never know.' His words are like stone. And I wonder if he really believes them. Is there comfort in not knowing why, not being able to blame yourself for something you didn't do?

I walk over to the cob and bury my face in his flaxen mane.

Rhys was just seven when he fell. A year after my mother. The unfairness of it all clogs my throat. How we've all carried on, wading through life like thick estuary mud, using all our strength to keep some normality, trying not to lose anyone else.

'Did I miss something, Dai? Could I have saved her?' I hate the childishness of my words as they spill out.

He walks over, closer than we usually are when the space between us is filled with dogs, horses, or sky, and pats me gently.

'No, love, no. But maybe it's time to let her go now.'

I wheel around to face him. The bay starts at my sudden movement. Dai sticks his arm between us instinctively.

'Think about the farm, Catrin. If you don't sell the land to Simon, you'll have to sell the flock anyway. Your dad won't go on forever. What's going to be left for you then?' He pats me again in the same way as the horses then walks outside leaving me standing in the straw.

He knows I won't take his advice, and I suppose that makes him a good friend. The anger towards my father sits in my stomach like a stone. He should have known what was wrong with my mother. He could have helped her or stopped her. Instead, he was back on the farm after it happened as if she'd never existed. Now this betrayal with the land. He deserves to be on his own. He'd probably be happy if I left too. Leaving him to sit in heavy silence while the farm crumbles all around him.

I walk out of the stable. Dai nods at me and tugs at his cap, turning to the next task in hand as if our conversation hasn't even touched him.

I whistle to Swift.

I'm going to say goodbye to Charlie-horse at least.

*

Charlie nods his head over the stable door in greeting. I take down the lead rope from the wall and clip it onto his halter. We'll go for a last walk together.

We amble out of the old stables and turn towards the back fields where Dai puts the brood mares out to graze. Charlie picks his way slowly along the path. Swift trots alongside us.

I breathe deeply, taking in the scent of the thick hedgerows and the dried mud. We could do with more rain, although my father won't want any extra today, he's still drilling the wheat in the top fields, and anything spoilt means less for us when it's time to harvest. We can't afford to lose anything else.

We reach the gate that leads to Dai's back fields. He doesn't use these now he has a smaller stud, but he'd never sell them. Farmers don't sell land. He should remember that.

I shove the gate open and let Charlie off the rope; he trots forward like a young colt before slowing and ducking his head down to eat. Swift threads between the long grasses at the back of the field following a scent. Four crows perch on the branches of the old oak that marks the boundary between this land and the next. I turn and look back down the slope towards the estuary.

I take out my sketchbook. This is one of my favourite views; just above the tips of the trees I can see the rising silver line of water spreading from west to east across the marsh flat, the white dots of buildings over the other side of the estuary, which may as well be a foreign land, and the lighthouse out to the far west, marking the last muddy point before the landscape transforms into rocky beaches and second homes.

I mark out the shapes in pencil, shading the clouds over the water. The wind is strong and I turn my back to shelter from the gusts.

Swift lets out a bark, I pocket my sketchbook and I walk over to where she's trying to stick her head into a small burrow.

'Come on, Swift, leave it.'

She ignores me and paws the ground over and over. I look

up and into the next field. You can see Mr Thomas' bungalow from here. His land stretches out before me, overgrown with weeds and wild grass. Now if anyone should sell, it's him. All that space and nothing put to use. His bungalow perches further up like a little white castle.

Swift yaps as Mr Thomas' slow form shuffles along the path next to his house. He's carrying a huge pair of shears. He suddenly looks our way and calls out, 'Catrin?'

I step back behind the thick trunk of the oak and count to ten, running fingers over the gnarled wood. I can almost feel his stare through the trunk. Accusing me of something. I shiver. I've never had any business with him, not since school.

I breathe out.

He moves back into sight, goes inside and closes the door to his bungalow.

A close call.

I click my tongue at Charlie, and he comes trotting over, head nodding. I spread my arms around his thick neck, allowing my body to lean into his.

We're halfway down the path when a heavy shape ambles towards us. It's Bev. She doesn't usually stray this far from the house. Dai prefers her not to be around the horses, says it's for her nerves but what he really means is if she's drunk, she can't be trusted.

'Catrin!' Her voice is slurred, and I grip the rope tighter.

She waves at me wildly and we slow to a reluctant stop.

'I saw Charlie's stall was empty. Thought he'd escaped.'

I nod politely and look at my feet. Bev is wearing baby-pink slippers, the bottoms now stained brown with mud.

'Just taking him for his walk. Nothing to worry about.'

She bursts out laughing, wiping the corner of her mouth with a loose sleeve.

'Oh Catrin, you and that horse. He's like your boyfriend. Always together.' She giggles again.

I glance around for Dai. Bev stumbles closer to Charlie-horse and he spooks away from her slightly. I pull his head towards me, stroking him gently.

'This horse, Catrin. This horse took my boy away.' Her voice is quiet now as if she's gone somewhere else. 'I should have let Dai shoot him. But then he'd have to have shot me too.' She looks up at me with sad eyes. 'He's the only bit of Rhys I've got left. Do you know how that feels?'

I can't answer her. I wish I could tell her that I do understand, I walk the estuary every day with my mother beside me, remembering her habits and moods. But when I look up from my sketchbook, she's never there. But Bev's tone, her sorrow, is too much for me. I'm just another person who wants to pat her on the arm and stop her from talking, stop the digging reminder of how I might feel if I really looked inside myself.

I lay my hand on her arm and hate myself for it. She looks at it and her mouth curls downwards.

'Is it fair? You tell me. Dai got you, the daughter he never had, and what did I get? This old horse. Everyone smiling and thinking *poor old Bev*. Do you know what that's like?' She pulls her arm away. 'It's worse than nothing, Catrin.' She turns and waddles off towards the house.

Perhaps Dai is right about not having people around.

As I close the door to Charlie's stall I lean down and kiss him on his nose.

'It's just for a little while,' I whisper, rubbing the white star at the centre of his forehead. 'It's alright boy. Dai says she won't last long, whoever she is.'

*

I choose the long route back home. Today of all days I can't face sitting across the kitchen table from my father in heavy silence. I should tell him about the letter and the offer. But what's the point? We stopped telling each other the truth of things after my mother died. Carried on as normal. I'll make a fire when I get home and use the letter for kindling. Better than empty hope, the kind that could leave you dead in a ditch.

As I cross the marsh road, the wind carries a flick of rain on it and I'm glad of the fresh mist on my face. The ponies have begun to pick their way to the higher ground near the road in readiness to wait the tide out. I slow to stroke their backs and hindquarters as they settle into position, pulling up grass next to the tarmac with a rip of their teeth. Swift snakes in and out of the reeds ahead, following one scent then another. I walk further out onto the flats and let the cockle-shell path change to grass then mud under my feet.

I close my eyes.

There she is, my mother, out there on the flats with her beloved camera, straddling a wide ditch, desperate to capture the half-light fading into dusk around her. The water is like silver and all around the curves and edges of the estuary are filled by the shadows coming to rest for the night. She stands up for a moment, glances around to check I'm okay, then clicks the scene into permanence.

I open my eyes, expecting to see her. I should know better. But there is a shape on the marsh. I start back. A tall and sombre person is walking out on the flats. I know his form; the held-in grief and bitterness towards life that makes him walk with long purposeful steps as if one day he'll find the culprit of it all. For a moment it looks as if he's coming towards me, then I watch him wade out towards the exact spot where I stood this morning.

I didn't think he knew where it was, let alone that he cared to go there.

He drops slowly down to rest his elbows on his knees, takes off his cap and wipes his hand over his face. Then he takes a small bunch of flowers and hovers for a moment, unsure of where to lay them, before placing them carefully on the sopping ground. I want to scream, 'You know she hated flowers,' but the hesitancy in his actions makes me want to rush over and hold him.

I do neither.

He stands up, places his cap back on and walks out the same way, looking only ahead. I drop into pace behind him and follow my father through the dusk towards our farmhouse.

4

The next morning, there's no sign of my father in the house. I'm not sure why I thought I might find him here making a pot of tea for us both, ready to talk. The sight of him laying flowers so gently last night ruffled me.

I take the blue biscuit jar off the shelf and open the lid. There are still only three fifty-pence pieces swimming around.

We're due a conversation. There has to be some other way for us to manage without selling the land.

Swift chooses this moment to amble down the stairs, taking each one with a heavy plop until she reaches the hallway and scurries into the kitchen. Even her old age doesn't stop the constant back and fore of her tail or the happy waggle of hind legs as she thrusts her wet nose into my hand and licks gently at my palm.

I ruffle her fur, lost for a second in the sense of comfort, then touch the side of the teapot – still warm. The only sign that someone else really lives here. We're nothing more than ghosts to each other now, silently eating together in the evening, offering the occasional polite question about how much wheat's been drilled or how the soil is holding up in the tricky fields that flood with tide-water near the marsh road. He'll ask me about the sheep even though he'll have checked them over himself. Not a man who can be still for long.

Should I ask him about the flowers? Demand to know what he was doing there.

No.

We reached an unspoken agreement long ago that we don't talk about her anymore. His silences eventually drowning out my questions until I found myself as hardened as him.

I pace the kitchen, taking a mug, pouring the lukewarm tea in, and stirring two sugars, a drop of milk.

I take out the letter and open it. It still doesn't seem real. My name printed in block capitals above the sentence, 'delighted to offer you a place.' A chance at something else. But what chance do I really have? A failing farm. Not to mention my father. I don't think I could look him in the eye and confirm what he's feared all along, that I'm the same as her and I want more, just like she did. What would that do to him? I've heard enough slammed doors and broken crockery to know.

I flip the letter back into my pocket. Somehow unable to put it down.

Swift gives a sharp yap and tilts her head to one side. I smile. She's right. No time for dreaming here, there's always work to be done.

'Come on then, old lady.' I move into the hallway, unhook my coat, and pull on my boots. 'Time to check the ewes before the beast arrives.'

The Jones' ram who does his once-yearly tupping is due today. My father marked it clearly on the wall calendar, giving us even less reason to communicate.

It's not a day I want to be part of. Watching the ram mounting one ewe after another, knowing it'll be them doing the work and the birthing, losing some of them without giving a choice.

Swift paws at the door. I throw it open and breathe in the cool estuary air.

*

It takes me a few hours to clean the barn, sifting the straw then wheeling the muck over to the heap. The sound of our flock's intermittent shuffles and calls soothes me. Swift lies on a pillow of clean straw snoozing. I walk over and heave the metal doors open, letting the ewes stream out into the bottom field close enough for when the Jones boys arrive. Swift used to trot behind them, head low, alert for any stragglers, but she doesn't even lift her ears at their noise.

I check my watch – nearly eight o'clock – they're already running late. I walk out with the ewes, touching my fingers to their thick waxen coats as they rush past. The sun breaks through the clouds, casting rays onto the field and further down to the estuary grasses.

I crouch down, balancing my sketchbook on my knees. A few minutes' work brings the ewes to life. I draw Swift as I'd like to see her, bounding after them full of energy, a black and white dart amongst the flock. That's the thing about art. You get to choose. My mother told me that. Always framing the perfect shot or testing the development time.

I sketch a figure at the back of the field holding a camera, bringing her back to life for a second. She faces away from us. The promise of her makes me ache. I scratch at the picture, turn her quickly into a tree, scribbling over the trunk again and again, until she is just a ghost of lines under the shading.

The wind ruffles through my hair. It's a good day for early October if a little breezy. We got the flock in early this year because there's promise of extra high tides over the next few days. Over seven metres; enough to cover the mud flats and rush all the way up to our doorstep. My father will have got the sandbags ready, never one to be caught out.

The sound of footsteps crunching through newly laid straw.

I jump up and stuff the book into my pocket.

In that instant he appears at my side. I glance at his face. It is etched with heavy tiredness, a weight he's been carrying since I was old enough to notice.

'Not like them to be running late.'

He doesn't reply but walks up to stand beside me, and stares out into the field. The warmth of his arm next to mine clenches my jaw. We are so rarely close to each other. Part of me wants to grab onto his arm like I used to, but my hands hang heavy at my sides.

He clears his throat.

'They're not coming.'

'Did the ram get out again?' I try to keep the scorn out of my voice but my father flinches. It's not unusual. I'm always cutting away at our life together with a thousand spiteful knives. Just like she did.

He shakes his head with the same passive acceptance he gave to my mother.

'I said not to bother. We'll leave it this year.'

For a second, I am stunned by his admission. I study his face for an answer but as usual he gives nothing away.

'Why?' My tone is accusatory.

He shrugs, takes off his cap and rubs his forehead with his hand.

How dare he? How could he decide like that without asking me first? First Simon buying the fields, now this.

He breaks the silence.

'We haven't got the money, Catrin. And we won't make it back with the lambs either.'

Dai's words ring in my ears about my father getting older and not being able to go on forever.

I am the daughter. I should be moving the farm on like the Jones boys have done for their family. Not having these fanciful ideas about making a different life for myself. Living off my drawings. The farm will become mine one day, and what then?

Generations of work hang heavy on both our shoulders. There is resignation lodged in my father's face. He sighs as if reading my thoughts.

'We can't cover it, Cat. We're short already and you won't do the lambs. I need to get the fields ready before the rain comes in. The flock is skinny this year. Likely they'll not all carry until spring. We can count our losses, sell the ewes on.'

His words sting with truth. Worry tracks are ploughed into his forehead and the weight of this life has curved his shoulders into a small stoop. He turns to me.

'Let them live out their days eating grass. Isn't that what she used to say?'

My mother's words.

'Bit late to take her side?'

He shrugs. 'Maybe.'

I want him to say more. Admit he could have given her what she wanted, let her be who she was rather than demanding that she fell into line as a farmer's wife. If he had, she could still be here with us now. Instead, he rubs his chin and smiles sadly.

'Well, she got what she wanted in the end.'

'You can't talk about her like that.'

'I need your help with the fields. I can't...'

'No.'

His hand trembles as he touches his forehead. I look away.

'Catrin.' His voice is softer now. 'We can lease out the lower fields to Simon instead of having the flock. Doesn't mean selling. It'll cover the basics.'

'I said no.' The words shoot out, a tightness forming in my chest. The ram isn't coming, and the ewes will be sold. I won't be able to walk the estuary every day. The place my mother and I jumped ditches and searched for treasure. The place where I can still find her if I try.

'You're not thinking.' The same words he used to say to her when she was in one of her furies. Him, sitting calm and cold at the table. Her body moving and whirring around him in a frenzy of accusations.

'Dai's had a word with Simon. He's interested.'

Finally, the truth.

'Fed up of cockling, is he? Wants to get into farming?' My words are furious, spat out with contempt.

I bet he's interested. Simon who's been buying up land all along the marsh road, making his cockle plant bigger and bigger every year while no one down here gets a look in. Well, he can't have our land. I won't allow it.

My father sighs, places his cap back on his head and walks away without another word. I stare after him. He's been leaving me like this my whole life.

*

Sweat drips from my forehead and snakes down my neck, I must have been marching so fast. I look across the open marsh, Swift trots over. I'm thankful for her. The horizon is grey and there is the thin silver line of tide creeping its way towards me. I don't have long, maybe half an hour before it comes flooding and pouring through these ditches, covering the land I'm standing on. It's going to be a high one today. It's tempting to stay out here and let the tide float me out and away to anywhere but our stuffy farmhouse.

I pick up a stone and hurl it towards a far ditch. There is a satisfying splash.

My father doesn't like change. For him to even contemplate renting the land he must be worried. I pick at a thread on my jumper. If I just helped him more…

Swift noses into my hand and licks my palm. I bend down and hug her tight. What else is he thinking that he hasn't told me? A wave of anxious needling washes through me. I tease a couple of burrs out of the fur on her back. She falls to the floor and turns her belly up in the air, wiggling from side to side. I smile and rub her pink stomach. My throat contracts with love.

The faint trickle of water.

We should get back to safer ground. I whistle and Swift jumps to attention and careers off through the reeds, nose low in the grass, towards home. As I turn to watch her go, I see a flash of purple in the reeds further out. The colour is strange and garish against the greys and browns of the estuary.

Water gurgles and flows through the nearby ruts and ditches. I should go back, but it wouldn't hurt to take a look.

I jump and my left foot lands, then sinks into a piece of soft sand. I wouldn't usually go over this way. Too many new trenches being made by the sinking mud. I wait a second, push into the suction then withdraw my foot with a sharp pull just like my mother taught me.

I make sure the next two jumps are more careful, aiming for the clumps of sturdy reeds even though they prick through my clothes and jab my ankles.

Finally, I arrive at the side of a newly made ditch where the sand has sunk and given way.

There's a purple jumper lying half in and out of the small ditch. I lean down and grab it. One arm is heavy and soaked in muddy water, but the other is pristine as if it has just come out of the wash. No hoof prints or bird marks on it.

Someone has recently dropped this.

I look around. The tide has already covered the back half of the mud flats and there's no one in sight. The gulls call shrilly overhead, but no one is shouting for help. Whoever was here must have gone back to the road without realising they'd lost it.

I hold the jumper up to my face; my nose wrinkles at the strong smell of washing powder and perfume.

I turn the jumper over and search for a label – it's one of those expensive surf makes that most surfers can't afford. Inside there is a tag with a name on it, *Emily*, with a little heart above the I. The girl I saw yesterday flashes into my mind.

She was wearing something like this. A flutter of panic rises in my stomach.

Not here. Not again.

Swift gives two short sharp yaps from the road, pacing the tarmac, her gaze fixed on me. The gush and gurgle of water is audible now, fast and strong, the tide is coming. I've never been caught out before. I look over to the road and trace the safe route back in my mind.

I know this place.

Wait.

What if the girl has fallen? I edge around the soft mud, taking care to avoid any patches where I would sink down, and peer into the ditch. The cold tea and toast I had this morning burns back up my throat.

My mother's body sways into my vision. But there is nothing in the ditch except mud and shells.

Swift barks again from the road.

'Hello? Emily?' I call out, straining my voice.

No reply.

Part of me is mesmerised at the sight of the ditch filling with water as fast as if someone was running a bath. A cold tide seeps into my boots, sloshing over the top of my laces.

Time to go.

I tie the jumper around my waist and leap back onto more solid ground, splashing through newly formed puddles as I get back to where I started. The tide is coming in fast. I need to get back to the road but the strangeness of finding something out of place out here makes me take one last look around.

The horizon is empty apart from two of the ponies who

must have got separated from the herd and are already belly deep in water, stoic and ready to wait it out.

That girl can't have dropped the jumper yesterday – the tide has been up and down twice since then. Which means she's been back out here today.

I slosh through the rising water, ankles cold and boots squelching. I should have been kinder yesterday. Not taken my own frustrations out on her.

The grass that was in front of me is now a gently moving silvery-grey mass. I close my eyes and imagine the rivulets and dips underneath the water.

I know this place.

Deep breath.

I take the steps without looking and at last tarmac whacks hard underneath my feet. Swift pelts over to me, delirious, wagging her tail and circling. My feet squelch and slurp in my boots. The wind blasts my legs, turning them even colder.

My mother's face, blue and lifeless, washes through me.

Not again. Please.

I need to call the police and tell them someone could be lost out there.

From this point, our farmhouse and the village are about the same distance apart. Both ten minutes at a run and the tide will have covered the road before I'm halfway there.

I don't have time.

Mr Thomas' land reaches all the way down to the marsh road. It's the last place I want to go, but if I jump the fence and run up the back way, I can get to his bungalow in minutes. The idea of his strange stare makes me turn towards the village. But the road is silver already. Too late.

5

I clamber over the fence posts that separate the road from his fields. My boots slip on the wood and threaten to throw me into the spiky gorse poking all around. As I jump, more spindly brambles pull at my clothes, needling my skin with little jabs.

What if she's out there and this is my fault? I should have helped her when she asked.

Swift shimmies under with a grunt and pulls her body through the maze of gorse. I run towards the house, sprinting now, across fields slick with long grass swept over by the rain. My legs splay out like a newly born foal as I go. I catch myself twice, hands slipping in the mud, nearly falling flat, before reaching the bungalow. I pound the door with my fist. Struggle to catch my breath. I look back at the estuary, smaller from up here on the rise. Please don't let there be another body out there.

Swift whines.

I rap at the door again, the white paint sullied by the muddy stain of my fists. I must look a sight — covered in twigs, sprayed with mud, and soaking wet from the knees down. My dark curls swirl wild in the wind.

Come on!

I give the door one last shove. I should have gone to the village. Maureen would have been quick to react. She'd have phoned the police straight away with a dramatic air of panic.

The long grey stretch of water has covered everything now, including the road. I rub my chest trying to quell the rising panic. Swift circles around my legs. No more death, please. I don't think I can survive it.

I take a deep breath.

It's okay. Think.

I can get to Dai's land from here. In through the back field where I was walking Charlie yesterday. Dai won't let me down.

At the joining fence, a stitch stabs at my side, stopping me just before I jump over. Swift catches up, her body heaving from the effort, and shuffles underneath. A sharp slam of the door behind me and Mr Thomas is running down the field towards us. His face thunderous. He stops short, a metre away, hands on his thighs, breath shallow from the effort.

'What are you doing here? You can't be here.'

'Someone is missing on the marsh,' I shout back, my voice louder than I mean it to be and shaking with emotion.

His expression changes to horror. He shrinks away as if I'm one of those skeletons the tide throws up.

'That is a sick joke. Are you part of it? I've told them I don't want to sell. Why are you doing this, Catrin?'

Hearing my name in his mouth chills me. What did I ever do to him? Something about the way he looks at me isn't right. Desperate.

I step back, remove the jumper from my waist and hold it in front of me.

'I found this out there. Someone is missing. I need to call the police.' I don't mention Emily or the fact I saw them together yesterday.

His body jerks with something between fear and anger. I edge a little further towards the fence, prepared to jump and run at any sign of trouble. His gaze drops down to take in the jumper.

'The police?' His voice shakes with the word.

My body pulls me backwards, willing me to turn around and hop the fence. Swift shifts and lets out a high-pitched whine.

I shake the jumper at him.

'The girl. From yesterday. I think it's hers.' I shouldn't need to say more.

His eyes snap up to meet mine and they are full of fury, widening then narrowing again as if clouds are blowing across his face.

'Another silly thing she's done,' he snaps, pulling the jumper from my hands.

How dare he be so dismissive. He must have seen the state she was in.

'The tide is up. She could be...' I can't finish the words. Can't say it out loud. 'It's dangerous.'

He steps back as if I've slapped him.

'And *I told her that* yesterday.' He peers at me again as if something is slowly dawning on him. 'Why can't you people leave me alone. That's all I want. Threatening me with this, is that the idea? It won't work.' He turns his back on me.

'It's not a threat!' I shout after him. 'I need your help.'

He stops and glares.

'You came to me, Catrin. Remember that. Tell him that.' He shakes his head and clutches his arms around his body as he stalks back to the house. As he reaches the door he turns sharply to shout.

'Call the police. For all the good it will do.'

The whole house shudders with the slam of the door.

I stop for a second. The jumper. He snatched it out of my hands before I had a chance to think. Should I go after him? I hesitate for a moment, caught in the fear of wasting more time. What does it matter? I already know her name.

As I plunge over the wet field, Swift barking and galloping ahead, I can't shake the feeling that if I turned back, I'd see Mr Thomas watching me from his window.

6

Dai's head shoots up from the inside of the stallion's stall.

'Didn't hear the gate.' His voice is irritated as if he's found yet another thing he's going to have to forgive me for. There are rules here. You don't go pissing about in other people's fields. Unspoken of course but everyone knows it. Only poachers and thieves hedge hop.

He scans my face.

'What's happened?'

It's all I can do to get the story out straight between gasps.

'I think there's a girl out there on the marsh. Lost. I saw her yesterday. Crying.' A stitch jabs at my side. 'She was talking to Mr Thomas. I found her jumper in a ditch. She could be cut off out there.' My words are all gabbled.

Dai nips out of the stall and puts a steadying hand on my arm.

'Let's go inside. We can call the police if we need to.'

I nod, grateful to be led into the house like a small child. With Dai everything is alright.

He takes me through the porch. Swift plonks herself at the door, knowing better than to try to go in the house. No animals inside. Dai and I stop, stumbling to take off our boots and hang our jackets on the peg with more hurry than normal. He gestures me into the lounge.

It never fails to surprise me, the strange floral haven Bev

has made of their house. Everything soft with draped materials, cushions, pastel colours, as if she needed an antidote to the starkness of life at the stud.

Bev rushes in, her cheeks pinked with the telltale signs of daytime drinking. There is a clumsiness about all her movements as if her mind is just a second or two behind her. This is why Dai likes her to stay in the house. No visitors. Her trips up to Maureen's shop are the most freedom she's allowed. To protect her. Like one of his prize horses, only let out to graze under supervision.

'This girl, what's her name? Her parents?' Dai hovers at the phone waiting for a surname which would unlock a phone number known by heart. But she's not one of ours.

'Emily. It was written inside the jumper.'

Bev gasps and turns around to face the door. Dai's eyebrows lift so far up his forehead they look like birds about to take off. Bev wheels around again. She pats her forehead with her hand.

'I told you it was odd she hadn't come round today. What did you say to me, eh? *Don't worry, love, she'll have overslept. You know how these kids are.* Well, now look.' Bev stamps her foot, a ridiculous gesture for a grown woman, but it makes Dai stand up straight.

'We don't know anything yet.' His words are rushed.

Bev is the only one who can blow his usual composure.

'Who is she?' I blurt out.

They exchange a look which tells me everything. She's the girl. The one who meant I got sent away. A childish thought stabs at me. Good. I'm glad she's lost. I can get back to Charlie-horse and my routine. Nothing needs to change.

'She's been helping us,' Dai says carefully. 'Her mother was our cleaner for a while, and she needed a favour. It's only been a few weeks.'

'Weeks?' I echo his words with shock. Why did he only tell me yesterday? I know I've been busy with the sheep but it's not like Dai to be so secretive.

He looks at the wall.

'Wanted to test her out before…'

Before he sent me away.

'I could have shown her everything.' My voice is petulant. I want to silence myself. Clamp my mouth shut and stop these childish whines from coming out. A girl is missing, and all I care about is why she was more important than me.

'Didn't want you…' Dai loses his train of thought which is not like him. He looks to Bev for help but finds none. 'Told her to keep a low profile. Didn't want her upsetting anyone.'

By that he means me. Is everything Maureen says about me really true?

'Lovely girl,' says Bev pointedly.

Dai gives her a warning look which she ignores.

'I wanted some help. Someone I can chat to. *For me*. It's about time I got something I wanted.' Her face burns red and Dai looks at the floor.

'Whoever she is, she might be in danger. It's up high today.'

'She didn't come to see us this morning,' Bev repeats a little too loudly.

Charlie-horse was clean yesterday so she must have been finished when I saw her. On her way to somewhere else.

'I saw her with Mr Thomas on the flats.'

Dai's shoulders stiffen. Bev shouts out, her eyes shining as if this whole adventure is thrilling.

'Ring Lorna, quick. See if she came home.'

Dai stabs the numbers into their phone pad.

'Lorna, it's Dai. Is Emily with you?' He listens to the answer. 'No, the tide's up full. I can't look for her. We've found her jumper out on the flats. We'll call the police. You should let Bryn know.' He slams the phone down then picks it up again and dials three numbers. Bev has gone stone quiet, watching his every move like a bird. He explains the situation again and puts the phone down.

'They'll be on their way as soon as they can. Put the kettle on, Bev.'

'Shouldn't we look for her?' My head swims with a memory – my mother's dark curls heavy with water.

Dai shakes his head.

'You know as well as I do, there's no getting through that tide until it's right down again. She won't be out there. She's not like that.'

Like my mother, he means. Or me. Looking for solitude. Happy in the elements.

'Didn't you warn her?'

He looks away.

'Didn't think she had any reason to be going out that way.' Bev wails.

'She got the bus, you knew that. She'd have to walk along the marsh road to us every day. You should have told her, Dai. Now she's gone!'

He balls his left hand into a fist and leaves a pause before he speaks.

45

'Be a good girl and make us all a cuppa, eh, Bev? It'll sort itself out once the police get here. She probably dropped it on the way to the bus and didn't realise.' His voice is firm, but his face doesn't look so sure.

Bev pads out of the room obediently, catching her arm on the doorframe as she goes.

Dai turns to the window and watches the sky for a moment. He's not a man who can be contained for long; like my own father, his body seems to lean towards the nearest exit if he has to be inside. The room heaves with awkward silence.

'If she's out there…' My voice rises, chest tight. The hours I spent splashing through the outgoing tide after my mum disappeared. Shivering with cold but unwilling to give up. Until I found her body.

Dai stays silent and gestures with a flick of his hand for me to calm down, but I can tell by the small vein raised in his neck that he's riled. Both of us stare out of the window, willing the police to hurry up. There is a loud clink of cups from the kitchen followed by a smash. Dai half turns as if he's used to the sound, like a gust of wind or one of the dogs yapping. I catch his eye, and he shrugs.

'Thought it'd be good for her to have some company. Thought she could handle it now.'

'I could have…'

Dai sighs and looks me in the eye.

'Someone she could talk to, Catrin. Up at the shop all the time. I'm not having her buying things for the sake of a chat.' He shrugs.

I open my mouth to make a comment about the bottles of gin then close it before a word comes out.

I wish Swift was here. Instead, I count the flowers on the curtains to stay calm.

Forty-five daisies.

We spend the next half hour in silence twitching at every sound. I lose count and start again. Dai ducks in and out of the room to keep an eye on Bev.

Finally, the sound of tyres on gravel.

7

I jump at the sight of PC Quinn striding up Dai's drive.

Why her?

The weak mug of tea Bev eventually made jerks in my hand. I place it on the table, rubbing the drips away with my jumper.

Dai greets them at the front door.

PC Quinn bounces into the room as if she is about to give a chat on road safety to a group of schoolchildren, all false enthusiasm and desperation to be liked. She breaks into the same toothy smile that made me want to slap her across the face almost three years ago to the day.

'Catrin!' she calls out in mock surprise.

I doubt she remembered my mother's anniversary yesterday.

I turn back to her, eyes sparking open as I search her face for proof she might possibly remember and regret what her incompetence cost me. She stares back with an impassive smile, benevolent as ever, jauntily pulling out her notepad and flicking it open. Waiting for details she's either too stupid or lazy to act on. I look at my feet. Anywhere but her face.

Her partner is not so attentive; he looms in the hall with Dai, chatting loudly about the height of the coming tides and what the cocklers will do if the blight comes back this year as casually as if they've bumped into each other in the local.

PC Quinn sits down and gestures to me to do the same. Finally, there's a small shake in her hand, giving away her awkwardness at us being brought back together under such similar circumstances. That's what I'd like to believe at least.

I stay standing. She gives a small shrug, losing her smile for a split second.

'Talk me through what happened.' She nods with all the authority of her uniform behind her this time.

'I think Emily is lost on the estuary. There's a high tide just in. You should be out looking for her.'

'We'll decide what's needed.' Her voice is cajoling. 'Tell me, what were you doing out there today?'

'Walking.'

'Right.' Her eyes flick up to my face and I wonder if she has finally remembered my mother.

'Is that something you do often?'

'Every day. You might remember that from last time.'

Her forehead creases for a second but she never loses her smile.

'You like to exercise then?'

She doesn't want to remember.

A burn of hatred glowers in my chest. How lucky to have the option of forgetting. I'd like to rub out the memory of sitting opposite her, my father looming over my shoulder, twisting his cap in his hands and saying nothing. Her cheerful jokes when my mother was out there missing, suggesting it was more likely she'd gone shopping with friends and lost track of the time. 'Happens to every mother once in a while,' she'd said to me in a sickly-sweet voice even my father recoiled from. If she'd just listened to what *I'd* said about my mother; how she was *different* and there was only one place where she'd lose track of time, they would have started looking for her out there sooner. She might be here now.

I fix her with a steely glare.

'I like to remember my mother. While I'm *exercising*.' I let the last word drip with sarcasm and watch as her pen pauses over her notepad.

'You always were very active,' she gabbles.

'Why aren't you looking for her?' My voice rises again and I notice a stillness in the hallway. Dai, always alert.

'Catrin, when someone has a history of running away and turning up a few days later, we have to be cautious. She's not been gone long enough at this point to classify…'

'Your caution didn't help my mother,' I snap.

Silence falls in the room. Dai strides in through the door, nods at PC Quinn. The atmosphere changes to one of brisk efficiency.

'Catrin, tell her about the jumper and Mr Thomas. We don't want to leave anything out.'

I take a breath, about to relay the strange conversation I saw between him and Emily on the flats, when Bev stumbles in. She's obviously had a few more while we've been waiting for the police.

'The mother is a right one,' she slurs.

'Bev.' Dai growls a warning.

She rounds the chair and leans down to PC Quinn who shuffles backwards ever so slightly at the smell of her, but doesn't lose her composure.

Bev sneers.

'It's no wonder she's run away. If you had to put up with that vicious woman day in day...'

'That's enough, Bev.' Dai grabs her by the arm and propels her towards the door.

'And why was that old man talking to her, eh? Doesn't look good, does it? He doesn't usually bother talking to anyone down here. Mr Too Bloody Good for this place.' A shrieking giggle escapes her mouth, and she clamps her hand over it like a child as Dai pushes her out of the room.

PC Quinn's partner shuffles in awkwardly to avoid the heated conversation in the hallway. He's a burly man with a deep tan line on his neck that marks him out as someone who works outside when he's not wearing a uniform. Perhaps he'll understand.

'I saw her yesterday on the flats. She was crying.'

'She say why?' The partner's words are blunt and uncaring, going through the motions. Just another silly girl.

'Someone promised her something. Didn't turn up.'

He rolls his eyes. I ball my hands into fists. If he'd just seen her, he'd understand. A flick of guilt in my stomach. *You saw her, Catrin, and you didn't even bother to try. Left her standing out there.*

'Why did you give Mr Thomas the jumper you found?' PC Quinn arches her eyebrows.

'He *took* it,' I spit back at her. 'I went there to call for help. He was furious... or scared.'

'About what?' Her partner again, muscling in.

PC Quinn sits up straighter.

'I couldn't make sense of it. He thought I was threatening him.'

'Were you?'

'No. I wanted to use his phone.'

'Where did you find the jumper?' PC Quinn cuts across him. There's a quiver in her voice that says she won't give up control to her partner.

'I could show you when the tide goes down.'

'No need for that. You tell me exactly and I'll write it down. Pass it on if we need to.'

Of course, the paperwork is the most important thing. Why would she care how impossible it is to describe a place on a landscape that is constantly moving and changing. I close my eyes for a second and picture the marsh. How many steps was it? Where did I stumble and nearly fall in? Usually I'd remember every detail, but the sound of the rising tide had panicked me.

'I ran for about two minutes in a straight line before I got to Mr Thomas' bottom field. Before that I'd jumped over three or four ditches heading east towards the village side. There's one big trench that's been there forever and some new ditches falling into place. I picked it up there – half in the big ditch. I checked to make sure she hadn't fallen in.'

'Could she have fallen? It's flat, isn't it?'

She's testing me or perhaps torturing me in the same way I am her.

'The sand is soft. Dangerous to walk on. Gives way under you.'

She smirks to herself. I dig my fingernails into the palm of my hand. No one believes you when you tell them the first time. Not if they've never been out there. What looks like a harmless stretch of grass could suck your foot so hard, you'd never get out. She's never had to plan her routes and routines based around the rise and fall of the tides like we do.

'Do you remember my mother's body?'

Her partner's face jumps in shock, but PC Quinn remains composed.

'Of course I do, Catrin. That is not something you forget easily.' She snaps her notebook closed.

'This must be upsetting. The idea of someone being out in the tide after what happened to your mother. But I can assure you this is different. The girl has run away a lot. The jumper could be a coincidence. Troubled family. We will look into it, of course. But she always turns up.'

I open my mouth to say something, but her partner interrupts.

'Bit prone to drama, y'know.'

I hate them both. For my mother and now for Emily. I'll look for her myself.

'Just one thing. Do you know Mr Thomas?'

PC Quinn's cloying voice is starting to make my chest tighten. The desire to get out into the open air sweeps through me. I shake my head.

'Not exactly.'

'Then why did you go to his house and not to the phone box? You said you saw them together yesterday. Did you see something that made you think Emily might be with him?' Her tone says it all. Silly young girl. Older man.

Could she be right?

Colour rises to my cheeks. I'd like to tell her that the three Jones boys ripped out the phone and its cord from the box with their tractor about a month ago, went charging up the marsh road trailing the receiver, leaving it clanging and banging against the tarmac. The horses bolted and birds flew away. I'd been standing out on the mudflats, saw it all and smelt the weed wafting afterwards. They call it the Wild West out here; sometimes they're not wrong. But PC Quinn doesn't care about how things work down our way.

'I thought it would be quicker,' I say.

She holds my gaze for a second then looks away.

'Do you have something against Mr Thomas? Why did he think you were threatening him?'

I squirm under her glare. What can I tell her? That he was a supply teacher at my comp; he wore jeans and black polo necks and got excited about Shakespeare, love, and poetry. All the mothers called him charismatic except mine who said he *had an air of tragedy about him*. It certainly felt like a tragedy when he made us jump up and down to let our emotions out; all the rushing and surging feelings there for everyone to see. But that was four years ago. Before he appeared on our marsh. Now he's someone to be avoided.

'He was my English teacher for a year,' I say grudgingly. I never gave him a second thought until he turned up here on our estuary, a strangely broken version of the man who'd proclaimed sonnets so passionately. I can't imagine him jumping on chairs anymore.

'Why do you think he was so angry?'

'I don't know. For trespassing?'

She laughs again, a little snort to herself, showing the snobbery of policing a community she'll never bother to understand.

'Yes, but you had a good reason to be there. You told him that?'

'He wouldn't listen. He was very upset.'

'So, you ran away?'

Her eyebrows are raised as if she's talking to a naughty child.

'Yes,' I spit out sullenly.

'To this farm?'

I nod.

'Because you know Mr and Mrs Morgan?'

Her partner has been shuffling from foot to foot throughout our exchange and he finally lets out a long hard huff. Dai walks back in, his face sheepish. Her partner rolls his eyes for Dai's benefit.

'Come on, Rose. These people have got work to do.' He nods at Dai. 'Let's hand it over and get on with the paperwork. She'll turn up soon enough.'

PC Quinn's face changes to a bright pink. Her partner seems to take up the whole room now, puffing himself up like a mating bird. He gives me a nod.

'Thanks, Catrin, you did the right thing in reporting this.' His tone is so patronising I half expect him to offer me a sticker for being such a good girl.

'If she's out in the tide, she's in danger.' My voice is hard.

He shakes his head and swaggers towards the door.

'We've got no reason to think she is. She's probably tucked up cosy somewhere with her latest fella or out joyriding with her friends. You said it yourself, she was waiting for someone. You know the type.'

'She's fifteen.' Dai's voice is clipped. 'What if she got into trouble on the way home?'

He flicks a puzzled look at Dai.

'You know as well as I do, there's a big tide today. No one would be that stupid. They'd see the water coming and turn straight back around. We can't be calling out the coastguard on a hunch.'

I flinch at his words. Rage wells up from my stomach. My mother was out there because she couldn't get back to the road or didn't want to. No one was looking for her.

'What about Mr Thomas? What if he saw her?'

'Yeah, well, we'll 'ave a word with him now. Let's keep calm though.' He winks at me.

PC Quinn stands up and shakes my hand with more force than is needed. Her palm is cold and stiff to the touch.

'Thank you so much, Catrin, you've been very helpful. As we're dealing with the disappearance of a minor, we shall follow every lead meticulously. If we think we need to call the coastguard, *we will*.' She cocks her head at her partner. 'Come on, let's stop gossiping about cockles and do our job.' With that she's out of the door, leaving him speechless inside the lounge.

He calls out to Dai in an overly deep voice.

'Better go, don't want to upset the boss.'

Dai looks away from him as he holds the door open.

8

Dai drove me and Swift home via the top road. I think he was glad to get out of the house and away from Bev, though he never said. Always loyal. As he dropped me off, we heard the chug and whirr of the coastguard helicopter overhead and he smiled grimly before getting back into his pickup and driving off. Perhaps it's a good thing PC Quinn's partner is an idiot and left her with a point to prove.

I stir the soup I'm making. The act of peeling and chopping a few potatoes and carrots has calmed me down. Kept me from calling the police station for an update.

'Something smells good.'

My father's form fills the kitchen doorway. It's not like him to come back to the house for his lunch. Dai must have stopped off at the top fields and told him what happened.

'Soup?' I say ignoring his compliment, reaching for a bowl from the wooden dresser.

He doesn't answer. I turn again, irritated to find him staring at me.

'What?' I say, my hackles rising.

'You alright?'

It's not a question he's asked me for a long time. Dai must have told him seeing PC Quinn rattled me. Words choke up in my throat but what would be the point of being honest with him now? Too many silences have passed between us over the last three years.

'Fine.' I nod and turn back to serving the soup, ladling the steaming chunks into two bowls. I suppose we can eat together at least – while there's still food in the house.

I take the bread out and saw off a thin slice. He's still watching me. I lay the food out on the table in our usual positions. We never sit opposite each other. Instead, we use the same places as when *she* was still here. The chair next to him and opposite me permanently empty. Her absence a constant barrier between us. There are times when I've had to stop myself setting a plate for her too.

'Thanks.' He nods at me, and we eat in silence.

Swift butts at my legs under the table and I rest my free hand on her head until she settles. I could ask about his day but the subject of selling the fields has wedged itself between any last remaining neutral space we had.

The phone trills out from the lounge and we lock eyes. Dad rises from the table, knocking the spoon off the side of his bowl in a rush to answer it. He usually leaves that to me. Women's work, talking. I stroke Swift's head as the mumble of his voice takes away any appetite I had.

Please don't let it be bad news. I should have tried to help Emily when I had the chance. If I hadn't been so caught up in my own thoughts. Worrying about the letter. About what to do. I stroke at Swift's fur over and over in the same place.

My father comes back in slowly, pauses in the doorway the way he does when he's sure he's going to say something I won't like.

'They didn't find anything.'

Swift licks at my hand. I say nothing. I'm not surprised. They don't care what happens down here. Bare minimal sweep over the water to do the paperwork and nothing more. My mother lay in a ditch when they told us not to worry, they'd done all they could, she'd turn up. Well, she did, but not in the way they'd imagined.

My father checks his watch and scoops his cap off the table. He'd usually be outside at this time having stopped to eat his sandwiches up in the fields. I suppose I should be grateful he came down at all, but I'm not.

He draws his cap neatly over his head, ducks down to move his bowl to the sink; the tremble of his hand almost invisible but a clear reminder that Dai was right – he's getting too old for this. He moves to the door and puts his wax jacket on, fiddling with the zip.

'They'd classed her as low risk. They wouldn't have looked at all if it wasn't for you. Whatever happens,' he calls out.

My head snaps up. It's not like him to say so much. *Whatever happens*. What does that mean? Prepare yourself in case you see another body and I can't help you. The irony of his half-hearted care so late in the day makes me scoff.

'Did the police say what they would do next?'

He turns to face the window, ignoring my attempt to draw him on PC Quinn's incompetence. His eyes dart back and fore checking the clouds for any changes in the weather.

'It was Dai on the phone.'

I take a deep breath. Of course it was. This place.

'How does he know?'

'You'd have to ask him,' my father replies, ever the master at avoiding conflict. 'Right,' he says with false jollity. 'Time to check the fields, you coming?'

He already knows the answer is no and doesn't wait for a

reply. Instead, he nods curtly and heads out of the door. I wait for the slam, then jump up and stalk over to the phone. I punch in the digits of the local police station, chasing away the reason I know the number by heart.

'Hello, can I speak to PC Quinn please? It's Catrin Roberts about the missing girl.'

After a pause she comes onto the line. I can hear the patronising smile in her voice. It must be her defence against reality.

'Catrin, what can I do for you?'

'They didn't find her?'

She sighs.

'No, we didn't but we can safely say she's not got caught in the tide.'

'How can you say that?'

She clears her throat.

'The coastguard made their sweep and let us know, so...'

'That doesn't mean anything. You know that. She could be under the water or in a ditch. There are some places you could shelter or...' My voice is coming out fast and she cuts me off.

'Catrin, your information was helpful, and we've eliminated the risk of her being in danger. Now we'll see if she turns up.'

'And Mr Thomas?' He must have had a reason to be so angry, first with Emily, then me.

There's a pause on the line. She's not going to tell me anything.

'He was very happy to answer all our questions.'

'Her jumper?'

There is an awkward silence. My stomach starts to dip as if

I'm in the car and we're driving over a big bump on the marsh road.

'Catrin, I know this must be hard for you.'

'Did he give you the jumper?' My voice is like stone.

She sighs, and I picture her already scanning the next task in her notebook.

'Did he?'

'He says there was no jumper. He said you were upset and rambling hysterically about someone being caught in the tide. He was worried about you. Now, I know it was the anniversary of...'

'No.' I cut her off. 'I picked it up in the ditch. It was purple. It had her name inside. She was wearing it the day before.' I pace the room with the phone jammed to my ear. The cord stretches and threatens to break.

'I know.' She continues as if talking to a crying child. 'The anniversary of your mother's death must be very upsetting. Perhaps you panicked and imagined...'

'What? A jumper that belongs to someone else?' Doesn't she realise how ridiculous that sounds?

'Catrin, we can't discuss any specific details. But I can tell you that we have no reason to suspect that Emily is in danger.'

'He's lying!' My voice is desperate, and I try to imagine what she's thinking, how I must sound to her, but I can't control myself, can't stop it from coming out. 'I saw them together. She was crying and he was there. He took the jumper. He must have something to hide or...' My voice catches as I gulp to take breaths.

'We are continuing to support her family, so you don't need to worry.' She's like a pious robot.

'You didn't look for my mother and now she's dead. How can you do this again?'

I slam the phone down.

*

There's a damp feel to the air. The tide has washed everything with grey water from our lane all the way to the village. It was a high one and there are still more to come this week.

I quicken my pace, driven by the rage of knowing Mr Thomas lied. That chases me all along the marsh road and up the lane to his house. I'll go in the front way this time. Demand he tells me what game he's playing.

I hammer on his front door. Swift sinks her bottom down in the grass, knowing something important is going on.

The door flings open. The same startled face stares at me with two creased eyebrows in the middle of his forehead like the drawings of flying birds you make as a child.

'Catrin. I knew you would come.' He smiles, looking almost hopeful.

'The jumper?' My body is fizzing with rage.

'I'm sorry. But you had to come to me, do you see?'

He's not making any sense. I study his face. It is hardly still, changing expressions from concern, to fear, to hope, then back again, like a storm cycle that won't stop.

'I did come to you. For help. And you took the jumper then lied to the police.'

He looks shocked then goes silent for a second.

'Yes, I suppose it does look like that. Actually, I have something of yours. You dropped it.'

My hand reaches instinctively for the envelope in my jacket pocket. It's gone. Colour floods my cheeks.

'What?' I clamp my mouth closed, trying not to give anything away.

He licks his lips, seeming to choose his words carefully, lining them up one by one for inspection before he speaks.

'You were always very creative.'

He's read it.

'Give it to me.' I hold out my hand.

He sighs as if I'm not following his lead, won't go where he wants me to.

'Just a minute.' He scowls with irritation and ducks back into the bungalow.

'And the jumper,' I call after him.

A few seconds later he returns and holds out my letter. I snatch at it, but he doesn't let go.

'What course is it? I recognised the college's address.' He smiles as if we've just bumped into each other at the shop.

My chest is tight. If my father finds out from anyone else… His worst fears confirmed. I'm just like her. Everyone says so.

'Your mother was an artist, I recall.' He tries to say it lightly but splutters over the words. He wipes his mouth with his other hand. Still, he won't let go of the letter.

'Are you…' He falters. 'Are you following in her footsteps?' His tone is strange.

'I hope not.' There it is – my fear. That I'll end up like her: bitter, frustrated or dead in a ditch, because people like us aren't allowed to have dreams. To escape.

'I could help. If you need anything. I'm a bit of an amateur…'

'No.' I snatch the envelope back and shove it into my pocket again. 'And the jumper?'

'I would have thought better of you.' He sighs. And there we are, back in the classroom, his teacher's voice convincing me it's my fault. But I'm tired of teachers and police officers and all the people who are supposed to help you but don't.

'Why lie about it?'

He shakes his head vigorously.

'I don't want any trouble. I needed to give you the letter.'

'Then why lie?' I insist.

'Why send the police to me?' He spits his words out. 'I suppose that was *their* idea, was it?'

I don't know who he's talking about. 'You took the jumper.'

'You expect me to believe it's about that? What a coincidence. I'm promised trouble and suddenly the police are at my door.'

'Trouble?'

'You think this will convince me to do what he wants? I don't respond to bullies. I can tell you that now.' He raises his hands, a manic look washing over him.

'I... don't understand.' I falter.

He gazes at me intently.

'Really trying to rattle me, aren't they?'

'The jumper!' I shout at him, trying to get his attention back.

'It doesn't really matter, does it? She's not coming back.'

His words send a chill through me.

'She's not in trouble, Catrin, not in that way. You, though, you need to get out of this place.'

My head spins with the strange, riddling way he talks. He

doesn't resemble the smiling man who answered the door now. Something about our conversation makes anger burn off him like water spilt on a hot stove. His chest moves up and down rapidly, face wrung with some kind of rage I can't quite pinpoint.

'What were you arguing about? You and Emily?'

'I told her not to put her happiness in someone else's hands. To go home and sort her problems out. To get off the marsh because it's dangerous out there.'

'What problems? Is she okay?'

He takes a step back, shakes his head at me and slams the door so hard I close my eyes at the thud of it.

9

The grass on the flats is still damp from the morning tide. If I ring the police station again and tell PC Quinn about Mr Thomas lying, she won't believe me. It'll be my word against his and I know how that will go.

Without the jumper the police aren't going to waste any more time searching the estuary. Emily will become another pile of paper on the missing persons' desk. Until her body turns up like my mother's did.

I need to keep walking. It's the only way I'll feel better.

But thoughts stab at me: the guilt of not helping Emily when she asked, the anger at everyone else's incompetence, or my own. And the letter. My own pathetic fear about telling my father the truth. About admitting that I want something for myself, just for me.

I know this place, every ditch and rut and river. There are places you can hide or shelter – old arms stores and defences from the Second World War, an abandoned car with its wheels eternally stuck in the mud, the lighthouse far out to the west. I can look for Emily myself.

I have to rule out the fact that she could still be out here. Alive or dead.

I head out west towards the war shelters.

At first glance they look just like a smooth curve of a rock face, although there are no rocks out here, and it's only once you get up close you can see they're hollow. They were used for storing weapons but now they just play host to the odd lost lamb. There are still unexploded shells in the sands out here.

The inside of the shelter smells of must. A smattering of white graffiti covers the curved walls.

I showed this place to Greg, one of the Jones boys, months after my mum died. Helped him write his name in tippex on the wall along with all the others. Nothing sentimental, just his name. Then we fumbled with each other's clothes and bodies. I'd thought how strange it was he hadn't written both our names in a heart or something. It was over before I even had a chance to realise what that meant. He never came to call for me again.

I run my fingers over the spot where his name would have been. Three years of tides and weather have left the stone blank enough for another teenager to scrawl their indifference. He would have broken my heart if it hadn't already been snapped tight like a shell. I didn't care. Wanted to feel something. Anything. That was the last time I really tried, unless you count the drunken New Year's Eve mistake with Mac, but the less said about that the better. Came down our way to celebrate on the cheap. He said he'd come to see me. But you never know where you are with him. Better forgotten.

There are no signs of anyone having been in the war shelter recently. I climb out, steadying myself with a palm on Swift's back, and the sun blinds me for a second.

'Look out!' a voice shouts, as a quad bike skids to a stop within a foot of me. I jump backwards, pushing Swift out of the way and smash into the hard stone of the shelter. A sharp pain strikes between my shoulders. The bike grinds to a final stop and the driver jumps off.

'You alright?' A young man around my age looks me up and down with concern. He hovers with his hands out in front of him as if uncertain whether to help or not. I don't give him the chance. His quad is loaded up with nets and pans ready to bag a few sacks of illegal cockles – he shouldn't even be out here.

'Cockling zone ends there.' I gesture to the part of the estuary towards the lane, snatching my hand into my pocket before he can see it shaking. With the other, I search for the scruff of Swift's neck and pull her close.

His shoulders square up.

'What's it to you?'

There's something about the way the cocklers treat this place, dredging up shells to make money, never thinking about the estuary or the birds – what it means to the rest of us. Flashing around in their 4x4s talking about holidays in Marbella and new cars for their kids.

'Just letting you know.' I hold his gaze longer than I should. My father tells me I don't help myself with people, but I gave up trying a long time ago.

He glances around.

'And you, what's your excuse then?'

'Do I need one?' I snap. 'I live here.'

He shrugs and gestures to the bike.

'It's not mine, it's borrowed. Whatever you're angry about it's nothing to do with me.'

'You have to have a licence for picking,' I say. 'They're like gold dust.'

He gives me a sharp look. 'Who said I was picking?' His tone is serious but there's a twitch of a smile at his mouth that says he might be playing with me. He sweeps his dark fringe from his forehead with his finger.

'I'd better get on.' My tone is flat, but he smiles nervously.

'Busy day?'

'I'm looking for someone.'

He studies me for a moment. 'That makes two of us then.'

'Emily?'

He nods.

'Nobody else is going to bother. Fourth time she's run away,' he adds with a shrug, then glances back at me. 'Why are you looking for her?'

I shift uncomfortably under his gaze.

'I know this place,' I say.

'Well, I know my sister, so we could make a good team.'

I look at my boots.

'You *were* right about me picking. Got a good instinct for truth.' He points at me jauntily as if it's a compliment then stuffs his hand back in his pockets, looking at his shoes. 'Got to bag a few sacks to pay my friend for the lend of the bike.' He shrugs his shoulders as if he makes deals like this every day. 'Multitasking,' he adds with a sad laugh.

I take another look at him; he's hard to place.

'You know the estuary, then?' I take a step closer.

He shrugs again, dips his head and looks up at me through his fringe as if he's trying to figure me out too.

'I was here before. Working the sands. About five years ago.'

He must be lying because no one gets to work the sands

without a permit and he's not old enough to have been more than a teenager.

'You'll know the way well then.' I walk towards the next war shelter, dismissing him.

'So, it's true,' he calls after me. 'People down here only look after their own.'

My mother said the same thing over and over again. How she was left out in the cold. Politely ostracised. It was one of her favourite complaints.

I turn around.

'Who said that?' It's silly to ask but there's something about him that's jarring just like she was.

He looks at me quizzically.

'My mam doesn't like your lot much.' He grins at the ridiculous sound of it, and I find myself smirking without wanting to.

'My lot,' I repeat. A smile breaking at the thought of us all being lumped together.

He scuffs his shoe in the dirt as if waiting for more. I slide my sketchbook out of my pocket, flick it open to the right page, careful not to show my other drawings.

'Can I ask you something, about Emily?'

He takes a breath in as if preparing himself for the worst and nods.

'Did she have a purple jumper, like this? A big flower on the front and a pocket?' I proffer the page, looking away. It's been three years since I showed anyone my drawings.

He stares hard and thinks for a minute. Perhaps he's suspicious of me too. It must look odd, someone out looking for his sister with no real reason.

'Yeah, she did. Wouldn't bloody take it off. Mam had to prise it off her to wash it.'

'I found it yesterday,' I say. 'That's why I called the police.'

'How do you know it was hers?'

'Her name was inside. Little heart on the I.'

He processes the information, hands in pockets.

'So, where is it?'

'That's what I'd like to know.'

'That's a good drawing. Shading and that.' He nods at me.

Heat creeps into my cheeks. I shouldn't have shown him. I'm struck by the fact that he doesn't seem in a rush at all. He's here on his own. How do I know he hasn't got something to do with his sister's disappearance.

'Good luck with your cockling,' I say, unable to stop the disapproval dripping off my words. He shakes his head.

'Tell your mate Simon from the plant I said hello. Ask him if he's still using kids from up town in the high season.'

'They don't do that.'

He laughs.

'They did once. When it suited them. Maybe they've got to play it by the book now.'

We face each other for a moment.

'They're not my mates. Can't stand the sight of them.' I say it more for myself than him, but he looks at me with renewed interest.

He kicks a stone and Swift launches out from under my hands in high chase. He watches her go with a genuine smile then turns to me.

'What do you care about Emily anyway?'

The words stack up one after the other in my throat and

render me voiceless. He takes my silence as a sullen rejection of his question.

'Forget it,' he says and climbs back onto the quad. 'If you do find her, try and be a bit friendlier. She's had a hard time of it lately.' With that he revs the bike and speeds off across the flats towards the village.

I follow Swift's shape darting in and out of the long reeds as we wander over to the next war shelter five minutes along the road. Nothing inside except some rusty beer cans.

This is hopeless.

I whistle for Swift.

If Emily's been working at Dai's for weeks, there's one person who'll know exactly what's been going on.

10

Swift slumps down in her usual spot under the trestle tables outside the village shop. There's a fresh pile of rhubarb stacked next to boxes of firelighters, both on special offer today. I take a deep breath and push the door open.

Maureen's head snaps up, eyes narrowed.

'Well, if it isn't our very own marsh detective.' She smiles and folds her arms across her chest.

My mother told me never to give Maureen the satisfaction of seeing how much her words irritate or hurt.

I nod at her in silent greeting, then turn my back. She hates to be kept waiting. Gossip is something to be served immediately. The longer I make her wait, the more likely she is to spill the beans.

I run my fingers over tins of tomato soup and spaghetti hoops, all with the same bright orange handwritten price label. Some electro-sounding hit from ten years ago blasts out from a tinny radio. Maureen hums along and shuffles newspapers behind me. She'll be winding herself up, waiting for me to break first and tell her some juicy piece of information. I move slowly around the shop. She drums her nails on the counter a little too loudly. Finally, she gives up and huffs.

'The police said you were helping them with their enquiries. I said, yes, if anything happens on that marsh Catrin will see it. She sees everything, don't you, love?'

I turn and prod a loaf of bread, think of the stale loaf back home we've got to use up. Her eyes follow my every movement like a cat.

'Don't you get bored of wandering around out there? Nothing but mud and wrecks.' Her voice is coy. Playing nice to get what she wants.

'No.' I learnt from my mother that the best thing to give Maureen is nothing. Nothing she can use or twist, so the worst she can say is you're a bit of a loner. Someone who keeps to themself. No one is allowed to get too big for their boots. Maureen will take them down in a flash. Her and the rest of them.

She tries again, restacking newspapers and fixing me with a smile that could curdle milk.

'It makes me sad to see you so lonely. At your age you should be out every weekend on the razz. What would your poor mam say?'

She takes her shot right where she knows it will hurt. Her eyes bore into me now, willing me to break and make a scene she could report on. She'd love to know about the offer letter. How *little Catrin* thinks she could be an artist. *Fancies herself better than us, just like her mother.* I can imagine her mockery; *well, what do you know, we've got our very own Picasso down here!* I walk closer to the till.

She huffs again. Patience is not her strong point.

'Why don't you take that bus driver up on his offer? Could do a lot worse.'

'No, thank you,' I reply. The faint memory of too many malibu and cokes washes through me, sickly sweet. His mouth rough on mine and stubble chafing against my face. Everything just a laugh, until it wasn't. I'd rather forget that night.

Maureen smirks, noticing the grim strain in my voice, glad to have caught a reaction however small. Now is the time to ask her about Emily. She's clearly having a slow day, bored of her own company, and won't be able to resist the chance to get involved in someone else's misery.

'Did you hear anything more about the missing girl?' I try and sound offhand but her eyes glint.

'Thought you'd have all the news, what with you calling the coppers and all that. What were you doing traipsing about out there anyway? Should know better with these October tides. You don't want to end up like…' She stops herself and shudders.

I give her what she wants. A bit of drama.

'It was the anniversary.'

It does the job. Maureen moves her hand to her chest and inhales deeply.

'Oh gosh, what is it…' She exaggerates counting numbers in her head, closing her eyes. 'Three years? Such a tragedy.' She opens one eye to read my face then closes it again, shaking her head with false pity. In another life she'd have moved to London and taken to the stage. She bats her eyes wide for effect and fixes them on me piously. 'You know, your mam wouldn't have wanted you to end up like this, love. She'd have wanted you to be happier than she was at least.'

My hands twitch and I dig my nails into my palms until they sting. How dare she. After her part in all of it, the sniping comments and judging faces my mother felt burning into her back as she walked around. *She's not from down here* always trotted out as the ultimate accusation. The one thing she couldn't change even if she'd wanted to. It was Maureen and the like who made my mother hard, pushed her out and into

75

the role of observer – further towards her photos for comfort and the estuary for company.

'So, have you?' I say, composed again.

'Have I what?' She pouts.

'Heard anything more about the girl?'

'Well, I have as a matter of fact, missy.' She smiles widely now, her teeth lining her mouth like little daggers. She sways behind the counter to the beat of the music, happy to be in control. I'll have to give her something first. With Maureen it's always payment before delivery.

'I met her brother. Just off the point,' I say, flicking a fly off the top of a newspaper. That's harmless enough. I don't say anything about his loaded quad.

'Didn't happen to notice if he was cockling, did you?'

'Strange thing to do when your sister's missing.' It's not a lie but my face burns anyway. I turn to look at the magazines trying not to think about why I'm protecting him, worried she'll see through me.

'That's funny. Simon's lads said they saw him with a quad loaded up for picking heading over your way. Not like you to miss something like that.'

'How do they know him?'

'Go way back, apparently.'

So, he was telling the truth. Simon is all about money, but using school kids as cheap labour is lower than I'd expect even of him. Another reason not to sell him our land.

'He was walking. Looking for Emily, that's all.' I don't owe him anything, but I wouldn't wish Simon and his boys on anyone. Or Maureen for that matter.

She stares keenly at my face for a moment too long. I finger the glossy cover of a magazine. If Maureen and PC Quinn swapped jobs, they'd both be happier.

She grimaces.

'Must have been one of those northern boys on the quad then. Coming down, thinking they can make money when we're not looking. Think we're bloody stupid, they do. God, the mess they made of the boys up west. Nasty bunch. Still, funny that Simon thought it was the brother.'

'Simon thinks a lot of things.' Like he can buy land from people who don't want to sell. I meet her gaze this time.

Maureen ignores my jibe and gives me a cruel smile, ready to deliver the real news she's been dying to tell me since I walked in.

'The brother probably went out looking himself because the police have called off the search.'

'Why would they do that?'

She smirks at my interest.

'Funny he got so far out your way without anyone else seeing him *walking* over the flats.' Maureen says her words with the flourish of a magician producing the trick card. She watches my face carefully.

Her gaze is like having molten lava poured on me. Colour rushes to my cheeks again.

'Not everyone is as nosy as you, Maureen,' I mumble. It's a low blow but the indignation distracts her.

'Want to watch where your loyalty lies.' She lowers her voice and stares at me pointedly. 'According to Bev, his mother's a right one. Not to be trusted.' She raises her eyebrows for effect. 'So, we don't know what he's about.'

'Why did they call off the search?' My tone is flat.

'They got a call, if you must know.' She picks up a pile of papers and starts tying them into stacks for return, clearly bored with our conversation. 'Said they'd had a tip off. The girl's been seen in the town centre drinking. Not missing at all, just playing about. They hadn't got far looking for her, mind, door-to-door as if they were selling biscuits. Those town coppers always afraid of getting their boots dirty.'

'And that's it? They've stopped looking because of one phone call?'

'Well, what do you expect?'

I think of Mr Thomas snatching the jumper out of my hands. Of Emily's tears about the person who had promised her something.

'It seems odd. She hasn't come home, and they've stopped looking.'

'What's *odd* is your father told Simon he didn't want to sell the fields this morning. Simon is tamping. Came in and forgot to say thank you for the walnut loaf I'd put aside, didn't even sign for his shopping in the book. Not like him. He thought they'd all but shaken on it. What would make your dad change his mind on an opportunity like that, eh?'

I'm struck into silence. My father listened to me. It's such a strange and rare occurrence that I can't believe it. We'll have to find another way to make things work.

Maureen trawls on.

'Probably needs time to think about it. *The benefits*.' She stares at me again, taps the credit book on the counter, reminding me what we owe. 'Dai's fuming too,' she adds.

'Dai?' I can't see why he would be bothered either way.

'Yeah. He's the one who approached Simon for your father.

Now, I'm not saying he was getting a cut or anything like that, but he did seem very cross about it when I asked him this morning. Waved me off like a mist of gnats.'

Why would Dai get involved in our business? He doesn't usually have anything to do with Simon; can't stand the sight of him since they got into a fight in the pub one night after Simon insulted Bev's drinking. Everyone was so disgusted by his comment they left it a good five minutes before they pulled Dai off him. I thought they hadn't spoken since then.

It seems there's a lot Dai hasn't been telling me lately.

I turn and walk out of the shop. Maureen's voice follows me with a hiss.

'A good day to you too.'

*

I place a hand on the cool metal of Dai's gate. I've never felt uneasy about scooting into his yard before. Swift has no such qualms and wiggles under as ever, bounding off in search of him. I climb over and lower myself down slowly.

The yard is strangely quiet, Dai's bustling form nowhere to be seen. I check in the stallion's box, but the big bay is alone munching his way through a pile of hay. He nickers softly, nodding his head in warning as he sees me.

'Where's he at, boy?' I whisper, not waiting for the reply, glancing around for Swift. If Dai's here, she'll have found him. Perhaps he's made a long overdue visit to see Charlie-horse. He never told me to come back and look after him after Emily went missing. I should have asked.

Poor Charlie.

I stride up the path behind the yard. I can take him for his walk and make sure he's not forgotten. Do one thing right today.

Charlie's stall is empty – his straw still dirty with manure, hay-net half full. He must have finally given up. My throat thickens and chokes. He'll have missed me too.

There's a shout from down by the house. Swift yaps. I run out of the stall and race down towards her, half expecting to see Charlie's poor body lying somewhere waiting for the knacker to come.

As I get to the end of the path, Bev and Dai are outside the house. Bev is shouting and Dai, both arms raised to quiet her, is repeating, 'Calm down' over and over. Swift jumps up at him, excited by the noise. He takes a second to realise she's not one of his own dogs and when he does he glances around for me, a look of panic in his eyes.

'Look who's here, love,' he says, trying to coax Bev into silence.

She turns, sees me, and charges up the path.

'He told you not to come anymore.' Her face is a violent red, flushed from shouting or crying or both. She eyes me furiously.

Swift springs over and puts herself between Bev and me, her head low and uncertain in the confusion. Dai walks over.

'Catrin, it's not a good idea coming here. I said…'

'Where's Charlie-horse?' I cut him off, my words fired out of the rage that's been building up in me since we last spoke.

'I've moved him.'

'Where?'

He sighs and Bev tuts to herself. They wouldn't send him to the knackers and lie to me about it, would they?

Dai relents. 'He's up in the old barn.'

Bev swings round and gives him a look that says he's betrayed her.

'Bev wanted him up there. Don't know why,' he adds with a shrug, his face tired as if he's had more than enough of whatever is going on here.

'I don't see what business it is of yours, Catrin,' Bev says, her tone clipped.

It's the first time I've ever felt uncomfortable here. Unwelcome. I've been coming in and out of their yard since I was old enough to climb the gate alone. The rejection stings. I clear my throat.

'I was worried. I…'

'Always worried about something, aren't you? Picking up things that don't belong to you. Creating problems for all of us. Want to try fretting about your own father, eh?'

'Bev.' Dai's voice warns her to go no further.

'I came about my father.' My tone is colder now, matching hers.

When they throw stones at you, you have to turn yourself to rock. My mother taught me that. Every nasty comment calcifying her further until she could repel all the gossip. Eventually she pushed me away too.

'I hear you've been talking to Simon on our behalf.' I won't let Dai get away with it.

Dai shakes his head.

'Look, Catrin. You should talk to your father.'

'I have. He's said no,' I hiss. There is a shake beginning in my body, an involuntary twitch making my shoulders and stomach jump. I don't want to fight with Dai. I used to feel safe here.

Dai looks at me solidly.

'He'll come round. Not much choice about the matter.'

'It's *our* land.'

He shrugs as if to say it can't be helped. When did he stop caring about us? We've always had shared lives. Where do I fit if not here helping Dai and ignoring my own father?

Perhaps he's angry because I brought the police to his house, rattled Bev. Reminded them of Rhys' death. A wash of guilt sweeps through me.

'Did you hear about Emily?' I offer, trying to control the rising panic pulsing through me. Even after all this I still don't want to argue with Dai.

'What about her?'

'She's been seen in town. Someone gave the police a tip off.'

Bev smiles widely. How much has she had again today?

'Didn't I tell you. All sorted in the end.' She smirks at Dai. He turns his back on us.

'Work to do,' he shouts over his shoulder, stomping down the path, back bristling with tension as he heads towards the yard.

'Her mother's a right piece of work,' Bev says. 'No wonder she ran away.'

I watch Dai's form disappearing for a second. Dai doesn't give up on people. He's not like my father who leaves gaping holes of silence in a room when he grabs his cap to leave. Dai stays. That's one of the reasons why I love him.

Bev babbles to herself.

'Dabbling in psychics. Says she can hear the dead. Oh, the pack of lies she tried to sell me…' Bev tuts. 'Spends all their money on it. Husband's left her and won't come back until she gives it up. Can't blame the girl for running off. Wherever she is, she's better off.'

'You know the girl's mother?' I don't really care about the answer.

But the question seems to catch Bev off guard. 'We did,' she says, the answer as closed as her face. 'But she's trouble. Nasty piece.' Bev spits the last words out with an expression I've not seen on her before.

I feel like I'm standing on the sinking sands of the marsh, not able to get a good foothold. Everything moving all around me.

'Can I see Charlie?' I ask, like a child longing for something, anything, to be familiar again.

'Best not, love. I've moved him up to the barn. I want to look after him from now on. Just me. For my Rhys. Should have done it before.' Her face changes. She smiles and puts her arm around me. 'Dai's not keen on the idea. You know he doesn't like change. But I've insisted. It'll give me something to do while I get ready. Did he tell you our good news?'

I shake my head. It seems Dai doesn't tell me anything anymore.

'We're having a baby.' She beams.

I watch my feet move one in front of the other as we walk slowly back down the path. A baby? Surely that's not possible for Dai and Bev anymore. She sees my hesitation and her face melts into a scowl again.

'What's the matter, Catrin? Worried you won't be Dai's favourite anymore?' She takes my stunned silence as a yes. Her mouth curls with distaste. 'Then you won't mind leaving us in peace while we get on with it. Dai doesn't need you now. You're too old to be hanging around here, playing silly buggers. He'll have his own child again. *Our baby.*'

She saunters off towards the barn.

11

Back on the marsh, I take a deep drink of fresh air. I'm an adult now. I should be happy for Dai and Bev. But something ugly throbs in my body. The thought of Dai not having time for me. He'll be just another person I'm an inconvenience to. Another place I don't fit.

I study the mud crusted onto my boots. Swift arrives behind me, panting, and pushes her wet nose into my hand as if to say, *I'm still here.*

'Thanks, girl.' I give her thick fur a rub, but my mind is elsewhere.

What was it Bev said about Emily's mother – she talks to the dead? I gaze out to the flats. What would I ask my mother if I could talk to her? What happened, of course. I'd know at last, and I wouldn't feel like my world was being turned inside out every time I think of her.

I look down at my boots again, unfurl my hands and study them one by one.

Something about this morning is all wrong. From the phone call about the girl to Dai and Bev's behaviour – everything is strange and confusing. I can't even think about the letter. About sending it back and filling in all those forms. All those questions about us and how we live. Admitting how bad things are. Not until I've found Emily.

The bus.

Of course.

If Emily has gone into town, she'd have got on the bus and Mac can tell me if he saw her.

*

I only have to wait five minutes before the hourly bus pulls up to the stop. It'll be Mac driving, it always is. Bored out of his mind, he's got nothing better to do except chat with his passengers all day.

The doors spring open with a whooshing sound. He beams down at me from his throne in the driver's cab.

'Now, what have we got here?'

I jump up onto the step and Swift follows. He raises his eyebrows, but I ignore him.

'Gone blind, have you?' He chuckles at his own joke and waits for me to do the same.

There are two ways to play it with Mac. Keep your head down and hope he gets bored, or give as good as you get. Anything in between he'll take as a sign you're flirting with him. I go for the latter.

'Wish I had.' I stare at him pointedly.

He looks away first. 'Charming as ever, Catrin.'

Swift ambles up the back of the bus, sniffing at the seats. He follows my gaze.

'Where you off to?'

'I'm going to look for that girl's mother. The one who was missing.'

'Was?' He looks surprised, obviously not been into the shop today for Maureen's latest news roundup.

'They had a call. Said she's been seen in town drinking. The police have stopped looking.'

He shakes his head. I'm not sure if he's dismissing the information or disgusted by it.

'Did you see her? She must have got the bus to town.' I keep my voice light and look at the change I'm counting out in my hand. It's never been anything less than awkward between us since that New Year's Eve, however hard we try at banter. I turn the fifty pence pieces to all face the same way. He stays unusually quiet. I look up and he's staring at me, blue eyes serious. I hope he's not going to try and ask me out again.

'Did you?' I repeat. He looks disappointed and glances out of the window at a car speeding in the other direction.

'Not on my shift,' he says, turning the watch on his wrist around twice. 'Maybe she got a lift.'

He laughs and we both relax a little.

'Strange no one mentioned it,' I push.

'Everyone knows everything down here, do they?' His words are mocking.

'Usually.'

'I hope not. Wouldn't want everyone to find out I messed up my one chance with you.'

It's my turn to look away. I call Swift back to me and pat her towards the side of my leg. Her warmth is reassuring.

'What do you care, Catrin? You know them?'

'I saw her. The day she disappeared. She was upset.' I sigh. 'I didn't stop and help.'

'Not like you to run out on someone.' There it is. A hint of bitterness. He won't let it go. Can't take rejection.

'It's called changing your mind.'

He shuffles in his seat. Any moment of frankness between us is lost.

'Right then, if you want her mother, you'll have to get off at the next one. A pound, please.' He jabs at the ticket machine, and I place two coins on the counter.

Nearly the last of the money from the jar. My stomach lurches with the thought of Simon and the land. My father has said no but how long can we really hold out?

I could ask Mac for a favour, but I can't bear the thought of owing him anything. He holds out his hand with a mischievous grin, all our history apparently forgotten. He's like that. Changeable. One minute your best friend, the next a cruel joker. Always a game. You never know which side of him you're going to get. I know what's coming next, it's happened to me a thousand times. I pick up the coins and place them into his hand. As I drop the last one in, he catches his thumb on top, trapping my hand in his. He gives me his best smile, the one that made all the girls at school go silly. He was three years above us then, Captain of the rugby team, and swaggered about with the confidence of knowing he could have whoever he wanted.

'So, how about that drink then?'

The first time he did this to me, I thought it was funny. Charming. I felt flattered by the attention. Everyone had fancied him at school, then he'd turned up driving our bus service. Said it was to tide him over until something better came along. It was after my mum, after I'd spectacularly failed my exams. He'd said we were similar, both waiting for something better to come along.

Now, his hand is slightly damp around mine, holding me

firm. I pull as hard as I can and snatch it away. The coins fly out onto the floor of the bus. Swift scurries after them, sniffing each one.

'Been there, done that. Didn't do either of us any good, did it?'

He sees the game is over and shrugs.

'Suit yourself. You used to be more fun, Catrin.' He hefts the bus into gear. 'Going to pay for your ticket, or what?' He cocks his head at the money.

I scrabble and pick it up, ignoring the blatant way he watches me do it. His idea of flirting, no doubt. When I slam the coins on the counter, he calmly takes them and presses the ticket button without another word. I rip off the paper and make my way to the back of the bus. He watches me in the mirror with a smirk on his face.

The marsh flashes past in a blur of brown, green and grey. It all looks so small from up here on the main road. So unimportant.

*

The bus pulls up sharply and nothing more is said between me and Mac. It was a stupid idea to try and talk to him about something serious anyway. I should have known better.

Swift eyes him as we get off the bus and I stroke her head, always glad she's here.

We call this the 'big village'. There's a doctor's surgery, two supermarkets, a butcher's and even a shoe shop; with two chapels and a fancy church it makes our village look tiny. People say they look down on us; our sorry existence where the butcher's van comes once a week on the day the library van doesn't, and we're lucky if the ice-cream van bothers at all. I'm not sure that's true. The truth is no one thinks about us at all. Our problem is we're stuck looking up at them.

I walk alongside the old stone wall that protects the road from high tides. It traps our expanse of water and sky behind it, making them nothing more than a backdrop.

My mother used to hold my hand as I would teeter along the top of the stones, perhaps the only time I had her full attention. Her fingers locked in mine rather than hovering over the camera's buttons.

Swift jumps up, two paws on the wall as if to leap over and make a break for the flats.

'Not now, girl,' I say. 'It's different here.'

The sands mean nothing to the people here. Worthy of comment only when they throw up the smell of rancid cockles or inspire a pint smacked down on the pub bar laying claim to *our* history – the golden age when women with baskets and donkeys could be found picking by the hundreds. It's surprising anyone wants to say cheers to that when only the chosen few earn their living off the cockles now.

If this was our village then a quick trip to the shop would give up anyone's family history and address.

The supermarket looks a lot more inviting than our village shop. Bright signage guides me towards automatic doors with a sandwich board shouting about offers and discounts propped outside. Our money would go a lot further here. I leave Swift sitting next to an advert for half price custard-creams. She looks at me with curiosity, sniffing at the sign before settling. It makes me uneasy to see her waiting there as the doors open and close and people rush in and out.

Maureen would have a fit if she saw this shop. She claims she hasn't, of course, but I can picture her driving past, mouth open, after closing time. It only opened a few months ago but she's already on the warpath with anyone suspected of having 'popped in' on their way home. She knows it's only a matter of time before people won't want to buy her overpriced tins; says she's charging for maintaining the community and we'll all be sorry when she's gone. Maybe she's right – I doubt they give credit here or would check on old Mrs Beynon if she didn't pick up her morning paper.

The smell of freshly baked bread wafts towards me as I walk in. A young man in a bright green overcoat kneels on the floor pulling the trigger on a pricing gun. The local radio station blasts out from a wall speaker. He's shooting labels onto the cans, sometimes two or three at a time. I imagine Maureen's horror at the waste of it.

'Excuse me.' As soon as I say the words, heat burns my cheeks. He stands up as if he's been caught smoking at school.

'What can I do for you, Madam?'

Impressive. He obviously wasn't trained by a Maureen. I force an unconvincing smile.

'Look, it's not about shopping.' My words come out gabbled. 'I need some information.'

He smirks. Why am I doing this? People are not my strong point. I swallow hard and try again.

'It's about Emily, the missing girl.'

He shrugs. 'I already told her mam, I didn't even know her that well. She gave me a right ear-bashing cos she saw us together once. You're not the police, are you?'

'No.' The thought of PC Quinn and her useless

investigation spurs me on. She probably hasn't even been in here asking questions. 'I'm trying to help her, and I just wanted to know a bit more about her.'

'Why are you trying to find her if you don't know her?' Smarter than he looks, he jabs the pricing gun towards me.

'Because...' I falter. The image of her tear-stained face comes back to me. 'Don't you want her to be safe? Maybe her mother was right to be suspicious of you.'

He reddens.

'No. Yeah. I mean, of course, who wouldn't?'

'Exactly.' I hold his gaze boldly, feeling more like Maureen than I'd like to. No wonder she always gets what she wants.

'Can you tell me where she lives?'

He steps backwards, not taking his eyes off me.

'I'll be back in a sec, yeah?' he says, and disappears in a flurry of green.

He reappears in seconds with an older woman dressed in an identical uniform, carrying a dripping mop. He deposits her in front of me and hurries off. There's an awkward pause as we size each other up. The woman seems oblivious to the pool of water gathering by her feet.

'You're asking about my daughter?'

Her face is worn and tired, framed by mousy hair sticking out at all angles. Her eyes dart to and from my face as if she can't quite remember what she's supposed to be doing. Nothing like the 'nasty piece' that Bev described.

'I found Emily's jumper on the marsh and called the police.' The poor woman can't have slept. She doesn't look like someone who's found out her daughter's been seen safe and sound. 'I heard someone saw her and just want to know if she's okay.'

She nods.

'I'm clocking off, wait here.' She walks back through the shop, water dripping behind her without noticing. Two minutes later she appears with her jacket on and a full shopping bag slung over her shoulder.

'Come on then,' she says, as if we'd arranged to go for a coffee together. I follow her out and whistle softly to Swift who jumps up with relief and trots behind us.

We cross the road in silence. She glances at me as we begin to walk slowly up the hill which crowns the village.

'I'm Lorna.' Her breath comes in shallow pants as the incline gets steeper and steeper. 'I asked them if one of the cockling boys had found her jumper, would have made sense.' She glances at me again sideways. 'They said it was a woman who was out on the flats a lot. Sounded a bit weird. Sorry, but it did.' She eyes me again. 'Now I've had a look at you, I'm not worried. I've got a good intuition for people. I can see you want to help.'

Lorna stops on the pavement, breathes in and out, and stares at me for a long time. Her neck is strung with five gold necklaces. Each one has an angel hanging in the middle. One with a clear crystal as its belly. Another solid with open wings. She seems to make a decision and grabs hold of my arm, pulling me towards her. She lowers her voice.

'They don't always tell you everything, the police, do they? I'm used to her running off. But this thing with the jumper. I mean, they must have been suspicious to send officers down there. Get the coastguard out. Then... nothing. Now a phone call. Something's off.'

We walk a few more paces then stop outside a small,

terraced house; one in a long line going up this side of the hill. Where you live marks out how well off you are – how far your kids have to walk for the school bus. We've climbed a fair way up before we stop.

'This yours?' She eyes Swift who is panting up the hill behind us.

'Yes.' I call her to my side, always glad of her warmth against me.

Lorna nods.

'Can she wait out here? Bryn will kill me if he sees a dog in the house. He's narky like that and I need him in a good mood when he arrives.'

I nod and gesture to Swift who's happy enough to plonk herself down for a rest on the doorstep. She sets her head on her paws and looks up at me with what feels like a warning.

It's too late now, I want to tell her as I follow Lorna inside.

12

I'd have imagined Emily lived in one of the detached houses at the bottom of the hill. There was something about the time I saw her on the marsh, the way she'd turned, face red and pleading, expecting me to solve all her problems with the right words, never doubting that I'd help, that made me assume she was privileged. Just like the immaculate girls who used to tease me about my clothes on the school bus – a spoilt daughter enjoying life within white walls, cream carpets, and the occasional holiday to Spain. Instead, Lorna leads me into a cramped hallway that smells of damp, with stairs running up to the first floor covered in unopened mail, phone directories and dust.

I follow Lorna through the chaos of discarded shoes and bags on the floor, turning this way and that to not unsettle piles of jackets and cardigans hooked precariously over a cold radiator.

There's a family photo on the wall; four of them standing on the prom with an ice cream. Each one looking uncomfortable in their own way. Emily stands next to her brother whose arm is slung over her shoulder with sibling affection, his dark floppy hair and bemused expression at odds with Emily's bright blondeness and serious face. Lorna stands in the middle, frozen in a grimace of something like desperation, and neither of the two children resemble the burly, dark-haired man at their side whose intense expression and grip on Lorna's arm makes me shudder. That must be Bryn, the husband who's left her. Looking closer, they are all standing poised to walk out of the photo as soon as it's taken.

Lorna doesn't notice my staring as she walks into the kitchen and announces she'll make tea. I follow her and try to ignore the overly sweet smell from a bin brimming over by the back door. She sighs to herself as she flicks the kettle on, takes two mugs from a pile of dirty dishes in the sink, swills them, waits, then fills them with boiling water. She spoons four sugars into one of the cups.

We sit at the table in the corner of the room. There's an open notebook scrawled with different names and numbers. The word 'jumper' with a question mark next to it, and PC Quinn's name, are underlined in red. I watch Lorna wring out the teabag and use it again in the second cup. We have a lot in common.

Lorna looks at me enquiringly. 'So then?'

'Catrin.'

'Right. Catrin, do you have any idea where my daughter is?'

'She's in town, isn't she?' I ask.

Lorna snorts with laughter.

'No, she's bloody not. *Been seen up town drinking?* My arse she has. Emily doesn't drink. Never has. Smokes a bit, but I count myself lucky as a mother, because for some strange reason she just doesn't like the taste of it. Doesn't pass her lips. So, when they said that I thought, *fat chance.*'

'What did the police say?'

Her laughter rings around the kitchen again as she smacks the mugs onto the table.

95

'What do you think, Catrin? Do you think they'd believe that about a fifteen-year-old girl who's run away four times already? Don't you think they took one look at this house, at us, and pinned us right there onto the page with all the other *troubled families*. They don't give a monkeys about people like us. We're not worth anything to them.'

She's right. PC Quinn didn't care about us either when we needed her help.

How many times has Lorna sat here explaining she doesn't know where her daughter is only to be told not to worry? *She'll turn up when she's ready*. Exactly what they said about my mother.

The image of her bloated body floods in. The putrid smell of ditch water. I blink away the memory.

'It takes an hour and a half to get to town and you have to know the timetable. You can't just jump on a bus anytime,' I blurt out, even though it's the same route for both villages. She probably knows, but I want to show that someone cares. 'I asked the driver, and he said he hadn't seen her.'

Lorna nods sagely.

'Exactly. Not likely, is it? She's been mad about spending time down your way lately. Why would she up and start some nonsense in town? Unless she's got a bloke.' She picks up the pen and scribbles across the pad, jagged lines that cross out PC Quinn's name. 'No. She's never had the money to go messing around in town. Someone wants us to think she's there. To stop looking for her. Any idea why?'

Lorna looks at me hard, her hand still making unconscious scribbles on the paper, tearing into the page little by little. 'Come on, tell me what you're thinking.'

'Mr Thomas. His reaction was strange.'

She shakes her head.

'Don't know the bloke but they can't be trusted down your way. No offence. It's all too tight and tidy, but only if you're one of them.'

I'm not sure how to respond. She takes my silence as agreement.

'And my boy, Roddy. He was down there looking for her. They're close, you see. Thick as thieves those two. She's always running off, then he finds her. So, what if he knows something? He wouldn't go to the trouble of rubbing his mates up the wrong way, asking to borrow the quad again, if it wasn't important.'

'Wouldn't he tell you if he knew something?' The question escapes naturally but she glares at me hard.

'You tell your family everything?'

I shake my head. Think of the letter I have to post before the end of the week. The conversation I still need to have with my father. How let down he's going to feel. I don't want the farm. Not like he does.

Lorna sighs. 'Family is complicated, isn't it?'

She leans forward.

'The living are not to be trusted, Catrin. Too many emotions. Too much baggage. The dead, now the dead you can rely on.' She drops the pen on the pad and reaches across for a pack of cigarettes, lights one and takes a long drag, staring at me again. She gives me an appraising nod.

'Someone close to you died, didn't they?'

I pick at a fingernail, not able to look up at her.

'I've got an instinct for these things.' She takes a long draw on the cigarette. 'If you've lost someone close, I think it makes you *open* to it.'

She's waiting for me to ask her more. I battle my curiosity. What about Bev's comment. *Nasty piece of work, that woman.* They can talk with all this newfound secrecy. Lorna seems honest at least. What if she can speak to the dead?

Lorna senses my hesitation.

'It's scary at first,' she says in a low voice. 'The idea that there are things we can't explain. But there are. Losing someone makes you think about it. You're cracked open.' She clenches one hand into a fist and smacks the other one on top hard. Opening the hand underneath, she smiles. 'Like an egg. And once that happens, there's space to let the questions in. Anything is possible.'

I lean towards her. I've never heard anyone talk about grief or death like this before. The most I've ever had is a consolatory pat on the arm and the words, *it takes time.*

'Who died?' I ask, my voice shaking a little at asking so directly, at finally leaving behind the euphemisms that exist only to make other people feel better – *passed away, no longer with us.* There's a feeling of teetering on the edge of something and Lorna wanting me to jump off with her.

'My father.' She reaches past me again; this time I pass her the packet of cigarettes. Her hand plants itself on top of mine for a second and she smiles, turning the pack to offer me one first. I shake my head; she snaps one out and lights up.

'Good bloke he was. Looked after me and Roddy when the boy's dad walked out. His heart wasn't up to it though. Always said he had a big heart. A kind one. Big enough to scoop us up and take us in. Roddy adored him. Then one day.' She clicks her fingers. 'Gone. No warning. Nothing. One day life is all routine and the next there's this gaping hole. *No warning,*' she mutters again before taking a deep drag in.

I know exactly what she means; that feeling. One day I was worried about my exams, wanting my mother to ask me how the revision was going. The next, she was dead. *No warning.*

I sip my tea. It's sour on my tongue.

'I'm sorry about your father,' I say. Surprised I can't manage anything else. That in the moment there isn't ever anything to say except how sorry you are, no matter how flat or pointless it seems when people say it to you.

She gives me a grim smile.

'And you?'

'My mother.' I seal my mouth around the words one by one, afraid if I say anything else a tidal rush of words and feelings will come tumbling out and I won't be able to stop them.

'Have you spoken to her since?' Her face is earnest, serious, although it takes me a few seconds to get her meaning.

'No... I... How...' I trail off.

'Didn't you ever see things afterwards? Signs everywhere?' She waits for me to confirm that I did.

I've heard about this before – white feathers floating in the breeze, people being saved from terrible accidents with a feeling of peace, but all I ever had was an empty, gaping hole and the doubt about whether my mother ever loved me at all.

I shake my head. She tuts at me as if I'm a child.

'There'll have been something. My father loved mints, Polos. Always crunching at them, drove me bloody mad.' She smiles to herself. 'That smell, I'd know it anywhere. After he died, I'd walk into the kitchen and smell it, be at work and get a waft of peppermint. He was with me. Then I'd find them in my pockets. Or a pack of them would roll out from under the seat in the car just when I was having a moment.' She chuckles at the memory. 'They don't let go quickly, see. Not when they love you.'

Her words stab at me. The comfort of them. What did I see of my mother after her death? Nothing. All I had was the marsh, the chance to feel close to her again, to what we were before she changed and locked me out of her world.

Lorna stubs out the last of her cigarette.

'Course, they do go eventually, they have to. That's when you need help to get in touch again. A conduit.'

The psychics.

Part of me wants to tap her on the arm and say, don't they just take your money, isn't it all a scam? But her face is so happy, so utterly convinced that I can't say it with confidence. What if she knows something I don't?

'Is that why you go to the psychic?' I ask, then wish I hadn't.

Her face breaks from a beatific expression to one of scorn.

'Bev been gossiping, has she? She never could believe, that one. Her little boy sending her messages from beyond and her just crying like a sop, then tittle-tattling to Dai about me.'

'Dai?' My voice is full of disbelief.

'Yes, mister logic himself. Convinced the poor woman I was messing with her. All she bloody wanted was to know her boy was alright and say sorry.'

'Sorry?'

Lorna's face snaps shut. She seems to come back to herself. She stands up and snatches the cup from my hands, swilling them both under the tap again, cleaning inside with her fingers.

'Well, we all want to say sorry for something, don't we? Don't you?'

What would I say sorry for? For not looking for her sooner or trusting the police to do their job. No. The real guilt comes from how I sulked over my homework as she left the house each day for an evening walk, too resentful at being left out to ask if she was alright, to find out what had changed. Or perhaps I should just say sorry for being born, for tying her to the farm and my father. Lorna's right, there's always something you want to apologise for.

A musical knock at the door makes us both jump. Lorna smiles for the first time, wide and genuine.

'Roddy,' she says breathlessly and her body straightens as if she's regained all the energy drained out by Emily's disappearance. She moves off to the hallway and shrieks with delight.

I feel like an intruder and look around for something to hold my attention. The open notebook pulls my gaze. Before the scribbles she'd also written Dai's name with a question mark and circled it twice.

I stand up too quickly as they come back into the kitchen. The ashtray scuttles across the table. I lunge to stop it, but Emily's brother snatches it up in his hands.

'Reflexes.' He laughs.

Lorna laughs too but her manner has changed. More careful and restrained like a child wanting to behave well. I wonder what they said in the hall and if there's any more news about Emily. Lorna ushers him in and makes a fuss so he sits down opposite me in the chair she was occupying. She puts the kettle on but this time she has all the vigour that was missing from earlier. She calls out over her shoulder.

'Catrin, this is my son Roddy…'

'We met yesterday,' he says, picking up the notebook, scanning it, then flipping it closed. 'Although we didn't get to names.'

I must have seemed so rude. His eyes search my face.

'Find anything?'

I shake my head.

'Me neither but those cockling boys gave me a good chase.'

Lorna tuts from the sink. He rolls his eyes and winks at me. I want to tell him it wasn't me, that I didn't tell anyone where he was, but I can't get my voice out.

Lorna plonks two teas on the table then goes back to make another for herself.

'You can't afford to get into trouble, lad. You've only just…'

'Alright, Mam, we don't need my life story, thanks.' He tries to sound light but there is tension in his voice.

'You'll need to go back for your cockles then,' I prompt, trying to change the subject.

He laughs.

'If you're willing to break the cockling code of honour and tell me where to find some, I will.'

Our eyes meet, we both smile and I look away.

'Catrin is worried about Emily.' Lorna leans on the counter, one hand in her mouth biting at her nails.

'We're all worried, Mam. Where's Bryn?'

'Driving up and down like a madman after the police got

that tip off. I told him, you won't find her in town. She's down on that bloody marsh somewhere. Messing about trying to make me feel guilty. Pure spite, and now we'll all be here worrying until she gets tired and turns up.'

Roddy looks at me apologetically. He doesn't seem at all surprised by Lorna's words and something about his easy presence lets me relax. I've seen worse, after all – at my own table watching my mother smash plates and my father stare at the wall. I found my mother's dead body. For some reason I want to tell him all that.

He breaks my thoughts, turning to Lorna with a gentle expression.

'What does Lisa say?'

Lorna falls silent and turns her back to us. Roddy shakes his head with sad resignation. He reaches into his pocket and pulls out a wad of ten-pound notes. There must be at least a hundred pounds there.

'Brought you this for the phone bill.'

Lorna runs forward, swipes the money, and cradles his head in her hands.

'Oh, you're a good boy, you are. I don't care what anyone else says.' She kisses his forehead and beams at both of us. 'I'll put this where Bryn won't find it.'

We listen as she clumps up the stairs. An awkward silence hangs between us.

'It's a long story but Lisa is...'

'The psychic?' I cut in wanting to spare him the explanation.

'And you're still here?' He laughs and I wonder how he can be so cheerful about this strange life when his sister is missing and his mother wants to speak to dead people. He looks at me seriously.

'Why *are* you here, Catrin?'

I shift in my chair.

'I saw Emily out on the marsh. She was upset. Crying. She asked me…' My voice trails off. She didn't actually ask me for help, but I could see in her eyes she needed it. I saw it and I left her. 'She asked me a question. I wasn't very helpful.'

'Sounds out of character.'

My head whips up at his sarcasm but he's smiling at me, playing. I look away.

'I should have stopped and tried to help her.'

'Why? You don't know her.'

'She was on the marsh. I told her it was dangerous.'

'She knows that Catrin, she's not dull. We're not complete townies you know.' His expression is mischievous.

'I didn't mean… It's dangerous out there. Easy to make a mistake.' I glance up at him; his face is serious now, listening fully, and he hasn't dismissed my warning as exaggerations or nonsense like most people do. I want to tell him more, but if I start I might never be able to stop, the words will come gushing out of me like water.

I pick at my fingernail.

He reaches over and squeezes my arm. 'Don't feel bad.'

His hand is warm on my jumper. For a second I can't focus on anything but the sensation. I slide my arm away, fold both of them over my chest. He leans back as if in apology.

'Emily was trying to get away from here. You can probably guess why. Although this isn't the half of it to be honest.' He sighs. 'She wanted me to help but I've…' He taps his fingers against the mug. 'Well, let's just say I haven't been around lately. So, I suppose that's two of us who feel guilty.'

He looks lost but I haven't got the courage to lay my own hand on his arm. I've learnt the hard way it's better to stay quiet when people are upset or risk their wrath turning on you. He carries on.

'Usually I'd know where to look, or she'd tell me where she was kipping but this time… nothing.'

'Mr Thomas is lying about the jumper.' I blurt this out. One of the only things I can say I'm certain of. 'The things he says don't make any sense. There's something odd about him…'

Roddy nods to himself, puzzling over something in his head.

'She didn't want to go down there. Mam sent her. Insisted. This Dai bloke owed her a favour or something. Emily wanted a nice little job, not shovelling horse shit. She was raging about it. Then a week later, everything was rosy. Something changed. She couldn't wait to get out of the house every morning. Don't know what it was.'

Perhaps she found a welcoming place at Dai's. Jealousy stabs at me.

'What do you know of this Dai bloke?'

'He wouldn't hurt anyone.' I'm quick to defend him, and Roddy smiles thinly.

'Friend of yours?'

'Yes, but I know him. He's…' I think about Dai's name circled twice in the notebook. 'He's kind,' I manage, which sounds feeble as it dissolves in the air between us.

Roddy shifts away from me and looks out of the window. I've lost his attention. Shown him that we only look after our own, just like he said. He seems to consider something important, then turns back again, his voice a little colder than before.

'Catrin, do you really want to help?'

The shame of his obvious disapproval washes over me. I've felt it so many times. Always disappointing people. My mother, then my dad, my teachers. Now this. I liked him and I've ruined it already. My nails dig into the palms of my hands and I long to get outside and breathe in fresh air. I nod anyway. Maybe I can still win his trust.

'Do you know what Mam is doing right now? She's on the phone to Lisa the psychic. Probably asking her to find Emily. She'll come back down with a head full of clues and no one will be able to convince her it's a pile of shit. Not even me.'

'What can I do?'

'Stay with her, she obviously likes you. And that is not normal, believe me. Do whatever you want, just keep her busy, off the phone. That was the last of my cash. Those phone lines are a pound a minute and I need Emily to have something to come back to.' He shakes his head in resignation. 'She thinks Emily running off will bring Bryn back, but if he finds out she's still ringing the psychics, he'll go ballistic. She'll do anything to get him back on side. Why do you think she was working today?'

'Take her mind off it?' I offer in shaky defence of Lorna.

He scoffs at my naivety.

'Trying to cover it up, pay the bill so Bryn won't know she got cut off again.' He picks at some fluff on his sleeve. 'Sometimes I think she wants us both to run off and leave her with Bryn. Stepdad number three. Third time lucky.' His laughter falls hollow into the room.

A door slams upstairs followed by the tap-tap of Lorna moving through the house. Roddy jumps up, face grim, just as she comes into the kitchen with a big smile.

'I'm off, Mam.' He tries to sound cheerful but there is a strangle of emotion in his voice. 'I'll leave you with Catrin. Have a chat. Wait for Bryn to get back. Let you know if I hear anything. Alright?' He pats her on the shoulder.

Lorna beams at him.

'Thanks, love, you go and see what you can do. Don't worry about me. I feel better now.'

A heaviness washes over Roddy's face. He looks at me meaningfully.

'Catrin knows all about the village, so maybe she can tell you what made Em cheer up so much.'

As the front door closes behind him Lorna whirls round to me, her face a frenzy of happiness.

'Right, so where shall we start then?' She taps the table and her eyes seem brighter, more able to focus, as if she's actually here in the room for the first time. 'Lisa told me I was right. Emily is lost, but she hasn't gone anywhere. She said I'd go on a search to find her. Said Bryn would finally find peace at home once we're all together again. So, we best get going.'

She claps her hands together a little too gleefully. 'Where shall we start?'

I pause, not sure what I'm getting myself into. It can't do any harm to take her out and show her the marsh. I still need to find out why Mr Thomas lied, and he might tell the truth if Lorna is there.

'Mr Thomas is hiding something.'

Lorna nods fervently.

107

'If something doesn't smell right you can be sure it's got a rotten bit somewhere.'

'The whole place is rotten.' The words are my mother's, bitter on my tongue, and I regret them instantly, but Lorna leans forward with a delicious smile.

'So, let's go and give it an airing.'

13

Lorna and I are parked in the passing spot of the lane that leads all the way down from the main road to the marsh road. She bombed it down here, full of theories about what's been going on. Swift lies on the backseat, confused at all the activity and quite happy to sit it out.

Lorna's animated and talking fast.

'I knew something was up. I knew it. Now it makes sense. Emily was going to Dai's. This man, Mr Thomas, saw her over the fence one day and started keeping tabs on her. Maybe he got her talking and started luring her in. He's a paedo, y'know. They're everywhere these days. He might have given her that new jumper. Not many young boys could afford that, right?'

I nod warily.

She grabs my arm, pinching the skin under my jumper so it stings.

'This man sees his chance and he tries it on with her, but she runs away. He chases her, and her jumper fell off, or she dropped it.' She rubs her mouth with the tips of her fingers, and I wonder how she doesn't remember that Emily was talking to Mr Thomas on the marsh. Coincidence or not, she wasn't running away from him.

Lorna wheels around to face me, her eyes aflame with ideas.

'So, she's gone and running. But she knows he's following her, so she leaves her jumper to throw him off then hides somewhere.' She falls silent, chewing on her already jagged nails. 'No, wait, that doesn't make any sense.' Her eyes darken. 'No, maybe he's got her, and *he* left the jumper so people would think that she'd just run off, then later he could ring and say she was in town, and we'd all stop looking for her. That's it!' She claps her hands together and the pleasure in her face at this deduction is disturbing.

'Why would he take it back and lie about it?'

Her face falls.

'Maybe you weren't meant to find it. At least not yet.' She sighs. 'Oh, I don't know. I've got to tell Bryn something, Catrin. This time it's different, he'll stick around. He can't leave me with all this going on.' Her voice is desperate, pleading as if I can find a way to make Bryn stay with her.

I want to tell her, when I said something didn't *feel* right, I meant Mr Thomas knew something, not that he'd done away with Emily and planted false evidence.

'Why don't we go and ask him?' I want to get this over with. Get back to how things were because Lorna's paranoia is catching.

She jerks up.

'Lisa mentioned an older man with a lot of anger in him.' She stares at me, doe-eyed, waiting for an answer. 'The question is,' Lorna continues, 'what did that anger make him do?' She snarls at the idea and shoves the car door open.

*

There is a rectangular strip of overgrown grass where Mr Thomas' car would usually be parked. I've seen enough of

Lorna to know this will convince her of his guilt. The older man absconded with her daughter.

Lorna takes a moment to realise his absence for herself then bounds up to the front door and hammers on it.

'Where's my daughter? Where is she?' Her hand smashes against the wood and I'm thankful there's no one to see us. My father might be right. I should think things through before jumping in.

'Catrin!' Lorna calls me with a hiss before disappearing around the side of the bungalow. I follow quickly and see her bobbing up and down at each window.

'He's gone. The bastard. Think he's done a runner?'

I sigh with relief. Lorna can go home and tell psychic Lisa she's still searching for the angry man, although judging by the photo I saw it could quite as easily be Bryn. Roddy can take care of his own mother and I can look for Emily on my own. Apologise for not helping her the first time.

'Come here!' Lorna has gone round the back of the house. She has her arm thrust through a window next to the back door, reaching for the door handle inside.

Don't open. Please don't open.

It clicks and the door swings inside. She looks at me, her eyes alight with glee.

'Go on then. I'll stand watch at the front.'

It's my own fault. I didn't stop to think and now the mother of a missing girl wants me to break into my old schoolteacher's house. Maureen will have a field day if this ever gets out.

I stalk past Lorna and shove the door open.

There's no going back once I set foot inside. I pause in the doorway. My heart is racing. What if he comes back, what will he say? But he had no right to take the jumper then tell the police it didn't exist. I turn to Lorna, more sure of myself.

'If he comes back, keep him talking at the front door and pick me up on the marsh road. I can run down through the fields if I hear him.'

Lorna nods feverishly. I stop.

'What if I can't find the jumper?'

She considers my question for a second then rubs her chin, nodding wildly to herself.

'Find some evidence.'

The way she says the last word makes me shiver. What could a man like him be hiding?

I take a deep breath and walk into the darkness.

*

The bungalow is dimly lit as if Mr Thomas doesn't want to look fully at his own life. Whenever I see him on the marsh, he has this constant look of desperation about him as if he's searching for something he's never going to find, and he knows it. Anguish. That's the word.

Whenever he catches sight of me, his face twists into this strange expression. Something between disgust and desperation – as if I'm turning a sharp knife in his heart.

I creep through the back hall, aware of the rapid thudding of my pulse. I'm not sure if I'm expecting to find Emily's lifeless body stuffed under the bed in one of the rooms, or if it's just the heavy guilt of being here. If I get caught my father will kill me. It's one thing to run onto someone's land in an emergency but quite another to break into a neighbour's house. Even one as disliked as Mr Thomas.

A floorboard creaks underfoot, and I stop. What if he's here? Behind one of the doors, listening and waiting to jump out at me.

Come on, Catrin.

The lounge is inoffensive and there is nothing amiss, red plush settees with slightly mismatched cushions and a walnut coffee table. No television, just a hi-fi player and a stack of cassettes on the sideboard.

I wander through the house like a ghost.

The bedroom is sparse; a green bedspread smoothed carefully over the wooden frame; every pillow in its place – a man of order. There are packets of open pills on the bedside table and a pillbox with the days of the week marked out. I shake it and it rattles.

A creeping sensation crawls across my back.

There's someone in the room behind me. I wheel around to face the door but there's no one there.

Breathe, Catrin.

'There's no one here,' I whisper out loud in a bid to calm myself, but the tinny sound of my voice in this strange space is disturbing. My hands itch with sweat and I hurry through the last door in the dark corridor.

I take a sharp breath in.

There is one huge, floor-to-ceiling panoramic window filling almost the entire space where the wall facing the estuary should be. That's why he's clearing the trees out of his garden. He has a near perfect view from here.

The two sides of the estuary are visible – from our village

on the east right out to the far point of the western lighthouse. The window is so wide you can see the way the light arcs into the grey horizon between tide and sky. I never knew it was possible to see the whole marsh from one of the houses.

The estuary looks like a beautiful painting.

Timeless.

I take a step closer, half expecting to see my mother out there with her camera slung over her shoulder.

A miniature version of our marshland plays out in front of me. The reeds sway hypnotically if I stare at them long enough. Tiny black dots turn into birds; little smudges of grey and brown are the marsh ponies. The light illuminates ditches filled with water like metallic circles and the sun glints silver off the bonnet of the car wreck.

I imagine the mini version of myself walking the flats. How many times has he seen me out there? Watched me wandering for hours. Is that why he marched down to tell Emily about the danger of the tide that day? With a view like this you'd notice that bright purple jumper on the ground.

I finger the heavy wooden desk set to the side of the window, skirting over papers but unable to take my eyes off the view. A flock of starlings flash across the sky. My mother would have loved this view as much as I do.

I pull my eyes away from the marsh and down to the papers in front of me; academic words loom out of what must be essays or exam papers about Shakespeare and sonnets – his passion for poetry hasn't changed even if he has. The wood creaks as I pull the top drawer open.

There are only shadows. The drawer is full of discarded pens and paper clips.

I pull at the second one – notebooks and blank paper.

Then I crouch down to open the last drawer. The faint scent of fresh washing powder wafts towards me. I start back – the purple jumper is curled into the drawer like a sleeping cat.

My hands are heavy and clumsy as I reach down to touch the material. It shakes in my grip and gives off the same pungent flowery scent as before, mixed with the must of dried marsh water.

PC Quinn's pitying words come back to me: *The anniversary must be difficult*. I run my fingers all around the soft fabric until I touch the nylon of a label, pulling the material through my hands. I already know what I'm going to see but when my fingers trace the neat handwriting and the heart above the 'I', relief floods through me.

I should take the jumper and shove it in PC Quinn's face, but that's not the solution. They need to find it here. They need to know he hid it from them then lied. I stuff the jumper back in the drawer and slam it shut.

The crunch of tyres on the drive. A car door slams.

I step carefully back out of the room and hope Lorna can manage her part.

Mr Thomas' gruff voice thunders out, questioning her. Lorna is high pitched in return but friendly. I tread soundlessly towards the back door and pause just in time to hear Mr Thomas change his tone back to that of the polite teacher and assure Lorna that he wasn't arguing with her daughter that day on the marsh. *Catrin must have been mistaken. A troubled girl. So sad what happened. Been having problems with the people down here as a matter of fact. Pressure to sell land. Threats.*

I step out of the back door, click the latch closed as quietly as I can, and run.

14

Lorna and I sit in her car, an air of unease settling between us. Swift, glad to see me again even though it's only been half an hour, has her nose over the back of the passenger seat nuzzling into my hair. The marsh draws down the last of the afternoon light; a few final rays cast themselves over the yellowing grasses. Sheep cover the road in front of us, picking over the tarmac, chewing and eyeing the car.

Lorna and I are silent. Neither of us can fit the pieces together.

'Why didn't you just pick it up, Catrin. I don't understand.' Her mouth is tight, and she taps the ash of a smoking cigarette out the window.

'We need the police to find it. To know he was lying...' My voice trails off. It made sense to leave it there. Mr Thomas isn't going to tell the truth off his own back.

Lorna gives an irritated sigh.

'We can't tell the police we broke in. Roddy's just got out and I don't want to go making more trouble for him.' She taps her fingers on the steering wheel. 'But we have to tell them something, give them a reason to go and search his house.' She inhales a long drag. 'You said he used to be a teacher. I could tell them Emily said he was helping her with homework. She was going there to visit him.'

'They'll ask you why you didn't tell them before.'

The gloomy silence resumes between us. A crow skirts close to the windscreen on its way home to roost.

'Did he say where he'd been?'

'Said he was taking legal advice. Reckoned he's had trouble from your lot down here about some land. Said you might be part of it. *Harassment* was the word he used. Bloody nerve. He's a good liar too. I would have believed him if I didn't know you.' She stabs the cigarette out on the dashboard.

The sheep startle and herd together, running towards the village. Black and white shapes dart in between them, and a low whistle trills out from further up the road. Swift swivels her ears towards them. The Jones boys have left their flock out late this year. My father won't approve. Not with the high tides forecast. He'll see it as putting the herd in danger for a few more weeks of fattening up. Running the farm into the ground for profit, he'll say.

'We need the police to find the jumper.' Lorna thumps the steering wheel. 'What's Bryn going to say about this? Police thinking she's done a runner and that man stood there lying about it.' She bites her nails. 'It's different now. It hasn't happened like this before. Something's wrong, I can feel it. They have to do their job.' She looks at me for help.

I should have taken the jumper when I had the chance. If someone else had found it the police would be in no doubt he was lying, but because it was me PC Quinn can dismiss it.

A troubled girl.

That's what she'd called me when I insisted they look for my mother. When I was making a fuss. Without the right accent or nice clothes, I was easy to dismiss.

I glance out of the window at the tiny dots the sheep have

become in the distance and throw my hand up to scratch Swift's neck. Lorna smiles grimly.

'Dai Horses owes me a favour. Let's go see if he can sort this out.'

I can't imagine Dai owing anyone anything, but Lorna skids the car back in the gritty lay-by and pulls us sharply back onto the marsh road.

*

I've never seen Dai look uncomfortable before. He's the person who is always in control, sorting things out, reassuring us; one warning look from him and people fall silent.

To see him in front of Lorna, he's a different man. Face grey and taut. He closes the stable door, holding it tight with one hand. The bay cob looms behind us as we crowd around the buckets of water and salt lick. Dai talks in a low voice, the one he uses to call a disobedient dog into line.

'I can't do what you're asking me, Lorna. You know that.'

Lorna snorts.

'I'm telling you, Dai. This man, we know nothing about him, do we? He's not local. Well, he's got my daughter's jumper and God knows what else has gone on. She's not up town; that's nonsense. We need the police to know.'

Dai shoots me a dark look. Of course, it's my fault. He's conveniently forgotten he brought Emily here. Changed things. Not me.

'And how are you going to explain how you know that, Lorna? If you tell them you broke in, it'll compromise whatever it is you saw. You're going to get yourself into trouble, gal.'

'That's why *you* need to tell them you saw Emily going over there after she'd finished with your horses. Tell them she was carrying something as if she was going to give it to him. Going over the fence. Wearing make-up. You were worried he's been taking advantage but didn't want to gossip... whatever. Just tell them you saw her on his land. You think she knew him. They'll take it from there. Please, Dai.'

He looks away. 'I can't do that, Lorna.'

'Why the bloody hell not?'

We all shoot a furtive look at the gate; no one wants to upset Bev. Dai sighs and puts both hands on the stable door, looking straight out into the yard.

'Because I've already told them what I know. I don't want them coming back, upsetting Bev. It's taken me days to calm her down. The sight of their uniforms, all those questions... reminds her of Rhys. She's delicate, Lorna.'

'She's half-cut, Dai. Let's not rose-tint what's going on here.'

I open my mouth to say Bev can't be drinking in her condition, but Lorna goes in for the attack.

'I *trusted* you with my daughter.'

Silence falls between them. Dai shakes his head.

'I didn't want her here and you knew that. And I don't want any trouble now.' His voice is low and full of warning.

'And what did you tell the police *exactly*.' Lorna's question is loaded. There's something unspoken between them like that moment just before a thunderstorm when the air is thick with electricity.

'I told them the truth. I let her help me out as a favour to her mother. She came with a long face and wasn't any use with the horses. Started turning up late and leaving early. Head like

119

a sieve. The most I could do was to get her walking Charlie-horse around the top field.'

'And…' Lorna is studying Dai's face hard.

'One morning she didn't turn up. Thought it was typical, just like her mam, does what she wants.' Dai directs the last part at Lorna, but she doesn't flinch.

'Didn't tell them you owed me?' She smirks at him, daring him to react.

Dai's hands grip the door tighter, his knuckles white, but he stays silent for a moment. When he looks up again, I know him well enough to see this is going to be the last word he says about it.

'What difference does it make, Lorna? Let her cool off and come back to you when she's ready. Nothing more than that. Bev liked having her around…'

'I trusted you and Bev with her. Thought it would cheer Emily up. She's been crying for months about the fact Bryn has left us. Why do you think I wanted her down here in the first place?'

'Thought you needed the cash.'

'But that's not it though, Dai, is it?' Lorna charges on, her eyes alight and voice rising. 'You didn't tell them because you were afraid. Worried they'd ask about the details. Why would you let a girl who doesn't know a horse's head from its arse hang around? That's it isn't it?'

Dai opens the stable door and nods at Lorna to leave. She shakes her head and titters.

'Did Bev talk to the police? You know how she likes to chat once she's had a few.'

Dai rounds on her, bringing his face close to hers.

I reach out, laying my hand on his shoulder. His back is rigid with tension.

'Leave her out of it, Lorna. She's suffered enough.'

She leans towards him.

'I *know*. Remember.'

Dai stares at her hard then whacks the door open with the palm of his hand.

'I'll make the call, anonymously, but I don't ever want to see you or yours in my yard again.' He stalks out without a backwards glance, the stable door bouncing against its frame.

The colt looks up nonchalantly. There's a clatter of metal in the yard. Swift barks and I nip out to see what's wrong.

Bev is kneeling on the concrete trying to catch hold of one of the metal buckets that has rolled out of reach. The hose is loose and spraying water everywhere like an angry snake. Bev is soaked but she doesn't seem to notice.

'Here again? Can't take the hint?' She reaches further and topples forwards.

I rush over to help her up. Lorna comes out of the stable.

'Up to your old tricks, eh?'

Bev grabs hold of my arm and heaves herself up off the floor. Her cheeks are red and the loose smock she's wearing is sopping with water.

'Thought we wouldn't see the likes of you again,' she snarls at Lorna.

'If you hadn't lost my daughter, I wouldn't have set foot in this shithole.' Lorna moves forwards like a horse straining at the bit.

'Perhaps if you'd been a bit nicer to her, she wouldn't have run. *Again*. Girl needs a decent mother.'

Lorna flinches.

'Any idea where she is?'

Bev straightens herself up and brushes down her clothes.

'Heard she was up town drinking her sorrows away. Might take a while.'

'You'd know a lot about that, but my Emily doesn't touch the stuff.'

'Did you ever see her talking to Mr Thomas?' I jump in, wanting to spare Bev more of Lorna's jibes. She doesn't deserve it.

She makes a face at me.

'Brought your own private detective, did you?'

'At least she's helping.'

Bev grabs the bucket from the floor, scraping it along the ground before thrusting it under the running tap.

'Is that what you call it? Bringing the police down here. Asking questions.'

'He's got her jumper,' Lorna whispers.

Bev stares at us both, thinks for a few seconds, then says, 'As a matter of fact, I did see her talk to that man. He used to come up close to the fence looking for Catrin. He's got a thing for you. We all know that.'

I open my mouth in protest. I've never spoken to him through the fence and never would either.

Bev is talking fast now. 'She was up there two or three times a day. Trying to keep up the same habits as this one.' She nods at me. 'So, if she got mixed up with him and got more than she bargained for, then ran off to town in a fright, you've only got yourself to blame, Catrin.'

She bends to pick up the bucket and I rush forward to take it from her.

'Careful, you shouldn't lift in your condition, Bev.'

She slams me away from her, breath heavy with gin. I stumble back and knock into Swift.

Dai appears, hurrying back down from the house.

'Right. That's done. Now off with you both.'

I look at him, hurt that my welcome here has disappeared, but he gazes at the buckets.

'What are you doing, love?' he says quietly to Bev, picking up the bucket and hauling it up the path. 'I don't expect to see anyone in this bloody yard when I get back. Got work to do,' he shouts over his shoulder.

'If you've come sniffing around for money, there's no more. Not for you,' Bev sneers at Lorna and shuffles back towards the house, wringing the water from her dress.

Lorna stares after her.

'Maybe Bev's right.' She turns back to me, her face struck with something like shock. 'Emily had a run in with the old bloke and went up town. I should tell Bryn.'

'But you said she...'

'Doesn't matter,' Lorna snaps at me. 'Dai's made the phone call. You can go home. Police will do the rest.' She turns and watches Bev let herself into the farmhouse.

'The police don't care... you said so.' My voice is petulant.

'If there really is a jumper they'll find it.'

I kick at the remaining buckets, sending them scattering and rolling around the yard with a clang. Swift jumps up with a bark.

'Let's go.' I march out of the yard, not looking back for Lorna.

15

I give Mr Thomas' front door a short sharp rap. It's hard not to hammer on it, take out all the frustration that has built up inside me. He lied. But worse: he lied about me to PC Quinn. Gave her more reasons to put me in the category of unreliable witness and say my mother's death was a terrible accident they couldn't have done anything about. Having her scorn me for a second time burns a deep rage in my stomach.

Mr Thomas inches open the door, his face furtive and tired. After taking a long look at me he blinks and invites me in.

'Catrin, I shouldn't... Oh, come in then. Bring the dog, it's a cold day.'

Swift follows me through the hallway and into the lounge. Can Mr Thomas guess that I've been here already? That I know Emily's jumper is sitting in his desk drawer? He seems oblivious – a completely different man, fussing around with the cushions. His face is pinked where a moment ago it was grey and drawn.

He gestures for me to sit on the sofa and takes his place opposite on the armchair, patting at Swift with a half-smile as she walks past. I click my fingers and summon her to my side where she leans into my legs and her warm weight calms my thoughts.

'Catrin, I feel as if we know each other. That sounds silly, doesn't it?' He is all politeness as if he's warming up and returning to the role of teacher. Only I don't want to go back to class.

'I remember you from school of course, you never much liked my lessons.' He pauses as if waiting for me to protest. When I don't, he gives a little shrug. 'You were clever but couldn't apply yourself, that was the trouble. Sad too.' He pauses and rubs his hands together. 'I thought I could talk to you at school at least.' He clears his throat. 'I wanted you to know that someone was thinking about you. I hope you knew that.'

Bev's comment creeps in. *He's got a thing for you.* Then the memory of his hushed voice in the corridor as he pulled me aside to offer his condolences. The time he sought me out in the art room, the only place I felt happy, and asked if I needed anything. The way he peered over my shoulder at my sketches as if he had a right to look. Twisting his hands over and over as he stood there, insisting he would do anything to help. I was relieved when he disappeared. Replaced one day by another teacher, one who didn't care quite as much. I never thought about him again until the first time I saw him out walking on the marsh. Maureen said he'd already been here for months, keeping to himself, thought he was too good for the likes of us.

'Why did you lie about me?' My voice shakes slightly.

He looks at the palms of his hands, turns them over, examines one finger closely then looks up at me again.

'It was survival instinct, I suppose. I am sorry about that.'

His apology catches me off guard. I'd expected him to be angry like the other day, or at least deny it. Instead, he seems perfectly glad that I came. Happy to talk. The rage in me deflates like a balloon.

'Survival from what?'

He smiles thinly.

'People. Gossip. Nuisance.' He wipes at the side of his mouth, the tremble of his hand at odds with his calm voice.

'PC Quinn thinks I made it up. Emily could be in danger because of you.'

He stands up and paces over to the window, lifting the net curtain slightly then brushing it back into place.

'I'm quite sure that Emily is alright.'

'Do you know where she is?'

He shakes his head at me with a rueful smile and I'm transported back to the classroom. *Wrong answer, Catrin, try again.* Except we're not in his classroom anymore.

'Do you?'

'I know she's not in any danger.'

'How do I know you're not lying?'

He holds his hands up.

'That's fair. What can I tell you to show you I'm not the person in the wrong here?' He ponders this question for a moment.

I shuffle in my seat. It's too much like a game.

Finally, he speaks.

'I did know Emily. She liked to walk the old horse over the field, and she was a lot friendlier than you. She didn't hide when she saw me for a start.' He gives a sad laugh.

Oh God. I never knew he could see me.

All the times I've avoided him, turned my back, headed back down to the barn with Charlie-horse if I caught sight of him in his fields.

He notices my embarrassment and laughs.

'No, don't feel bad. I'd stay away from me too. Sometimes I wish I could.' He sighs, attention wandering, and stares into the distance for a moment.

I stand up.

'What did she say, when you talked to her?'

'She's a chatty little thing. Never stopped talking really. I think I might have been the first person to ever really listen to her.'

I imagine him encouraging her to express herself like he did with us in class. The way he always wanted to know our hopes and dreams – to trust in him as if he was different to other adults.

'Do you know where she is?'

He mulls my question over, then stands.

'If she wanted to be found, I'm sure she would be.' He walks towards the kitchen. I stand open mouthed as he goes. As a teacher he was always eccentric but this talking in riddles is ridiculous. I charge after him.

In the kitchen he pulls down two mugs from the rack and places them on the side.

'Now, I was rather hoping to talk to you about that letter.' His tone is chiding. 'As I was once your teacher, I hope you'll heed my advice. You should take the opportunity. It's not as if there are many of those about down here.' He pauses what he's doing and thinks to himself for a second. 'What's the alternative? Scraping around the farm like your father? Wasting your talent.'

'That's nothing to do with you,' I mumble.

He turns to me and smiles as if remembering something from long ago.

'I'm sorry, I overstepped. Sometimes you remind me of her, it's almost too uncanny. Takes me by surprise.'

'Who?'

He waves me away and carries on with the task of making tea. His hand trembles as he tries to pour boiling water into the cups, it sloshes and spills over the sides. He smacks the kettle down with a sigh.

'I suffer with my nerves,' he offers by way of apology.

I don't care about his ailments. What I came here to find out was what really happened with Emily.

'Why were you arguing with Emily?' I ask.

He raises his eyebrows. 'I'm not going to betray her confidence. Or make any further trouble for myself.'

'You'll have to tell the truth when the police arrive.'

He turns to me with a slow smile and leans back on the counter.

'I'll tell them what I've told you. I have nothing else to add.'

'That is a lie.' I say it through gritted teeth.

'No.' He smiles at me. 'It's a question of language.' He seems almost amused at his own cleverness. 'And I would suggest you leave before someone sees you here. I've been having terrible trouble with the locals.' He says the last part with mock indignance.

I exhale slowly. Losing my temper isn't going to help. Perhaps if I appeal to his better nature. The schoolteacher's responsibility.

'If you saw her that morning walking Charlie-horse, you may have been the last person to see her.'

'I doubt that.'

'Why?'

'She was going to meet someone.'

'In town?' I think of the phone message. Could she really be there?

'No. Somewhere on the marsh. Again. That's why I was so cross the first time.' He sighs. 'She shouldn't have been going out there. The tide is very dangerous, you can get caught out in a flash.'

'You lied about the jumper.'

'I told you. I thought it was more of that nonsense about selling my land. Those thugs won't take no for an answer.'

There is a sharp rap at the door. He raises his eyebrows at me.

'Am I to assume that is the police, Catrin?'

I nod. He looks away and shakes his head.

'Your mother was right, they're all out to get you here in the end.' He laughs to himself and wipes at the counter with a cloth.

I stare at him, mouth open. He catches sight of my expression and a dawning realisation of what he said turns his face pale.

'Excuse me, I have to get the door.'

'You knew my mother?'

He dashes past me into the hall, gabbling.

'Yes, parents' evenings and what not.'

Swift bounds out of the lounge at the sound of our activity. He throws the door open and there is PC Quinn and her partner. Her face is grim.

'I'm sorry to bother you again so soon, Mr Thomas. We've had a call and need to ask you a few more questions about Emily Davies. Is that okay?'

He nods enthusiastically.

'Of course, come in please, officers, but I don't know what I can add. I certainly haven't had any unexpected visitors. Except for this one.'

PC Quinn walks down the hall and catches sight of Swift and me hovering in the lounge doorway.

'Catrin? What are you doing here?'

I open my mouth and nothing comes out. Mr Thomas rushes back up the hall with his well-practised smile and eloquent voice.

'She just popped in to ask about Emily. She's still looking on the marsh for her and is *very concerned*, aren't you, Catrin?'

All I can do is nod. PC Quinn eyes me harshly. She stops herself from saying what she thinks, takes a deep breath.

'It's our job to be concerned or not about Emily based on the information we have and whether we deem it reliable.' She emphasises the last word with a raise of her eyebrow. 'Let us handle it, please.'

'The way you handled finding my mother?' I spit the words at her.

'I'm sure your father wants you back home. It's late.' Her voice is steel but her expression kind.

'Best not tell him what you've been up to.' Mr Thomas exchanges a look with PC Quinn. 'She didn't mean any harm.'

I rush out of the front door just as her partner lumbers in. I hear the last strains of Mr Thomas chatting away to PC Quinn.

'Just out of curiosity, was the caller male or female? I'm having a spot of bother with someone. Land issues. People are so very sensitive about what you should do with it down here, you'd think it was gold.'

'Male,' she replies. 'But if you have any problems with anyone harassing you, male or female, just let us know.'

I rush down the porch steps, propelled by shame, grab Swift by the scruff and herd her hurriedly between my legs, racing to get as far away from these people as I can.

*

In the semi-darkness of the marsh road, I finally stop to catch my breath. Gnats skim past my face. There's the familiar shuffle of birds settling to roost, and behind that the hush of the landscape. I breathe it all in for a minute, let the cool air touch my neck and face; the unseen expanse in the darkness calms my racing thoughts. Two streetlights throw halfhearted pools of light, one at the turning to the lane and the other at the start of the village to the east – the rest is darkness.

Swift and I walk slowly back home through the shadows. She noses at my hand. I reach down and stroke her.

'Sorry, girl,' I mumble. She deserves better.

Mr Thomas knew my mother. *Parents' evenings and what not?* That can't be true. There was only one, and that comment about everyone being out to get you, it's not the kind of thing my mother would have said offhand. She was always guarded, protecting herself.

I take my time walking home, wandering over and across the flats in aimless zigzags, making the most of the darkness to guess what the shadow shapes are. A resting pony. A thicket of brambles. My mother and I used to play this game, and the comfort of her imagined presence slows my steps and my breathing.

If I try hard enough, I can bring her back. Imagine a rustle in the dark is her impatient form returning from further out on the flats, full of satisfaction at having caught the last photo before the light went. How I'd know she was close by, then a gloved hand would reach out and rub my shoulder and she'd whisper, *good girl,* because I'd waited exactly where she'd told me to no matter how long it took, then, *let's go and put the kettle on,* as she planted a kiss on top of my head. Somehow even in the darkness, she always knew exactly where I was, and I never felt afraid.

Then, later, when everything changed, she walked out there alone. I would sneak out, stubborn as gorse, following her silently until she'd sigh and snap, *Catrin, go home before I get cross.* Then it was up to me to find my way back to the farmhouse in the dark, chest clenched with fear and legs scurrying. It was those nights that taught me how to be alone with myself.

*

My father is waiting in the kitchen when Swift and I arrive. Still dressed for the fields; I sometimes think he sleeps in those clothes. Swift rushes past me to the warmth of the fire. Another stab of guilt. My father's cap lies on the table, the only sign that he has finished for the day. A glass sits next to it; not his usual tea, but a dark shot of whiskey. I haven't seen him drink for a long time. Emily's disappearance is affecting us all.

We never speak about my mother, but Mr Thomas' strange words make me bold.

'Did Mum have friends in the village?'

The question hangs in the air. He takes a sip of his drink.

'None that she told me about.'

Something heavy lingers between us. My father looks up with tired eyes, showing him up for the old man that he is. He nods at the bottle on the table.

'More in the pot.' It's a feeble attempt at a joke but I'm tired of all this talking in riddles, all these concealed things. He leans forward and shakes the bottle at me. I turn my mouth down in distaste and he shrugs and pours himself another glass.

There have been times when I've felt sorry for him, aware of his loss. Then I think about the silences I've endured, the questions that remain unanswered, the fact my mother's name is never spoken in this house. The cruelty of it, of not even having the comfort of remembering her with someone, and my heart snaps shut with contempt.

He's watchful as I pass behind the table, spark the stove into life and warm up lunchtime's cold tea, pouring myself a mug and heaping in two sugars. I open the breadbin, and butter the last sorry crust. When he thinks I've settled he begins.

'Dai phoned.'

'Something stopping him sleeping?' My voice is cold.

My father is used to it. He shrugs and I can see he's tired of it all too.

'The police didn't find anything at Mr Thomas' house. Clean as a whistle, he said.' He braces for my reaction. 'Said it's best to leave it all alone.'

'Well, if Dai says so.'

Swift chooses that moment to amble back in from the fire, breaking the tension. My father reaches down to her as she shuffles towards her food bowl. I throw the buttered bread in, and she gulps it down.

Clean as a whistle. And Dai knows already. How long was I out wandering on the flats? I glance at the clock, it's gone eleven.

Hours.

It's like an addiction, being out there. Maybe I'm no better than Lorna and her psychics.

I slump down opposite my father. My hands itch for my sketchbook, something to keep my mind busy. I could tell him now. Come straight out with it and say the college has accepted me, but I can't find the words, not on top of all this.

My father sips his whiskey. His mouth curls up at every taste and I'm grateful it's so unfamiliar to him, that he never turned to the bottle after Mum died, not like Bev. I study the solemnity of his face. He used to laugh but I can't even remember what that sounds like. He slugs back the last drop.

'You were in that man's house? You saw the jumper?'

I nod.

'That changes things.' There's no reproach. No lecture on trespassing or what the neighbours will say. He rolls his neck to one side and looks at the ceiling.

I stare at him. He doesn't usually sit still for this long. I edge towards another question – the fact that there might be something about my mother that I didn't know. I thought she told me everything.

'He said something about Mum, as if he'd known her.'

'I don't want you talking to him.' He smacks the glass down on the table. Pushes himself upright in the chair.

'Were they friends?'

'Your mother was a mystery to all of us, Catrin.' It's a practised line. One I've heard a lot over these last three years, but this time his voice breaks a little as he says it.

With a few strides he's out of the kitchen and the front door slams. We have that in common, the desire to be outside when things get tough. Me in the wildness of the estuary and him comforted by things that can be planted, herded, or harvested.

I take out my dog-eared sketchbook and lay it on the table, glad of some peace. With the tip of the pencil, I sketch soft lines across the paper. The estuary slowly comes to life as I shade in the low clouds under an evening sky. Everything falling into shadows, mere suggestions of the ponies and sheep amongst spindly reeds. I draw the outline of two figures standing close and looking out at the flats. A quick flick of the pencil and my mother has her camera in her hands.

We used to tell each other everything, didn't we?

My father made us take a torch if we ever went out late; my mother gripping it solemnly, suppressing a giggle as we walked arm in arm down the drive. As soon as we were out of sight, she would click it off with a conspiratorial smile and the world around us would fall into darkness. *Better like this*, she'd say. The next morning we'd walk down and compare what had been a looming monster from the night before, to the harmless tree stump it had now become. She seemed to love the monsters more than whatever peace the daylight could bring.

I look at my work for a moment, at the smaller figure by her side, then close the book. This place makes no sense to me anymore. I stand up and whistle to Swift.

'Time for bed, girl,' I say, and hope I'll be rid of the monsters in my mind by morning.

16

The early morning air is fresh on my face. Small droplets of rain fall intermittently. Swift noses at the trestle tables outside Maureen's shop, hoping for a scrap of something tasty, but she's out of luck – two rows of round pumpkins take up all the space. A handwritten sign reads, *local produce*. I wonder which farm has given in to the fancies of Halloween to make ends meet.

I couldn't sleep last night, kept waking with nightmares of Emily and my mother, one or the other calling out for me in muffled screams, their fingers clawing at mud and reeds, begging me to hurry, warning it was nearly too late.

When I woke for the third time, tangled in sheets and gasping in panic, the idea came to me. Why not use the worst of this place to get to the bottom of things? Maureen is the one who loves to deliver all the juicy gossip. Why not let her do just that?

Maureen is preening herself, holding a compact mirror and staring at her reflection. She touches up her coral lipstick, pouts, then lifts her eyes as the door chimes.

'It's not Tuesday, so this must be a social call.' She snaps the compact shut and places it on the table. 'And to what do I owe this very early pleasure?' She looks at her watch to make a point.

'What do you know about Mr Thomas?'

'Not a fan of pleasantries, are you?' She turns away from me haughtily and hefts up a stack of newspapers tied with plastic. She gives me a sharp look then begins to slowly sort the papers into piles.

I sigh. 'Sorry. I didn't sleep well.'

Her eyebrows raise for a second at the apology, mouth twitches into a thinner line. But she's still cross at me. She places one paper on top of another. I try again.

'All of this is… with Emily Davies…' I search for the right words, trying to play Maureen at her own game, but where has being guarded really ever got me? Perhaps my mother was wrong about that. I might as well tell her the truth. 'It's getting to me. I thought you might be able to help.'

Her eyes snap up in surprise. She puts her hands on her hips.

'You alright?'

My throat chokes up. Maureen has never asked me that. Not like she meant it.

'Nightmares,' I mumble, taking a deep breath. 'I don't want the same thing to happen to Emily…' I stop myself. Any further and I might crack.

'Now then.' She reaches over the counter and pats my arm. 'You know what they say, lightning doesn't strike twice. One terrible accident is enough. The girl will turn up.'

'It's Mr Thomas.' Now I have her full attention. 'He's been saying funny things.'

'Like what?' She can't hide the disapproval in her voice; no one likes him down here. He hasn't done himself any favours by keeping to himself.

'Like he knew my mother.' I look up at her hopefully.

137

Surely, if there's something to say Maureen won't be able to resist.

Instead, she bites her lip and picks up a newspaper, carefully stacking it on top of another one, smoothing down the creases.

'Have you told your dad?'

I nod.

'What did he say?' She moves the pile of papers to one side, starts sorting another.

'Not a lot. That she was a mystery to him.'

Maureen scoffs at that.

'Men,' she whispers under her breath.

She fixes me with a stern look. 'Don't let Mr Thomas play silly buggers with you. He's an odd one. Best give him a wide berth.' She chocks the papers into a clean stack. The inner door swings open and her daughter Jade bounds in, dressed in her school uniform.

'I'm off, Mam.' She rushes over to give Maureen a kiss on the cheek.

'If you miss the bus, you'll have to wait 'til lunchtime. I'm not closing shop because you were too busy watching breakfast telly.' Maureen's tone is chiding but she smooths Jade's hair as she speaks.

'He won't go without me.' Jade wriggles free, grabs a chocolate bar with a grin and heads out of the door, giving a small wave as she goes.

The bell trills out.

'Who does she think she is, the bloody Queen?' Maureen chuckles.

'Mr Thomas. Was he friends with my mother?'

Her attention turns back to me. 'What really matters is what you do with *your* life, Catrin. Your mother's gone. You're the only one with a future.'

The comment stings even if she means well. So much for Maureen loving to gossip.

The doorbell chimes again and Bev stumbles in, looking bright.

'Morning Mau, usual please,' she says, beaming at me as if the other day's events had never happened.

'Someone's looking pleased with themselves,' Maureen exclaims, relieved to have someone else to play with, someone more entertaining.

'We've got a lot to celebrate.' Bev leaves the sentence hanging, waiting for Maureen to catch on.

'Sold another mare, have you?' Maureen asks over her shoulder as she takes down the three bottles of gin that form part of Bev's order every week.

'No. Nothing like that.'

Maureen sighs as if she's humouring a child.

'Then what is it? Catrin's dying to know.' She rolls her eyes at me.

'Catrin already knows.' Bev smiles, pleased to be able to beat Maureen at her own game for once.

It works. Maureen can't hold back the scowl that crawls across her face.

'Spit it out then, haven't got all day.'

'We're having a baby.' Bev bursts into happy laughter, looking from Maureen to me and back, grinning all the while.

Maureen's mouth drops open. She glances at me to see if Bev is pulling her leg.

'But...' Maureen stutters over her words. 'Love, aren't you,

you know, past all that?' Her voice is softer; she wouldn't hurt Bev, not with that particular knife, not after what happened to Rhys.

Bev shrugs.

'I thought so too, then I was sick and now I know why. These things happen sometimes out of the blue. Like in the magazines. A miracle,' she says with such finality that there is no room for questions.

Maureen nods slowly and looks Bev up and down.

'Is that right? You look well on it, love.' She stares at the bags she's just packed. 'I'll take these out though, you won't be wanting them anymore, will you?' She studies Bev's face carefully as she reaches into the bag and takes out the first bottle of gin.

Bev's jaw clenches for a second, then she smiles.

'I hadn't thought of that, you're right. Get rid of them, all of them!' Her voice has a hysterical note to it.

I stare at her stomach and Maureen catches me looking.

'How many weeks then?'

'Oh, it's still early days. We're only telling close friends. What would you think about being Godmother?'

Maureen lifts up the countertop with a grin, slips through, and hugs Bev tight. Bev is caught off guard at first, her face a picture of surprise, then she wraps her arms around Maureen, tipping her from side to side and giggling. I've never seen Bev so happy.

Maureen straightens up and grasps Bev's hands.

'Now, you look after yourself and this one. Keep yourself straight.'

Bev's smile slips for a second.

'Course I will. I know my Rhys sent this baby to me. It's a sign. He wants us to be happy again.'

Maureen crosses back to the other side of the counter, her eyes stern on Bev.

'Make sure you see the doctor then, want to make sure you're taking advice from the right people.'

Bev ignores her and turns to me.

'I was telling Catrin that now we'll have someone to leave the farm to, she won't have to worry about us anymore. Better start sorting her own affairs out.'

The words hit hard, but I smile back at her. After losing Rhys they deserve some happiness. I hope the gin stays behind the counter. Bev catches my glance at the bottles and changes the subject.

'I heard Mr Thomas was questioned again. Strange that. What happened to the jumper you found?'

'I don't know.' It's true and the safest thing to admit.

Bev tuts.

'Emily told me she had a boyfriend. An older bloke. Giddy she was.' She stares at Maureen, enjoying their new camaraderie. 'I never imagined it could be him, but it's obvious now, isn't it?'

'Police don't seem to think so.' Maureen yawns.

'Well, Catrin found that jumper, he took it, then she saw it in his house and now it's gone. No one can say why, but it must have been him – the boyfriend. No other explanation.' Bev looks pleased with her theory. 'Emily must have scared herself. Thought she could handle it, but it must have been a shock, an experience with an older man like that. Too intense for a girl of her age. No wonder she legged it up town. Probably scared about what her mam would say if she found out.'

'Does the mother know about him? You seen her about?' Maureen peers at Bev.

'She came down here blaming us, shouting all sorts. Dai sent her packing.'

Maureen sucks in a breath through her teeth.

'Sounds like that Thomas bloke should do one, we don't want troublemakers like him around here either. Thought it was odd him giving Simon gyp about the land. Calling in his solicitors just because someone makes you a polite offer. He's not right in the head.' She picks up a pen and chews the end of it. 'My Jade is a year younger than Emily. Can you imagine? Not safe to let her out while he's roaming around.' She glances up at me. 'You stay away from him, Catrin, you hear? Nothing but bad news.'

'He says he just chatted to her. That she was meeting someone else.' I feel the need to defend him though I'm not sure why.

'I bet he did,' sneers Bev. 'Not going to own up to it, is he? It would be better for everyone if he moved.'

'You saw the jumper in his house?' Maureen slaps the pen on her notepad.

'Yes.'

She nods savagely, her mouth turned down at the corners. I should be pleased that finally someone believes me, but something in her tone says she's the one who's about to make trouble.

'Well, we didn't know about that. And her getting it from her *boyfriend*.' Her fingers hover over the phone. There's no doubt that she's going to make sure everyone knows. I have to tell Roddy before he hears it from someone else.

*

Mac is sat in his driver's cab, doors open, reading the paper. Alright for some. He looks up as Swift and I get closer to the bus stop.

'Ay ay. Twice in one week, must be my lucky day.' He folds the paper shut, shoving it out of sight. 'Would I be getting my hopes up, if I thought you'd come to see me?' He flashes me a mischievous grin and a wink.

This is what he's always been like, a little bit too much so you don't know whether to feel flattered or stupid.

'Sorry,' I say, trying to make it sound like I'm matching his banter when really I want the marsh to swallow me up. 'I'm off to see Emily's lot.'

Swift jumps up onto the first step. I grab her collar and hold her back, pushing my hand deeper into my pocket. There's only one fifty pence piece left. It could be a pint of milk or a loaf of bread. I draw it out and smack it on the counter.

'If that'll get me there.'

'Things that bad, are they?' Mac pushes the coin back towards me, keys something into the machine and plucks out a ticket. 'On the house. For old times' sake.' He smiles.

'Thanks,' I mumble, picking it up, not wanting to think about the last time he looked at me with the same earnest expression. I nod at Swift and she hurtles up the aisle, settling under our usual seat.

'Give a bloke a chance, eh, Catrin?' Mac starts up the engine, switches into gear and sets off.

I catch sight of myself in the wing mirror. This is how it had started. Casual banter on the bus. Me hanging next to the driver's cab, staying for an extra stop or two. His questions – someone who was actually curious about my life. I'd told him where I'd be for New Year. When he turned up, he acted like it was a coincidence, but I knew he'd come for me. Felt flattered I suppose that someone would make the effort.

'What business you got with her lot, then?' He glances at me.

'What do you care?' I say, turning towards Swift.

'You're not very trusting, are you?'

I look at my feet. Say nothing.

'I've been keeping an eye out for her, after our last chat.' He crunches a gear and the bus shudders with the change.

'Why?'

'You're not the only one who's concerned. I would have told you last time if you hadn't been so short, but she caught the bus, we exchanged a few words here and there, said she had a lot of problems at home.' He lets the end of the sentence hang in the air.

'Did she tell you she was going to run away?'

He swats a hand at the indicator then pulls in at the next bus stop, halfway between our village and Emily's. It's no more than a lay-by, no one gets on or off here anymore.

He turns off the engine and opens the driver's cab. Just for a second we're close enough for me to smell the citrus twang of his aftershave, notice the way his tattoo pokes out from under a shirt sleeve. My cheeks start to burn at the memory of my hands on his skin.

I step away from him. Swift lopes over and places herself between us. He doesn't notice and steps off the bus, patting his trousers for a packet of cigarettes. He lights one and takes in a long drag, leaning over the sea wall.

So much for being in a rush.

Reluctantly I jump off the bus. My eyes follow the curve of light on the distant water, a line of silver in a grey green landscape.

He fumbles with his cigarette.

'You've got a bit friendly with her mam?'

'Not really.'

'The thing is, Catrin.' He takes a dramatic drag, then blows smoke over the wall. 'She's a real piece. I didn't know whether to say anything before. I know you're still angry with me about...' He waves his cigarette and looks the other way.

I'm not angry, just embarrassed. How can I explain that to him? I acted like a scared little girl.

'I'm not...' I clear my throat. 'It wasn't...'

'Doesn't matter. All water under the bridge. You're too good for me anyway.' He leans back and studies my face for a reaction.

'No...' I stumble. I was stupid. Numb. I wanted to forget everything, blitz out my own existence with the warm feeling of alcohol. Let someone love me. I thought I could handle it. 'I'm the problem,' I manage.

He drags on his cigarette again.

'You, Catrin, you're a star. Top bird. Always have been.' He nudges me with his elbow. 'I shouldn't have pushed it, but I couldn't believe my luck.'

'Yeah, right,' I say and jab him back like we're at school again. I was the one who felt lucky. The fit rugby player all the girls in class used to moon over, interested in *me*.

He rests his elbows on the wall.

'Do you ever think, is this it? Like, they used to tell us at school we could do anything, be anything, and this is where we end up.' His face is earnest.

'No one ever said that to me.' I reach down to stroke Swift. She nudges her head towards me and licks my palm.

He stubs the cigarette on the wall and leaves the butt smouldering.

'Right. Enough of that philosophical shit. Now I know you don't hate me, I can tell you the truth.'

'About what?'

'Emily's mother, Lorna; she's the problem.'

'I know about the psychics.'

'Oh, you do, do you? Sorry, smarty pants. If you know everything, you won't want to hear this.'

'Go on.'

'Not even a please?' He lowers his voice and smiles, enjoying the upper hand. I shrug and whistle to Swift, moving away from the wall towards the road.

'Where you going?' he asks in surprise.

'I told you, to see Lorna. Haven't got all day.' I walk away but he grabs my arm and pulls me back towards him.

We're as close as we were the first time he kissed me in the beer garden of the pub. I'd gone outside to avoid the New Year countdown – another year about to begin without my mother. He'd slipped out, handed me a drink and a compliment, pressed his lips to mine, told me I tasted sweet.

'Get off your high horse, I'm not the bad guy here.'

'Who is?'

He brings his face closer to my ear, warm breath on my skin. 'Her mother threw her out. Didn't tell anyone. Not you. Not the police.'

146

My eyes flicker in shock. He smiles, pleased at the reaction, taking my silence as a sign I trust him. I look at his face, study it for signs he's playing with me, but his gaze is serious, no jokes now.

'You didn't tell the police?' I whisper.

'My word against hers, didn't fancy that. Thought the girl would turn up, families fall out all the time. Kicking myself now.'

My mind races and I turn away from him, rest my hands on the wall and look out over the grey water.

'Why?'

He settles into the same position. The heat of his arm against mine.

'She told me all sorts. Mother was the jealous type. Didn't like how much her dad doted on her. Always putting her down. Paranoid about being left out. Didn't want her to have a boyfriend either. Poor girl couldn't win. She started seeing someone, her mother didn't like it and threw her out.'

He offers me a cigarette. I shake my head.

'Was it Mr Thomas?'

He shrugs.

'Who knows. Could've been anyone.'

'Why did Lorna pretend to look for her, if she'd thrown her out?'

'Catrin, you're a nice girl. Trying to help everyone.' He shuffles closer. 'But that woman is mad. Proper mental. Wherever Emily is, Lorna is glad she's gone. Let them take their drama somewhere else.' He reaches up and moves a strand of hair from my face. 'Don't waste your time on it. Bad lot, all of them.'

'Not all of them.' I'm thinking of Roddy. I have to tell him.

'So, what about that second chance?' Mac leans towards me.

'I've got to go.' I duck away from him and whistle to Swift. 'We can walk from here, thanks.'

He laughs to hide his disappointment.

'And there I was thinking we were having a moment,' he calls after me. 'If you change your mind, you know where I am.'

17

I hammer on Lorna's front door. She owes me an explanation after the risk I took for her.

The brooding man from the family photo appears and stares at me and Swift. His face is tired. Dark, puffy half-moons under his eyelids make him look as if he's been punched. He steps out towards me.

'You here about Emily?' He turns away just as quickly and calls back into the hall. 'Lorna come here!' He asks me again, this time a little quieter, 'Have you seen her?'

'No. Sorry…' What else can I say, that his wife has lied and we've all been running around for no reason?

He slumps, looking out beyond me into the middle distance as if staring hard enough at the gate could make her magically appear.

Lorna bustles out from the hallway. Her face drops for a second when she catches sight of us, then she immediately pastes on a smile.

'Catrin! This is the girl I was telling you about, Bryn.'

He studies me with more curiosity than before.

'You found this invisible jumper I've been hearing about?'

Lorna whizzes past him, taking my arm with a firm grasp.

'She did. On the marsh like I said. Then at his house.'

'Less said about that the better,' he grumbles, giving me

daggers. 'Question is, what's that old bloke doing, messing about with her clothes?'

Lorna lowers her voice.

'God knows. You know what she's like, Bryn, always fluttering her eyelashes to get what she wants. She had you wrapped around her little finger.'

'I'm her bloody father!' he says, horrified. 'He hasn't got any business talking to her or...' His voice trails off and he kicks at the stone step.

'Alright, love.' Lorna shushes at him. 'We don't know anything.'

'Know enough to go round and give him a piece of my mind. Give me one good reason why I shouldn't do that, eh?'

'We don't want any trouble with the police,' Lorna says in a warning tone. 'They won't help us if they have us down as a bunch of troublemakers. We've got to get things sorted.' She gives him a pointed look. 'For when she comes back.'

'Should have thought of that before you broke into his bloody house.' He puffs his chest out like an angry child.

'*I* didn't,' seethes Lorna.

Bryn turns his attention to me again.

'And what do you want? Come to tempt my wife into a bit more breaking and entering? As if we haven't got enough problems.'

'I need to talk to you,' I say to Lorna.

'Heard some more gossip, or what?' Bryn's face has turned a deep crimson, he seems determined to wind himself up.

'Cool down. Go and put the kettle on, will you?' Lorna tuts at him.

He gives me one last look of disgust and slopes away. Lorna watches him retreat then turns to me.

'Come on, spill it out, girl.' Her grip on my arm tightens.

'You lied to me,' I hiss. I need Lorna to tell me the truth herself.

Her face twitches in shock. 'Someone been sounding off? Have you found out something else?'

'There *is* nothing else. *You* threw her out.'

The words stun Lorna into silence. She glances behind then drags me further towards the front gate with a ferocious energy. Any hope I had that Mac was messing about disappears with her tight smile and the pinch of her fingers on my forearm. Swift barks and paws at Lorna who shoves her away. Her face is hard.

'Why are you talking nonsense?'

'Emily was seeing someone. You didn't like it. You threw her out. She didn't run away at all.' I repeat Mac's words.

She shakes her head.

'No, no. Who told you that?' The question is loaded. She reveals her lie in the way she studies my face intently, searching for clues.

'Why did you pretend?' I ask, desperate for there to be a good reason, for Lorna to need help or for there to be a way out of this.

'Bryn can't know.' She spells each word out to me like a naughty child. 'It doesn't make a difference anyway whether she ran or she was pushed. She's out there somewhere. It doesn't change anything.' Her voice is wheedling. 'We're waiting for her. Or... or looking for her.' She changes tack, grabbing at me again. 'Please, Catrin, he'll kill me if he finds out and I need him here.' Her voice turns from grave to petulant, eyes imploring. 'I need him to be here. Emily does

151

too. We'll wait it out. She'll turn up. It'll all be better. Can you understand that?'

'Do you really think she was seeing Mr Thomas?'

Lorna sighs and pushes me away.

'I don't know. I can't even bear to think about it. What matters is Bryn is here. He left me, y'know that? Now he's home again and I want him to stay here. While he's helping me look it gives us a chance to patch things up, talk things over.'

The man I saw leaning against the door didn't look too keen on talking about anything except Emily, but I keep that to myself.

'Are you going to tell him?' She fixes me with a stare.

'Tell me what? Tea's up.' Bryn stands in the doorway, taking up all the space again.

I open my mouth, but Lorna jumps in, her eyes wide with fright.

'Bryn, you won't believe this,' she calls out over her shoulder. Her face sets into a grim mask of determination. 'Catrin's managed to get him talking, haven't you?'

She has no intention of telling the truth.

'He's taken quite a liking to you, hasn't he?' Her mouth twists into a victorious smile. 'What did he tell you? You were there, weren't you, when the police arrived?'

I nod, unsure where this is going. The sensation of wading into a pulling tide, legs unsteady.

'And you asked him about Emily?'

Bryn looms impatient behind Lorna like a bodyguard.

'What did he say?'

My hand reaches down. Thankfully Swift's warm nose finds it. I stroke the top of her head.

'He lied. He didn't want trouble. He'd seen her.'

Lorna grabs onto my arm and drags me around the path. 'Oh my God, where is she? Where's my baby? Quick, Bryn, pass me my coat and my keys. Let's go!'

Bryn shifts his weight, stands straighter.

'Let's hear it then, detective. Where is she?'

I shake Lorna off, planting my feet on the ground.

'I don't know. He told me he'd spoken to her. Said she was going...'

'Let's go, Bryn. Come on!' Lorna grabs at him this time, trying to pull him towards the gate. He flings her hand away, sending her reeling in a circle. Bryn stares at me, cold.

'Why would he talk to you?'

'I told you, Bryn. He's taken a real shine to Catrin.'

'Let me get this straight. We don't know you. You turn up here asking Lorna to help; you break into a man's house. You're the only person who sees my daughter's jumper but rather than tell the police you get someone else to do it, then it disappears. Next, you're telling me you go and have a nice chat with this bloke, and he tells you something else he hasn't told us. *To you.* Only to you. And you expect me to believe that?'

He walks over to me then pulls up short as if stopping himself from doing something. I take a step back.

'Yes,' I say quietly.

'Let me tell you what it sounds like, love. It sounds like the dodgiest bloody person here is you.'

I open my mouth to say that Lorna is the liar, but he grabs me by the shoulders and turns me around with a sharp push.

'Right. Get inside.' He propels me through the door with a

shove between the shoulder blades that knocks some air out of me.

Lorna follows us in silence. Swift whines as the door clicks on the latch and she's left outside.

In the hallway, Bryn picks up the phone.

'Wait in there. I want to get to the bottom of this.' He punches the number of the police station.

Lorna bustles me into the kitchen to sit at the table.

Bryn bellows down the phone that he wants to speak to PC Quinn right now.

I look at Lorna, incredulous.

'What are you doing?' I whisper.

She shakes her head at me, fingers tapping on the table.

'I need him here. Long enough for us to make a fresh start. Get him back for good. It's nothing personal.'

Bryn slams the phone down, cursing about how useless the police are.

The front door clicks then closes lightly.

Lorna turns to the window and whispers, 'Here we go.'

For a second I think it must be Emily, but then Bryn, still in the hall, erupts.

'Who the hell gave him a key to this house? Lorna!' He shouts her name, and she ignores it, grasping at the sides of the kitchen table and looking into her lap.

Roddy strolls into the kitchen, smiling as if Bryn were invisible.

'Might have to repaint the front door. Your friend out there is giving it a good scratch.'

He doesn't have time for a response as Bryn storms in after him, face red with rage.

'Lorna! I said who the hell gave him a key to this house?'

Lorna doesn't answer but turns around slowly and smiles at Roddy even though her eyes are sad.

'Hello, love, any news?'

He shakes his head. Bryn looks from one to the other, but they ignore his hulking presence in such a way they must be well practised at it.

'I told you I didn't want him coming here anymore. And yet, here he is, letting himself into my house.'

'You don't live here anymore. Your choice,' she spits at him, losing her temper. 'My son knows he's welcome here. I gave him a key. Maybe if you'd let him visit more Emily would still be here.'

Roddy walks past Lorna, squeezing her shoulder, and sets about making tea. He shakes a cup at me and without thinking I nod my head. He turns his back to us, clinking and stirring the cups. Bryn roars and moves towards him, but Lorna stands in his way. She stares at him with a fire I've not seen in her before.

'I've got one child missing. I don't want another one gone. We're supposed to be rebuilding this family. What would Emily say if she saw you like this? No wonder she ran. No more. Do you hear me?'

He deflates and slumps his shoulders, mouth curling up like a sulky child.

'If anything goes missing here,' he spits over Lorna's shoulder, 'I'll know where to go looking for it.'

Roddy shakes his head with a smile. Lorna frowns.

'That's not fair, Bryn. He was blamed for something he didn't do, you know that.'

'I know that's what you want to think, Lorna. We all know you like a bit of make believe, don't you? What's the matter, that psychic lost her instinct, can't even tell you where your daughter is?'

'That's not fair.'

'It is when you're the one ringing me up, crying about getting cut off and asking me to pay the bloody phone bill.'

Roddy places a mug of steaming tea in front of me. His wide brown eyes show no hint that Bryn's words have affected him. He shakes a mug at Bryn.

'Tea, Bryn?'

The whole house seems to shake as Bryn slams the front door. I watch him storming down the path.

'Charming as ever,' Roddy offers to the room.

Lorna shakes her head.

'Don't start, love. He's been good to us, you know that.' She slumps as the adrenaline seems to leave her body. She smiles sadly at Roddy. 'It was going really well. Bryn's been such a help, you know I'm calmer when he's here. He's just bloody stubborn and won't say he's coming back for good.'

'He doesn't deserve you,' says Roddy, but there's no emotion in his voice.

Lorna pats him on the cheek.

'I need him here. Emily running off will show him that. We all want him back. He'll realise it eventually...' Her voice trails off. 'Think I'll have a lie down, love. Catrin can tell you what that old weirdo said.' She walks past me and pinches my arm hard, catching my eye and shaking her pale head in warning.

We sit listening as she clunks up the stairs.

Without her the kitchen suddenly feels smaller and I find

myself examining a loose thread on my jumper. Roddy takes his time cleaning up the countertop, comfortable with the silence. When he finally sits down opposite me, I jump at the sound of his voice.

'So, what's put a bee in Bryn's bonnet then?'

'Mr Thomas told me he'd seen Emily, been chatting to her.'

'Isn't that what he told the police?'

The truth is I never stopped to find out what he'd told them. Assuming when he fobbed Lorna off, he must have done it to them as well. It never occurred to me that he might have told them the truth. I falter.

'I… I thought he said he didn't know her. That's what he told your mum.'

'So, he didn't tell the truth to the pair who were breaking and entering.' Roddy's smile is wide and although his tone is mocking there is nothing cruel in his face. I smile back, glad of some warmth.

'I think our friend Mr Thomas has got bigger problems than you and Mam rifling through his stuff.'

'What do you mean?'

'Seen it before. Trauma. It affects the nerves. Can't keep it together. Life makes them shake no matter what's happening.'

'Where have you seen that?' I drag my eyes up to meet his.

He looks at me intently before answering, weighing up my ability to receive the information.

'A lot of blokes like that inside. The ones who are sorry for what they did. After they did it. Not all of them.'

It takes me a second to register what he's said. *Inside*. I try to keep my face neutral. He observes my silence and looks away.

'What did you do?' I blurt out.

He looks up, surprised at my directness.

'Theft. Had a record from my rebellious school days. Judge took one look at me and thought he'd teach me a lesson. Month or two inside, make sure I'd come out a different man.' His voice is tinged with bitterness.

'Did you?' I ask.

He laughs softly.

'Didn't need to. Took the blame for someone else. Paid the price. End of story.' He swigs the last of his tea. 'Emily used to tell me things, but Bryn wouldn't let her visit me. We hadn't seen each other in a while.' He studies my face for a reaction. Satisfied there is none, he continues. 'She couldn't hack it here with Mam. Wanted to get away. Before I went in, I told her to keep on studying. Wanted her to get to university, get out that way. Make something of herself. But she didn't believe it. Said her teachers laughed at her, told her to ask for a job in one of the shops in town. I was livid when she told me, but she didn't mind. All she wanted was to get out. I 'spose that's why she took the job with your friend.'

'I don't think Dai had much choice.' I jump in too fast as always.

He sits back, folding his arms across his chest.

'Your mum was very persuasive,' I add hastily. He must know what she's really like.

'He never heard of the word no?'

'He couldn't say no.' And I still don't know why but I've never seen Dai like that before. The vein rigid in his neck, hands gripping the stable door to stop him from losing it and grabbing hold of Lorna.

'One of Mam's favours?' Roddy's face falls.

I nod and wonder how much chaos Lorna has already been responsible for in their lives. He shakes his head grimly.

'So, Emily was dreaming of a job behind the make-up counter and got sent to clean up horse shit. No wonder she ran off.' He sighs, the guilt sagging his shoulders.

I can't keep it in any longer.

'Your mum threw her out. She didn't run.' I wait for a reaction like Bryn's, but he just looks thoughtful.

'Knew something didn't add up.' He smiles sadly. 'Any idea why?'

'She had a boyfriend. Older.'

He clears his throat, wiping both palms across his eyes as if it could help him to see the answers more clearly.

'Emily was at that stupid phase.' He catches my eye but can't hold it. 'Y'know, too grown up for her own good. Thinking she could bat her eyelids and get what she wanted. You can guess who taught her that.' He pauses. 'But she's still a kid. This Dai bloke. Think he might have taken a shine to her?'

'No.' My voice shakes with disgust.

'I know he's a friend of yours but...'

'He'd never hurt anyone.' I stand up, shoving my chair away.

'Sorry. I had to ask, I...'

'Did you? Why not ask your mother why she threw her own daughter out then lied about it? Why not start there?'

'Catrin...' He moves towards me, one arm outstretched.

I thrash it away.

'No. Dai and Bev don't deserve this. They've suffered

159

enough. You've no idea what they've been through. Leave them alone. Tell your mother to do the same.' I barge my way out of the kitchen towards the front door.

He doesn't come after me but his words, soft and sad, follow me down the hall.

'I would, if I thought it would do any good.'

18

I was lucky enough to catch the bus on its way back from town. Mac was distracted by some banter with a young lad who keeps failing his driving test. He waved me on without paying, glancing away from his conversation only to mouth, 'You okay?' I'd nodded back with a rueful smile, trying to tell him he was right, and I was grateful.

Right now, Mr Thomas is the only person I need to talk to.

I storm up his drive, Swift in tow, and hammer on the back door, the metal shaking at the force of it. There's no answer and I'm about to walk away when he approaches from the garden, blinking as if he's just stepped out from the dark.

'Catrin. This is becoming a habit.'

'Why do you tell me things and lie to everyone else?' The words come juddering out, giving away my own fear.

He lifts his chin to look at me. If I want to find out the truth, I'm going to have to play his game, whatever that is. He smiles and gestures for me to follow him.

We walk to the other side of his garden, where it meets the thick hedge bordering the lane down to the marsh. My skin prickles as we near an outhouse with boarded-up windows.

He turns to me. 'I shouldn't really, but...'

'What is it?' I demand, my hand stretching out for Swift.

'She'll have to stay outside I'm afraid. You've caught me at the right moment. I was about to shut myself in for the next hour or two.' He smiles as if that's the most normal thing in the world to say.

I study the building. The original door has been reinforced with plywood, covering it completely. He follows my gaze.

'Not a hint of light. But you know that. Come on, we don't want them to spoil.'

I signal for Swift to sit, wishing I could tell her that if I don't come back out she should go for help. Then I walk through the heavy door he's holding open for me. It slams shut and we are thrown into complete darkness.

I take a breath in. The panic of not seeing anything. Not even a shadow. Your eyes are supposed to get used to the dark, but this is different. It is heavy. You lose all sense of perspective, like being underwater and not knowing which way is up. Only sound helps. He shuffles next to me, fingers searching for something, then flicks the red light on.

I've been in a space like this before. In our attic. My mother's makeshift darkroom, held together by sheets and pegs. She'd tried her best but always grumbled that it wasn't right. She needed a space of her own. A place where she could work. There'd been arguments – which would come first, the money to make our old shed into a darkroom, or the money from her photos. *How could we pay for it*, my father had asked, *when it's the difference between a school uniform for Catrin or food on the table?* No answer. Only the slam of a door, and me, burning with the guilt of my existence.

Mr Thomas moves to the three trays laid out on the table and swishes the prints around with a pair of pincers. The pungent smell of chemicals wafts over. It brings her back so clearly, it's hard not to run out screaming.

'You can put the light on now,' he says. 'They were ready, but I wanted to double check.'

I turn and find the switch next to the door. The room erupts into white light, a moment of blindness after standing in the shadows.

'Did she come here?' I say, already knowing the answer. The last time I'd clambered into the attic to look for her and found it empty, the sheets taken down. Yet her photos kept appearing on the kitchen table when she came in from her evening walk.

'She needed a space to work.'

'Why here?'

'It was as good as anywhere,' he says lightly. 'She needed to be able to focus.' He glances at me. 'Work uninterrupted. She had talent and didn't want to waste it.'

The words *on us* hang unsaid. She didn't want my father or I distracting her, demanding that she be a wife or mother.

'She never mentioned you,' I whisper.

'Well, why would she?' He holds up a photo to inspect it, shakes off the liquid and pegs it on a cord hung between us. The white-backed paper faces me. 'I was only helping her out.'

'People talk about their friends,' I say, warily making my way around a table containing glass jars labelled with chemicals and warnings.

'Not always. But I hope that answers your question.' He pegs another photo. 'I suppose when I see you, I think of her.'

'What did you talk about?' I ask, rounding the space where he's working.

'This.' He gestures around him. 'We learnt from each other, although she was far better than I was.' He smiles. 'She was talking about an exhibition, before she… well, I suppose you know all about that.'

His words strike a blow. No. She never mentioned it. Stopped talking about her photos. Seemed only to tolerate being at home, moving through her life like a ghost, only half there.

I look up at the photo and gasp.

'What's this?' I cry out, grabbing it. An image of Emily and Charlie-horse looks back. She's holding his lead rope, looking into the camera, clearly happy to pose and smile.

'Yes, I was quite pleased with that one. I won't be able to use it now of course.'

I glare at him incredulously.

'You took photos of her?'

He looks offended.

'Just this one. She happened to catch me when I had my camera in my hand. Asked me to take it. Wanted to give it to someone, but I hadn't got around to developing it until now.' He gives the photo a wistful glance. 'She might come back for it, I suppose, one day.'

'Did you tell the police?' My voice rises as I take in the photo again. Emily, wearing the same jumper I picked up from the marsh.

He turns, irritated, snatches it from me and re-pegs it.

'I was hoping that would answer all your questions. You can see she's alive and well. What happened after has nothing to do with me.'

'Don't you think it's important? Do you know who her boyfriend is? The older man?' I try to hold his gaze but his grey eyes dance away.

'I want to be left alone, Catrin. That's all I've wanted for some time.'

'Where's the jumper?' I ask. 'You took it because you didn't want anyone to know what you were up to.'

'Is that really what you think of me?' His mouth curls in disgust.

There's no time to play these stupid games.

'Yes. It's odd. You... you stare at me all the time,' I shout, spinning towards the door, my leg knocking into the table. A foul-smelling liquid sloshes over the side of one of the trays. He grabs a towel and dabs at the mess.

'This nonsense with Emily. Well, look how it's brought us together.' He smiles at me. 'I haven't been able to talk to you before now, Catrin, don't you see?'

I don't. I want to get away from him, from the constant sensation that he's trying to reel me in like some kind of prize catch.

'The jumper. It's here. You're hiding it. You did something bad.'

He shakes his head and dabs the table.

'You're forgetting the police have already asked.'

'So, what have you done with it?' I launch myself at the door. If it's not here it must be in the house somewhere. He calls out after me but the door slams and muffles his protests.

I run back across the garden. I can't trust anything he says. Swift jumps up with a yap and canters alongside.

I throw open the back door and stalk inside the bungalow.

Swift and I rush into the office room. I'm caught out just for a second by the view from the huge window – evening light arcs across the estuary turning it golden. Swift barks. She's right. There's no time for this.

I pull open the drawers to his desk with such force that they come out completely.

Empty.

'For goodness' sake.'

I whirl around. He's standing in the doorway, tutting as if he was indulging a naughty child having a tantrum. Perhaps that's all I am to him. An old student. A game. A way to feel superior.

I inspect the bookshelves. Nothing. Anger propels me forwards. I can't stop.

I push past him and back into the hall. In the bathroom I open the cabinets. More pills. Then the bedroom. I open the bedside drawers: books, nothing more. Catching my breath, I turn to the wardrobe.

'No!' he says sharply from the doorway. 'That's quite enough.'

I lay my hand on the cool walnut wood of the door.

'I will not have you rifling through my *personal* things.' His tone is clipped but he remains in the doorway.

I've opened every other drawer and cupboard in the place. What's one more? I reach for the latch.

'What would your mother say, Catrin?'

I deflate.

She used to tear around like this in an uncontrollable temper. My father was always calm, but she smashed plates and dishes, slammed every door in the house, drove off and left us when life got too much. I don't want to be like that. To hurt people like she did.

He senses my lapse and strides into the room, standing too close. He might appear calm, but now I can see his breath is short, anxious.

'Out, please.'

I need fresh air. To walk and walk until I don't feel anything anymore.

'I assume you've answered your own question? It's not here.' He follows me down the hallway.

'Where is it?' I whisper, moving slowly towards the back door where Swift whines and paws to be let out, already knowing where we'll be headed.

'Gone. The same as her. And like her, it'll turn up again, you mark my words.'

'What?'

'I only wanted to help,' he says. 'My only intention was ever to help her. Give her some good advice. I've seen countless teenage rebellions in my time. Family trouble. Teenagers push the limits to get their parents to notice them. Mark my words, she'll come back when she's bored or runs out of options.'

'How can you be so sure?'

'There are undercurrents here, Catrin. Just like out there.' He nods his head towards the estuary.

The undertow that you can't see, pulling and shaping the mud. Sucking the twigs and branches down, turning them over then throwing them up in another place.

'This place. Your mother knew...' He looks at me exasperated. 'She was trying to capture it in her photos. All the hidden things. You mark my words. Emily will appear as if nothing happened, and we'll all be sorry we wasted our time. I want nothing more to do with it.'

We're at the door now. He shepherds me onto the porch steps.

'You mean she's still here?' I glance around outside, almost expecting to catch sight of her.

Swift jumps down the steps, happy to be free. The sight of the estuary swims in front of me. I glance back at him, puzzled. He seems to have drawn himself up to his full height, once again the charismatic teacher who holds the power.

'Our time on this subject is up, Catrin. I've been more than generous. Don't come here again.'

The door slams. My body hums with shame as if I've been singled out in the classroom and torn to shreds in front of everyone for not knowing the right answer. But there's no one here. The sky and the water are the only witnesses to this strange exchange.

I stumble with tiredness. Swift jumps at my side, her teeth softly nipping at my fingers. She can't stand this house either.

I glance up at the estuary; the familiar silver line of water is already covering the road, making it impossible to pass. Maybe it's time to go home, forget it all.

19

The sky is still half dark when I wake up the next morning. No nightmares, that's something.

Out of the kitchen window bulbous clouds hang low over the marsh. My head throbs as I make tea and toast, burning both pieces so I have to scrape them clean and swallow the bitter taste of ash against the butter. I turn the strange conversation from yesterday over and over in my head. It's been days since I found the jumper and I'm no closer to sorting this mess out.

My father is in the fields already, always the first out, checking nothing will be ruined, and no sheep lost to the rain he knows will fall later. I don't know how he does it. The same constant rhythm day in and out. Perhaps it's what holds him together – a tiny thread of consistency when the world is falling apart around him.

The deadline to respond to the letter is in two days. I smooth the envelope out of my jacket pocket where it's become dog-eared and dirty. The paper inside is still pristine. I think of Mr Thomas' words yesterday. *Your mother wanted an exhibition.* What can someone like me really do in a world like that, where I don't belong? What if it makes me as bitter and disappointed as she was?

I turn to throw the letter on the fire. Except it hasn't been lit for days. No wood. No firelighters. I should probably sort that out, ask Maureen for more credit until we can pay. I tuck it back into my jacket.

Swift is already waiting by the front door, knowing my moods better than I do. I stroke her head and gather her into my arms.

'We're alright as we are, aren't we girl?' I whisper, before opening the door and letting the cool air wash over us both.

We wander down onto the marsh road and criss-cross our way over to the spongy grass, still sopping wet after the tide. I pick up a stick washed smooth by the water.

Maybe Emily doesn't want to be found. Maybe it's just a teenage rebellion like Mr Thomas says.

I never had the chance to rebel. My mother was irreverent enough for both of us. Said we shouldn't be defined by where we're from, talked about doing things differently from her buttoned-up parents, the grandparents I never met. She said you should never conform for people; keep everyone at a distance in case they tried to take away your freedom. Sometimes I wonder if she really meant it; she didn't look free when she said those things, just lonely.

I stop to choose a stone, then launch it with all my might into a pool of water, revelling in the plop and ripples of something that makes sense. I count the ponies on the flats. All twenty of them are dotted around munching on grass. Rays of morning light push their way through gaps in the dark sky. Everything as it should be. I trudge on, looking at the details the way my mother taught me to. *A life-raft in the storm* she'd called them.

Swift barks sharply and I turn to see what's caught her attention. She proudly drags part of a small animal carcass out of the reeds. Nothing left but hanging bones and a bit of fur. By the size, it was probably a rabbit. Her proud swagger along the mud flats makes me chuckle.

We wander on further and she continues her sniffing. Two ponies lift their heads as we pass then settle back to the grass, flicking their underbellies with little kicks to keep the last of the autumn flies away.

Swift dives off into the reeds again and I lose sight of her. I scan the horizon then glance back up to the houses behind the marsh road. The hill where Mr Thomas' bungalow is perched. Is he watching us now – has he always been watching? The thought of it gives me a chill. But this is my place. I won't let him ruin it for me. I pick up another stone and hurl it into a pool of water. It lands with a hard splash and something about the action makes me smile.

Swift yaps again from further away, a sure sign she's found another bone. I whistle to her, and she bounds out of the tall grasses with a scrap of fabric in her mouth.

'Swift, come.' My tone is sharp.

She runs over obediently and sits, lifting a paw to placate me with an old trick. I take the wet material from her mouth and smooth her head.

It's purple.

I turn instinctively to look at Mr Thomas' house. He got rid of it. What a coward. That's what he was babbling on about yesterday. Rather than help with the search he washed his hands of it. This scrap must have caught in the reeds. Although, turning it over in my hands, the fabric is only a little frayed, meaning it didn't tear but was cut into pieces.

'Good girl,' I murmur to Swift, shoving it into my pocket

and turning towards the road. If I show PC Quinn this material, she'll have to admit the jumper existed, make Mr Thomas tell the truth.

A car speeds up behind me. The engine revs and the sounds of grit squealing from the tyres says whoever is driving doesn't know the road well.

I stop, drawing Swift quickly to my side. To my surprise the car pulls up alongside us and Roddy stares at me from the driver's seat. He leans over and opens the passenger window. His face is earnest, and I can't help but notice how his black T-shirt hugs his taut muscles. I look away. He takes this as anger.

'Sorry about the other day. I shouldn't have suggested that about Dai. It was insensitive.' His eyes are wide, and he seems genuine, but I'm not used to people apologising.

I stand there awkwardly, the fabric burning guiltily in my pocket, not knowing what to say. Swift helps me out by barking and jumping up to the window, her paws on the door. I reach down to stop her, but Roddy laughs and leans further over to scratch her head. He eyes me uncertainly.

'Can we start again?'

I nod, unable to say more. He extends his hand out of the window.

'Hi, I'm Roddy. My family is completely messed up and my mother threw my sister out then lied about it. Now she's disappeared. I also offended the only person who's tried to help me and now I feel like a bit of an idiot.' His face breaks into a wide smile.

'Did your mum tell you the truth?'

'Aren't you going to introduce yourself first?' He proffers his hand playfully.

Surprising myself, I lean forwards and take it. The shock of his skin on mine nearly stops me but I manage to speak.

'I'm Catrin. My family...' I falter over the words, the smile dropping from my face. I can't even play this simple game. Heat fills my cheeks. '...sorry,' I mumble, looking at my feet, and clumsily let his hand go.

Instead of driving off he reaches across and opens the passenger door.

I put my hand in my pocket and finger the damp fabric. To anyone else it might not even be convincing. Bryn was so suspicious when I told him what Mr Thomas said. If I start telling people he's put the jumper, the one he denied existed, back on the marsh, I know what they'll think. An irritation rises in me. I want Roddy to trust me.

'Wait,' I say.

I take a furtive glance at the material in my palm. It's dried out, paler than before. No longer purple, more of a light pink. It could be an old cloth dropped by anyone. I close my palm tightly around the fabric and push it back into my pocket.

He shakes the door jovially to get my attention.

'Two heads are better than one.'

I nod and jump in, promising myself I'll tell him about Mr Thomas' photo of Emily if it feels right.

Swift jumps over my lap and into the back seat where she lies, head on paws, ready for the next thing.

'She's clever,' he says as he starts the car again, and I beam with pleasure.

'Bryn doesn't know I've got the car. Said he'd report it stolen if I took it again, but how else am I supposed to get down here? Your bus service is bloody ridiculous. I spoke to the driver. Said he couldn't remember Em getting on the bus to go home.'

If Mac knew Roddy was Lorna's son, after everything he'd heard about her from Emily, he probably didn't want to tell him anything.

'Seems weird he wouldn't have noticed her, given only one man and his dog use the bus. Not very helpful down here, are they?' He looks at me with a smile. 'No offence.'

I shake my head. *Tell him about the photo.* But I don't want to look stupid again. For people to call me *troubled* in front of him. What I want is for everything to disappear and just leave Roddy and I alone together.

'Catrin, is there anywhere we haven't looked?'

His face is so open and earnest. I desperately want to help him. I let myself relax and feel a small glow of happiness spreading across my chest – Roddy used the word *we* and that means everything.

'There is one place I haven't been yet, but it takes hours to walk out there.' It's also my favourite place in the world. I want to show it to him. To have something good to share for once.

'Can we drive there now?'

'Not all the way. We'll need to walk the last part. The tide is out so there's time.'

'Will you show me?'

I examine my hands carefully.

'Okay,' I manage, looking at my lap.

'You know Emily wasn't working for Dai because *she* needed a job.' He looks at me sadly. 'Mam told me today when she was off her face on pills. The doctor's got her taking stuff in the daytime to keep her calm. She's off sick from work and Bryn's had enough, which makes her even more paranoid. She's terrified of him leaving again.'

His words spiral out, hard to follow and keep track of. What's obvious is the weight he's carrying. It's his job to look after Lorna and he was trying to look after Emily too.

'Why was she there?'

'Mam sent her over. Calling in a debt. Money went straight to Mam; Emily never saw a penny.' He smiles sadly. 'Even though she owes money everywhere, Mam's never one to forget a debt.'

'Why did Dai owe her?' I try to keep my voice light. Dai's face was leaden when they spoke. It can't be about Bev's drinking because everyone knows about that. I glance at Roddy. His brow is furrowed as if he's weighing something up in his mind.

'She saw something she shouldn't have.' The omission about what it was hangs large between us.

For a moment my stomach swims as I imagine him telling me Lorna saw Dai with Emily. But that wouldn't make sense. All this deception is confusing me, jangling my nerves. My father was right, it's better to leave Dai and Lorna's business between them.

'Who did you cover for when you went inside?' I ask, changing tack.

He glances up, surprised.

'Someone who couldn't afford to lose anything else.' Another sidestep. Roddy is loyal. There's only one person I could imagine him showing that loyalty to.

'Lorna?' I say softly, the pieces fitting together in my mind.

He nods. Of course it was her.

'Lucky it was all circumstantial. I'd been with her, picking her up and dropping her off on her cleaning jobs. Wasn't too much of a stretch of the imagination, someone like me with access to all those posh homes. Bit of jewellery going missing. Plus, I had a record. She plays the grieving mother well, as you know.' He covers the hint of bitterness with a laugh.

He should have let Lorna be caught. They could have got her some help. Someone would have noticed her addiction. She would have got off lightly. How could she watch as he went inside for her? That's not love. I want to tell him all this, but the words get stuck in my throat.

Roddy stares at me as if he's trying to read my thoughts.

'She had a hard life,' he offers.

'That's no excuse,' I say. 'We should go. It takes time to walk there, and we've only got half a tide left. Head west.'

He nods, relieved, and starts the car. I glance quickly in the back at Swift who's fallen asleep as Roddy turns the car around and powers towards the lighthouse.

20

We leave the car parked up on a solid mudflat just off the path and walk the last part towards the lighthouse. I scan the horizon for anything that looks out of place.

Nothing. No sign of Emily. Part of me is glad.

The flats are shining muddy gold with the outgoing tide; they look solid enough, you'd never think that if you take a wrong step you could sink up to your knees. I whistle for Swift to stay close. She turns her head nonchalantly then carries on nosing through the dead crabs and shells washed up on the causeway.

The three of us follow the spine of rocks out to where the lighthouse stands rusting against a grey sky. I close my eyes and hear tiny hints of life against the vast silence of space; the plop of a crab falling into water and the crunch of our steps on shells. A gull shrieks with indignation as it flaps and takes off from its perch. This place has always been magical. Far from everything, as if real life can't touch you here.

Roddy's eyes are wide with delight. He runs over the rocks and marvels at the lighthouse.

'I reckon we can get up to the top.' For a moment he has the face of a child, blazing like a sun with possibility and imagination. He grabs the rusted iron ladder frame and hauls himself up. It's forty feet or more to the top platform. I raise my hand to stop him but he's already above the height of my head, staring at the top, taking one rung at a time.

I crouch down and take out my sketchbook. Turn to a fresh page.

I climbed up to the top of the lighthouse just once, with my mother. Knees shaking all the way, I tried to hide how terrified I was and be who she wanted. A fellow adventurer, co-conspirator against the world. When we reached the platform, she needed both hands for her camera and told me to wrap my arms around her leg if I was scared. I was. I stood hugging her like a tree, not daring to look around, the wind buffeting us gently, until she said it was time to climb down. She sighed with each rung as she guided me to the safe floor of the estuary, as if she longed to have adventures on her own, free of my childish hands always searching for her in panic.

I stand and scuff the shells with my boots, sending a spray of them towards the mud.

'Catrin!'

Roddy's shout comes from above, breaking my thoughts, and my stomach wrenches to see him up there so high. I stop the words, 'Be careful' in my throat before they can escape, waving with a smile instead.

'You can see everything from up here, it's amazing.' He throws back his head and screams.

A cormorant unfurls its large wings and elegantly flies off from the rocky scrub behind the lighthouse. I sketch its dark form on the paper, adding another bird further out in the water, calm and waiting.

There is a clang, a long scraping sound, then Roddy jumps down next to me, thudding hard onto the rock, feet first, knees bent. Swift barks and prances next to him.

'Hey, that's good.' He nods at my drawing.

I snap the book shut and walk around the large barnacled base of the structure. Roddy runs alongside me like a puppy, Swift cantering behind him.

'You should have come up. The view is like nothing you've ever seen before.'

'I reckon I have,' I say dryly.

He rubs his hands on his trousers to get rid of the brown rust stains.

'Not a soul out here. Nothing. Can I see?' He reaches for my sketches.

I let him take them. Watch as he skims through the collection. Eyebrows raising or mouth twitching at something.

'These are good.' He nods enthusiastically, and something about the way he always says what he feels takes away the sting of embarrassment.

'Are you studying art?' he asks, holding up a drawing of the lighthouse to compare it to the real thing.

'What's the point?' I say, thinking of the letter in my pocket.

'To learn,' he replies with a cheeky grin, closing the book. 'Must be great to have a talent like yours, make something out of nothing. I'd love that.' He looks around as if considering what he would draw if he could.

'They're not that good,' I mumble, thinking of my mother. Her critical eye on my GCSE art homework. Always something to improve. Never just a *well done, that's good.* Those words came from my father. He loved my drawings of animals. Liked to look over them in the evening and say silly things like, *Now I know exactly which sheep this is, it's Siwan the elder isn't it?* Then he'd let out a hooting laugh. I'd forgotten that. The sound of his laughter, always too big for the room we were sitting in. It was my mother who would smack the book shut, tell him he should take it more seriously.

I breathe out slowly. Put my hand out for the book which Roddy returns with a smile.

'So, where is *she*?' I ask, desperate to turn the attention away from me.

'Not here.' He walks off, shoulders sagging.

Why did I do that? Take his pleasure away.

'Apart from not having the money to move out, what problems did Emily have?'

Roddy shrugs and kicks at some pebbles, sending them flying.

'That not enough?'

'Was there someone she was scared of?'

He assumes I'm talking about Bryn and shakes his head.

'She's the apple of his eye. That's why he's so on edge at the moment.'

'Is he violent?' I remember the shove he gave me between my shoulder blades. How the air had been knocked out of me for a second.

'Wouldn't raise his hand to a woman.'

A heavy silence falls. Roddy sits down on the wet shells and pokes around them with a stick.

'Mam had me when she was just sixteen. Some big mistake she made with her shift supervisor – older bloke, married. Didn't want anything to do with her when she broke the news. We were alright though. Lived with my grandad. He was a character.' He smiles to himself.

Swift plonks herself shamelessly down next to him. He strokes a hand along her back.

'When he died, it all went downhill. Well, Mam did.

Couldn't cope with it. Said he was the only one who'd ever really loved her. Psychics, tarot cards, phone lines, you name it, she tried it all – *just to hear his voice,* she said. Kept insisting it was just one last time to say goodbye. Then she needed guidance. Had a difficult decision to make. Always something new. Dramas with men. Bryn came along like some kind of white knight and suddenly we were living with him.' He frowns and rakes his fingers through the sand. 'I was a chopsy kid by then – we didn't get on.'

'Then Emily came along?'

He nods.

'Fixed it for a while. They managed to play happy families for a bit. But not really. Mam is good at hiding who she really is, being whoever she needs to be. When Emily went to school everything changed. Mam had time on her hands. She was reading horoscopes in the paper, underlining things, using them to make decisions. Bryn thought it was funny. Used to call her Mystic Meg and ask her what kind of day he was going to have. He was laughing until the phone bills came in, and no matter what he said they kept coming. Emily grew up in all that shit.' He smacks the stick on the sand. 'And I tried to help but mostly I just got in the way. He'd give me a good hiding when it all got too much.' He looks up at me. 'Anyone would run away from that, wouldn't they?'

'You didn't.'

'Couldn't leave Mam, could I? My grandad told me to look after her. Be the man of the house.' He smiles. 'Fat lot of good that did. Nothing's changed. Not even with this shock of Emily disappearing. Thought if I could help her pay it all off for good this time, she'd give it up.'

I remember how Lorna snatched the money out of his hands in the kitchen. There was nothing but hunger in her eyes.

I sit down next to him, so close that our arms brush against each other as we both reach for Swift's soft coat. He turns and smiles at me.

'That's enough of my pity. Your turn.'

We laugh and both look out ahead at the marsh, wishing it really was a joke.

I take out my sketchbook again and study him. He pulls a face, and we giggle but my pencil brings him to life on the page. His kind eyes, floppy hair always falling to one side, *that* smile. I turn the drawing to him.

'Bloody hell!' He grabs at the paper, pulling me closer. 'Am I really that handsome?'

I ignore his question and let him have the book. I pick up a stick instead to write my name in the sand. He smirks, passing the pad back to me, then does the same. We scratch at letters in silence for a minute or two.

'What happened to your mam?' He says the words softly as if he's trying not to startle me.

My instinct is to put my hackles up and tell him it's none of his business, but I find myself looking into those brown eyes I've just taken such trouble to sketch exactly right.

'She died out here in the tide. Three years ago.' I say the number as if it will be as important to him as it is to me.

He doesn't flinch or look away but nods.

'Was it an accident?'

'What else would it be?' I push at the sand with my feet, making great holes with the heel of my shoe.

He shrugs.

'People do strange things.' The words hang between us.

For the first time I don't have to defend my thoughts – I can tell the truth.

'They said it was an accident, but some things were odd. Too off for it to be true... maybe.' I add the last word because I don't want him to think I'm making things up like his mother does. Unable to let go of a dead loved one. But maybe Lorna and I aren't so different. The idea annoys me.

I look back at him for reassurance. His face is open and expectant. It spurs me on.

'Sometimes I think she was disappointed in her life. In me. That she wanted to get away from us. Maybe...' I can't finish the thought. That I'm somehow responsible. Holding herself under the water until she got some final release.

'Why do you think that?' he asks.

'My mother knew the tides. She would never have been caught out without a good reason. Her camera. It was a precious thing to her. But it wasn't... it wasn't found with her... And she was holding flowers. I tried to tell people, but no one ever cared about that.' I feel my voice rising as the words tumble out and try to calm myself.

Swift stirs at my side and I place my hand on her head, fingers stroking her soft fur over and over. 'She hated picking flowers, said it was a waste of life,' I add.

'So, someone took her camera?'

The question is so direct it catches me off guard. I've always wondered where her camera could be, but it never occurred to me someone else might have it. It only belonged to her. My version always said she either had it or it was lost in the tide. I take a shuddering breath in.

Roddy rests his hand on mine.

'Sorry, I didn't mean to…'

Unthinking, I push him away.

'No. You're right. If someone has it, they would know what happened. I never…' My voice trails off because it sounds ridiculous. I've been so stuck in my self-pity of not being enough for her that I never even stopped to question if someone else was there. I've never changed my story.

Shame floods through me. A heavy swinging feeling rushing through my body. My mind races to Mr Thomas' darkroom and with it a slow wash of betrayal. Would she have trusted him with her beloved camera? I thought only I had that privilege.

I pull my arm away from Roddy and stand up.

'I have to go.'

His face drops and he reaches out to me, but I'm moving across the causeway, half running. I can't believe I've been so stupid. He shouts after me.

'Catrin, I'm sorry. I'm always saying the wrong thing. Let me drive you home.'

I shake my head, embarrassment smarting in my face.

Roddy catches up, puffing with the effort of sprinting. He takes my hand gently and pulls me to a stop. I can't look at him. For a moment we stand there, my hand in his, me looking at the marsh. He steps towards me slowly, my view changing from the green flats to his concerned face. I don't want to see pity from him. I couldn't bear it. His eyes are searching, and we hover there uncertainly.

I close my eyes. I like him. Please, don't let me mess this up.

It's no use.

My mother's face fills my thoughts. Blue. Not peaceful, as I try to convince myself that I remember it, but hideously bloated by water. Tossed around by the tide. Clothes torn, limbs stiff, lying in the ditch. The real memory makes me retch. I stumble away from Roddy.

'Sorry,' I mumble, but I'm not sure who I'm talking to. I whistle for Swift.

'Catrin?'

I can't look at him. I don't want to see his disappointment.

'It's not your fault, you know?' he offers.

'What?' I reach for Swift, feel the comfort of her warm fur between my fingers.

'What happened to your mam.'

'How do you know that?'

'I don't but I'd guess.'

I finally look at him.

'Whose fault is it then?'

He reaches for my hand again. 'Things happen to people, and you can't stop them, even if you want to. What our parents do, it's not our fault.'

He's talking about Lorna's addiction, how he'd do anything to pull her out of it if he could. He might be the one person who understands my guilt. But I can't stop the way I'm unspooling – I know she was there because of me, us, the need to escape once and for all, and I don't want to feel it. All I need to do is walk and keep walking until I feel empty again. I was so stupid to think I could have a friend. Could have anything normal people do.

I shake my head at him, pulling my hand away, and watch

as his face falls. That's what I do. Disappoint people until they leave. My mother did. My father in his own way too. Dai and Bev replaced me. And now this. At least it doesn't come as a surprise anymore.

'Mr Thomas has a photo of Emily,' I say as I turn my back and walk away from him. 'She let him take it.'

There's no reply. I've blown it. I'm better off alone where I can't hurt anyone. I keep walking and don't look back. Swift yaps and bounds at my side as we head towards the marsh road.

21

My father stands in the field checking the wheat he's drilled, scuffing the earth with his foot to gauge the moisture before he plants more. His breath clouds in front of him as he works, turning only once at the angry clang of the gate as I charge towards him, then back to the task in hand.

The sight of the tractor leaning to one side in the mud, threatening to topple over, stops me in my tracks. I say nothing to my father and instead walk over to check for damage. It gives me a moment to build up to my question. That and the fact we can't afford a replacement.

He calls over his shoulder.

'The rain's made a right mess of the field. Just need a couple of stones to get her out.' His voice has the tone of a petulant boy.

We have that in common – defensiveness. Both of us so self-sufficient that the mere presence of someone else is like an insult. Unless it's Dai.

'As you're here, you can give me a hand to get her out without ruining the engine.'

I nod. How long would it have sat there if I hadn't turned up? Probably until the next time Dai called in.

He tries to clamber into the driver's seat, but the tractor sways under his weight. I rush forwards. He gives me a warning look. No room for sentiment here.

I find a nearby plank of wood to give the wheel some traction, stick it under the tyre, and he revs the engine; in a second the tractor rolls forwards and settles at a normal angle.

My father switches her off and climbs down slowly. I let out a little breath as his feet touch the ground. His hands shake as he leans against the metal to right himself. I look at my feet, pretend not to notice. He nods to me and is about to carry on with his tasks when I stop him – my hand catching his arm.

'You alright?'

His eyes widen in surprise. When did I last ask him that? He pats my hand as if I was one of the ewes.

'Fine. It was the rain last night that mulched it all up.'

Standing together as the cool wind whistles past us from the estuary, and with it an occasional splat of rain, it seems hard to mention her. To sour the day after all his hard work. But I've been waiting for the right moment all these years and he's made it very clear there'll never be one.

'Did Mum ever go out onto the estuary with Mr Thomas?'

His eyes widen in shock. I've never been so direct before, always tiptoeing around the subject of what happened, or allowing him to leave gaping silences between us. His brow furrows like the field we're standing in. He takes his cap off and rubs his hand across his forehead, looks over the horizon to the tide which is now on its way up. I stand my ground with silence, refusing to fill the gap. Finally, he speaks.

'What's this about, Catrin?'

'Did she?' I insist.

He mangles the cap between his hands, twisting it continuously. His jaw is set, and his eyes wander out to the estuary flats. He looks back at me, eyes sad. Resistance fills the space between us. Why won't he tell me? He licks his lips, and I can see that he is choosing his words carefully, checking each one.

'Yes, she did…' His voice trails off and the sentence is left incomplete.

I squeeze my hands into fists, opening and closing them to get control of the repulsion I feel towards him. He sighs, realising that this time I won't storm off or run away to the estuary to hide from it all. I take a deep breath and wait. His shoulders sag.

'Catrin, it's not something you should hear…'

'No!' I cut across him. 'I'm tired of this. I need to know what was really going on – you owe me that at least.'

'Promise me you will not talk to him.'

I shudder. The child in me wants to close her ears, to keep the memory of my mother pure and free of doubt. But I can't live like this anymore; I need to know who she really was.

The sky darkens above us and a fat droplet of rain lands on my nose, then another on my cheek.

'Tell me,' I whisper as the rain starts to splatter on us and we stand there as if we feel nothing at all.

'Mr Thomas.' The name tumbles out of his mouth. He grits his teeth as if he could stop himself from saying anything else, but the words come out one by one like he's chewing on glass. 'He took photographs too, built a place to work on them…' Slow and painful he drops each syllable as if from a bloodied mouth. 'She used to go there, and they became close…' He folds his arms and stares at me defiantly. His face is taut, voice low and trembling. 'Catrin, promise me you won't talk to him…'

'I promise you nothing,' I spit at him with all the force of contempt I feel for the way he has kept these secrets.

I thought he was just some weirdo. The way he would stare

at me then give me a wide berth. He must have wanted to tell me all along. Wanted to talk about my mother, something I've never been able to do here, something my father has denied me since the day it happened.

'Catrin...' My father's voice is full of warning. He watches me putting together the pieces of the puzzle as if he's waiting for an explosion.

Mr Thomas will know what happened to her camera. He might have been there that day, know what she was thinking. Or...

'Do the police know?'

'There was nothing to tell. It's private.'

'And you decided that, did you?' I shout. 'What if he lied about Mum the way he's lied about Emily?' My breath catches in my throat, and I stop there.

My father stares at me, his face unreadable, eyes burning with something unsayable.

'I don't know...' he stumbles over his words, not used to speaking and thinking on his feet, unable to hide behind the long silences usually between us, 'what his involvement is with Emily. But I can promise you he's got nothing to say about your mother that you should hear.'

'You can promise me?' My voice is mocking. What is a promise from my father worth? 'He lies about everything. Don't you want to know?'

'No. He has nothing to say.' There is a grit in his voice that I'm not used to. Something hidden. My father's face is grey, eyes sparking with anger.

'I'm calling the police. This has to stop.'

'Catrin, they won't help you...'

'And you will?' I shout back.

His shoulders sag. The old man returns, all his fury seeping away, leaving him slumped like a stack of stale hay. He swipes his cap onto his head.

'Work to do,' he says in a voice so flat and devoid of feeling I want to pound my fists on his back. Make him feel the way I do. Make him feel anything. Instead, I turn towards the house.

*

Swift jumps up at me as I bowl through the door of the farmhouse. I brush her out of the way and head straight for the phone, punching in the digits. The line rings out. A formal voice asks how they can help.

'PC Quinn, please,' I say, no politeness in my voice. It has to be her. She's the one who missed a vital clue. The camera. I told her about it. She's the one who never stopped to ask the right questions.

The line crackles before a chirpy voice pipes up.

'PC Quinn here.'

'It's Catrin. I need to talk to you about…'

'Slow down, please, Catrin. You sound very agitated.'

'I am.' I will myself not to shout or cry. I just need to tell her the information. It's her job to make sense of it. 'It's about my mother, she had a friend. I didn't know about it at the time, but I do now. He could have some information…'

'Catrin, I'm sorry. You're referring to an accident that happened three years ago. I can't help you with that.' She doesn't sound sorry at all. Her voice is smug with an air of looking down her nose at us.

'I think he'll know about her camera. She always...'

A sigh at the other end of the line. I punch my fist into the cushion on the chair next to me.

'Catrin, there was no reason to suspect anything strange...'

'There was every reason to suspect something was wrong,' I shout out, losing control and regretting it immediately, my words streaming out like misfired shots. 'You were just too stupid to see it.'

'Now, that's enough...'

But I can't stop. The dam has burst.

'She always had her camera and she knew the tides. Who would pick their own flowers? I told you this and you wouldn't listen. She knew that place better than anyone. You should have been looking for her. She would never have been caught out. Ever. She either wanted to die or someone hurt her.' My throat is burning.

There is a pause. For a second I think she might have hung up, then she speaks gently as if to a frightened child.

'Catrin, people have been caught out before. The tides are dangerous and it's very sad. Your mother had a tragic accident. She might well have known her way about, but if she slipped and broke her arm, she wouldn't have been in a state to get out. I'm sorry you...'

'Broke her arm?' The room swims around me. They wouldn't tell me the details. Said I was too young. The shock of finding her body was enough. 'What do you mean?'

'Just that. She had an accident. What's this about?'

'It was Mr Thomas,' I tell her, playing my last card in a desperate fit of hopelessness. 'He's been lying about Emily; he could have done something to my mother too.'

She sighs again, this time deeply. Her tone quickly changing back to the schoolmarm voice I hate.

'Now, this vendetta against Mr Thomas has to stop.' Her words are clipped. I imagine her gesturing to a colleague, mouthing my name, and rolling her eyes.

'He has a photo of Emily, he cut up her jumper and put it in the marsh. He's hiding things. My father told me they were friends. Please, you can't trust him.' My energy gives up at the last words. They ring hollow and desperate in my own ears, so what must she think of me?

'I'm a mother, Catrin, so I'm going to give you a bit of advice. Light a candle and say a prayer. Go and visit your mother's grave and tell her you love her. I'm sure she knew, but it'll make you feel better. Then move on with your life. She wouldn't want you to be suffering all these years later. She'd want you to be happy.'

'If you'd just looked when I told you. Why didn't you believe me?' I whisper.

'We did our best. And so did you,' she tells me in clipped tones. 'Let her go.'

The receiver clicks and the phone gives out a long wailing tone.

22

I sit cradling the phone receiver when the front door slams. I haven't got the energy for another fight with my father. He appears in the doorway, cheeks pinked from the rush.

'Dai's coming. Emily's father is going after Mr Thomas. Something about a photo.'

He doesn't need to say more. I can guess what Bryn is capable of.

'Wait.' I jump up and throw my coat back on. I need answers from Mr Thomas about my mother while he can still talk.

My father prickles. 'It's not as simple as you think, Catrin.'

'Then you should have told me yourself,' I shoot back.

The screech of tyres in our yard sends us both running out to meet Dai. He's grim-faced and already turning the pickup around to head back to the road. He doesn't get out, just shouts, 'Come on' over the noise of the engine.

I run after them. Dai throws a few words out: *lost the plot, spoiling for a fight*. My father shoots a dark glance my way, but his step doesn't falter. I haul myself up into the back of the truck with Dai's dogs and no one says another word.

Then we're travelling down our drive, barely stopping for the corner, before we're bombing along the marsh, and I hug the dogs, inhaling their musty fur as we bounce around in the back.

The engine pulls to a halt. Two doors slam as my father and Dai jump out. Raised voices. Dai must have asked Maureen to send reinforcements.

Dai barks a command, and the five men march up Mr Thomas' drive. The sun is in my eyes. I can just see their outlines, black bristling shadows, as they disappear from sight.

Dai's dogs yelp at the loss of him.

I jump over the side, hoping Mr Thomas will be in his outhouse, and run.

*

I sprint as fast as I can up the path and veer behind the house towards the darkroom. If I can get to him first. Tell him he has to talk. But as I round the corner my heart drops: the back door is open. I speed up the steps and through the open hallway.

'Mr Thomas?' No reply. I walk through the house checking each room but they're all empty.

There's a shout from outside.

Then another.

I dash around to the front of the bungalow and immediately wish I was somewhere else. Anywhere else. Bryn is standing inches from Mr Thomas. Two shopping bags from the big supermarket lie scattered on the floor. Mr Thomas' face is grey, and Bryn is red with fury. My father has a hand on Bryn's shoulder, his knuckles white with the effort of holding him back.

'Where is she? You bloody pervert.' Bryn pushes Mr Thomas. 'Enough messin', you tell me where she is.'

195

Mr Thomas shakes his head and steps backwards. The shopping bags crack and squelch under his feet.

'I've told the police everything I know. I wish I could help more but…'

Bryn grabs him by the shoulders and shakes him fiercely.

'No, you haven't, you haven't told them everything, have you? Cos you're a bloody liar.'

Mr Thomas' head rocks back and forth. Dai steps up and takes his place at Bryn's other shoulder. Dai, always reasonable and fair, places his hands between them, separating them by a little more distance. Bryn tries to swat his hands away but Dai stands firm. Mr Thomas takes a breath in.

'I don't know where your daughter is. I wish she hadn't brought her problems to me. I thought I could help.'

Bryn snarls.

'Is that it? You thought you could give her a shoulder to cry on. Took advantage.' He swings again at Mr Thomas who just manages to move his body away from the blow.

'No, no.' He stutters, body shaking. 'I was a teacher; we're trained to listen. I just wanted to help.' He raises his hands to placate Bryn, all the polish and eloquence of his usual speech replaced with panic.

'But you're not a teacher anymore. Why's that? Did you get the boot for being over-friendly? Taking photos of your students?' Bryn's spit lands on Mr Thomas' face.

'I was ill.'

'That's right, because you're sick in the head, aren't you? An old bloke who's sick in the head was taking advantage of my daughter.' He screams out the last words.

Mr Thomas shudders. He stammers and stutters.

'Is this about the land? Getting rid of me? I won't sell...' He stares at my father hard. 'Did you put them up to this? You ought to take some responsibility for...'

Bryn charges towards him, shouting, driving him up towards the house. Each shove getting harder and harder; the only sound the thump of fists against ribs.

'You are not going anywhere until you tell us the bloody truth!'

Bryn gives him a final whack in the chest that sends him flying. He catches sight of me cowering at the corner of the house.

'Right! Let's have this out now, shall we?' He stalks over, grabs me by the wrist and drags me over to Mr Thomas, throwing me in front of him. I catch sight of my father lurching forwards but Dai stops him.

'She says you've got a photo of my daughter. Something you didn't tell the police.'

Mr Thomas' face has drained of all colour. Spit has gathered in the corner of his mouth. His eyes roll towards me as if he's seeing someone else. 'A photo?'

'Now is she a liar, or are you?' Bryn roars.

'Alright, that's enough.' My father steps between Bryn and me.

'And if it was your daughter missing?' Bryn grabs at me again. My father and Dai take one arm each and hold him still. Dai talks to him in a low voice. 'Let's keep it calm.'

The word ignites Bryn like a fury; he shakes both of them off and kicks Mr Thomas hard in the stomach. There is a dull sound of boot against body.

My father turns to me. 'Catrin, go home.'

I shake my head.

Bryn grabs Mr Thomas by the collar and hauls him to his feet. Mr Thomas is breathing hard, his face contorted in pain.

'Who's the liar?' he rages.

'I am,' Mr Thomas whispers.

Bryn's eyes roll in his head, and he throws him down to the ground viciously.

'You knew my daughter?'

'I talked to her. It's true.'

'Bloody pervert. What did you do to her?' He kicks him again.

'Nothing. She needed help.'

Bryn roars and kicks him again. This time Mr Thomas cries out with every force of energy he has left in him.

'She's pregnant!'

Everything stops for a second.

It's as if the whole world slows down at the sound of his words. Dai drops his arm from Bryn's shoulder and turns away, his face a picture of anger and disbelief. The other men exchange glances of fear. They move towards him in unison, knowing what will happen next. Trying to stop it. Bryn lurches, takes a step back to prepare himself for a hard kick.

'Was it you?' he screams.

Mr Thomas shakes his head fervently.

'No. No. I was helping her.'

Bryn kicks him hard in the stomach. A dull thud.

'Stop,' I shout out, running between them.

It all happens in a second. Mr Thomas' hand on my ankle. Me falling towards the floor. Bryn's kick landing squarely in my stomach.

All the air is gone.

No breath.

Pain radiates through my body.

Mr Thomas whispers to me through his weeping. 'No, Catrin. I deserve it, let him do it. I deserve it.'

Dai appears, running. His face is grim, blazing with anger and something else.

He knows.

I gulp in air as I stare at him. Dai knows Mr Thomas is telling the truth.

Then my father is at my shoulder helping me up off the ground. I gasp in a full breath, stomach and chest throbbing. My head swims and my legs are weak under me. My father pulls me in tight and hugs me. How long since we hugged each other? The smell of him fills my nostrils: wool and soil, warmth. I want to stay like this, tell him I'm sorry. For everything. But he stands me up and leaves me, dashes over to Dai who has Bryn in a headlock helped by two others.

When we get to the bottom of the path Lorna is parking up. Dai's dogs sit up and bark at the sight of him. He runs down the slope, Bryn pulling at him like a crazed stallion, resisting all the way. Dai lets him go and he finally stops fighting. He leans his palms on his knees as if someone has winded him. Lorna goes to him.

'Bryn?'

He wheels around to face her.

'Did you know? Tell me you didn't bloody know, Lorna.'

'What's happened, love?'

He doesn't answer her. Instead, he shakes his head and gets into the car, slamming the door so hard the whole body of it quivers.

It's Dai who turns to Lorna, can't meet her gaze.

'He said she's pregnant. That changes things.'

'My girl? By him? No. Not that, Dai, tell me it's not that.' Her voice is pleading. Dai gives her a long look devoid of all sympathy and shakes his head.

'Police and ambulance are on their way. Bryn's been up the stables with me the whole time. Okay?'

'No, it is not okay.' Lorna grabs his arm. 'My girl taken advantage of. How is *that* okay?'

The veins in Dai's neck are all lifted under his skin. Sweat drips down the back of his neck even on this cold day. He wipes his hand across his brow.

'That's not my problem, Lorna.' He shrugs off her arm. 'Talk to the police if you want to. You've had your fun with us. With Bev. We're done. This is your bloody mess to sort out.'

Dai nods to my father. They march towards his truck. I'm forgotten, any tenderness already lost.

Lorna and I are left standing between the departing cars. I cradle my stomach in my free hand, the pain of the blow still pulsing through me. Lorna is trembling, her hand covering her mouth. She turns again to Bryn who is slumped in the car, head resting on the steering wheel.

'I didn't know about this, Bryn. I swear to you,' she whispers.

He doesn't lift his head or say a word. She edges towards him as if he's a wild animal.

'It makes sense now why she ran away. Silly bugger. She's scared herself. She'll be back, she's going to need us now. Both of us.'

Bryn shouts at her from the car.

'You know what, love? You don't seem very bloody shocked.'

'So, what now?' she shouts, eyeing the men in turn. 'Do we just take his word that he isn't the father of this baby? Let him off the hook.'

Dai calls out from his cab, voice heavy with warning.

'He'll be lucky if he hasn't broken all his ribs, Lorna. I'd say he doesn't know anything else, wouldn't you? Enough now.' Something bigger and heavier than before remains unspoken between them.

'We're not looking for the father of any baby!' Bryn smacks his hands on the wheel and revs the engine. 'I want to know where my bloody daughter is. Get in, will you?'

'No,' Lorna hisses. 'He's going to pay for this. Someone has to.' She walks towards Mr Thomas' house.

Bryn stamps his foot on the accelerator and screams. I can't tell if it's the car or him making such a noise. He takes off along the road so fast the bonnet bounces open and shut on the bumps.

'He's going to kill himself.' Dai closes the cab door and races off down the road. The other car follows.

I'm left alone on the roadside.

Two sets of blue flashing lights appear further up the marsh road.

If anything happens to Lorna, Roddy will try and take the blame for her again. I can't let that happen. I run up the drive after her.

*

When I get to Mr Thomas' house Lorna is at the front door but there's no sign of him. He must have crawled inside. Lorna is banging and tearing at the wood like a wild animal. Her hair flies around her face, cheeks red with rage.

'Open the door, you pervert. You think you can get her pregnant then walk away, do you?' She slams her body against the house. She's sobbing so hard she can barely breathe but still she punches at the wood as if Emily was behind it.

'You've ruined everything, he's never going to stay now. I had it all sorted. So, it's your turn to pay up, you hear?'

The police car pulls up, followed by an ambulance. PC Quinn jumps out and runs over.

'I need to talk to Bev,' Lorna whispers.

PC Quinn nods and soothes her, rubbing her back, whispering over and over. She shoots me a look full of contempt.

'You *cannot* be here,' she hisses, leading Lorna past me and helping her into the car, before turning to head around the back of the bungalow with the paramedics. Lorna slumps against the passenger seat.

'It's going to be me, looking after a bloody baby again, Catrin. I've done my time. Don't I get to be happy, eh?'

When PC Quinn comes back out with the paramedics and Mr Thomas strapped to a stretcher she pauses beside me. 'He says he fell.' She spits the words out. 'I'd expect nothing less down here. This is not a game, Catrin. What you've done is spiteful and it will not bring your mother back.'

I open my mouth to protest, but she cuts me off.

'Next time it'll be you in this car going to the station.'

I watch as they pull away, then I walk around to the back of the house. I push the screen door open and go inside.

202

23

I wander down the dark hallway towards the study. The desire to look at that window one last time – at our marsh from up here on high – too overwhelming to avoid.

The afternoon light glows behind the panoramic window. Through the glass, the tide glints on the estuary. Everything in perfect miniature. Did he and my mother sit here and watch the estuary? Wait for the perfect moment to rush outside and take photos? I used to be her co-conspirator, the one she would show the first prints to, holding our breath and hoping they would come out exactly as she wanted. While she was swishing liquid over paper I would say, *be perfect, be perfect,* because I wanted to see her smile.

I glance at the lighthouse; a ray of sun catches the metal and shines like a tiny searchlight. I turn away from the window and march through the hall to the bedroom.

There is nothing in the room except the bed and bedside table. His boxes of pills lie next to a glass of water. I stoop to look under the bed. Nothing.

Just do it, Catrin. A see-saw sickness of unease sweeps over me. The idea of opening something that can never be closed again.

I walk over and fling both sides of the wardrobe open at once.

A mix of black, beige and brown clothes stare back at me, all carefully hung and ironed.

But there is an inner door on the right-hand side of the wardrobe, the old-fashioned type that would have housed shoes.

Squeezed on the five shelves are piles and piles of black packets. I know from the colour and smell of them what they are.

I grab one, tugging it gently to get it free of the others, and slide the photos out. There, framed perfectly in the reeds is my father, or the shadow of him, out on the marsh. My mother's style is unmistakable. He's walking away from her. The paper flaps with the tremble of my hand.

After her death I asked my father about her photos and he said they were gone. Didn't know where. No explanation. Does he know Mr Thomas has them?

I study my father's form in the image; his back is straight with what I know to be anger. What had they been arguing about to make him walk off like that? And her, more inclined to take a picture than go after him to fix it.

I turn the photo over but there is no date on it. Usually, she would write them on the back like little spiders huddling in the corner of the page.

I flick through the bunch and stop. The other photos drop to the ground, and I remain holding just one. It shows the face of a girl, wild dark hair dashing in the wind, eyes filled with delight or pride as she smooths the back of a marsh pony.

I close my eyes.

I can feel the coarse hairs under my hand again, remember the cold wind that had brightened our cheeks, the way I had won the pony's trust by standing as still as a wading bird with my hand outstretched until curiosity overcame him, and he snuffled a velvet nose against my fingers. And the first thing I did: turn to look for her, to show her what I could do, who I was. Instead of seeing her face, I heard the click and winding of the film, and I was satisfied.

I open my eyes to look again at the photo. That child cannot be me. There is joy in her face, an unrecognisable lightness to her features; something I haven't felt for so long. And something else, what is it? A pleading look. *Love me, please*. I wanted her to come over, kiss my head and join in with stroking the pony. But she was always the observer and with that came the distance of being observed.

I slide the image into my jacket pocket. Mr Thomas has no right to my memories. Our memories. And why didn't he want me to see this, to know he had them?

I used to think her photos were the most precious thing in the world, but now there is a dawning of something else. Of the child that wasn't seen. Of how much time I spent trying to please her, to win her attention. So focused as she was on her photos, I felt like a burden, unimportant unless I was in her lens.

Part of me wants to take a match to the whole wardrobe right now. The whole house. Instead, I take a deep breath and slide them back into place.

They are nothing but ghosts after all. He can keep them.

I run my hand over the packets. It's hard to admit I didn't know her. Not in the way I thought. Can we ever know our parents? The way we raise them up like gods only for them to come crashing to earth as we get older. But not her. She has always stayed perfect in my mind. It was only my father who had the privilege of failing me. Until now.

I check the last shelf. There's a box pushed so far back that I have to stick my whole arm in to drag it out. It's heavy and tips forward onto my knees. The lid falls to the ground. I jump up and away as a black leather case lands on the floor with a dull thump.

A camera spills out from the case, jolted by the knock. I look around, half expecting my mother to come running in at the sound of it.

The only noise is my shallow intake of breath.

I already know that it's hers. She showed it to me so many times, and I, like a child looking at a favourite sibling, marvelled over every tiny scratch and button, hoping some of its favour would eventually fall to me.

The camera shakes in my hands as I draw it towards me. There, the small dint where it dragged against the wall we climbed over for a better view of the church. Here, the scratch from a fall on the causeway near the lighthouse.

I run my fingers over the buttons as if I am touching my hands over hers; the deft way she wound on the film, clicked the adjustments without looking, never taking her eyes off her subject.

I place the camera carefully back into its case then pass the strap over my shoulder, hanging it next to my hip just as she did. I shove the empty shoe box back into the wardrobe.

As I pass the mirror, I take a sharp breath in.

A quick glance and I could be her. Same dark curly hair and green eyes. My body turns itself to the mirror and I take out the camera again. Holding it the same way she did. Seeing myself reflected through the lens. Without thinking I push my finger down on the curved button. It clicks with a clunk, and my thumb searches for the lever. It's light to the touch; there's no film inside. I lower the camera and look at my own reflection. So far now from the little girl who adored her.

I could call the police but what would they say? Mr Thomas would calmly tell them it was a gift from a friend and they'd believe him.

No. The camera will come with me. I need to show this to my father. It's the one thing we can agree on, she would never have given it to anyone else, not by choice.

I leave the wardrobe door open. A message to him for when he returns. I *know*.

24

I arrive home to find Dai and my father deep in conversation at the kitchen table. I twist the camera so it sits behind my hip, resting lightly on my back.

They fall silent at the sight of me.

'I walked,' I say, and they both look sheepish for having left me at Mr Thomas' without a second thought.

My father takes off his cap and rubs his face with his hands, staying silent.

'Sorry,' says Dai, sipping his tea. 'Got out of hand.'

I scoff.

'What did you think would happen?'

'We were there to stop it,' he reminds me.

'Does it hurt much?' My father won't look at me directly.

I hold up my jumper and show them my middle where a red mark is turning green and purple. They both look down at their mugs. My father eventually looks back at me.

'You were brave... to jump in like that.'

'He could have killed him.'

'We wouldn't have let it...'

'Out of hand, you said?' And I stare at them hard until they both look away.

My father shuffles in his chair, unusually eager to make peace.

'He doesn't know anything more about Emily. That's clear enough.'

'No but he…' I stop myself mid-sentence. I don't want them to know what he was whispering to himself. That he deserved to be punished. I'm not sure even I want to know what it means. They look at me expectantly, but I shake my head.

'Nothing. He lied and…'

'And he's more than paid,' my father cuts in.

We hold each other's gaze for a second then both look away. Paid for what, exactly? I try and read how much he knows but as always, his face stays impassive.

The phone rings and I roll my eyes. If Maureen dares call here looking for gossip… I stalk out and grab the receiver.

'It's Bev, is Dai there? She's gone, Catrin, gone.' Her voice is thick and slurred. I shake the receiver at Dai, wondering which of the mares has got out, and he jumps up like a man who's learnt to assume disaster when it comes to his wife. He takes the phone and I go back to sit with my father.

Dai's placating voice drifts in from the other room. My father sloshes his tea around. He's tired; we survive together on this mixture of silence and habit neither of us is willing to break.

Dai jogs back in and snatches up his jacket. He nods at my father and heads for the door.

'What's happened?' I ask. I hope Bev hasn't heard about the fight and drunk herself into a stupor. The last time she had to go to hospital and have her stomach pumped, Dai told everyone it was gallstones.

'Something to sort back home.'

'Bev alright?' My dad raises his eyebrows.

Dai shrugs.

'She's not making any sense. You know how she gets.'

'Did she let the mares out by mistake?' It wouldn't be the first time Bev's let the horses get loose, saying she'd gone to get Rhys' horse for him.

'I don't know what she was thinking, Catrin. Honestly, I don't. This is all a bloody mess.' He stops himself from saying more and curses.

My father and I exchange glances.

'Let me help with the horses.' I stand up.

'I'll deal with it.' He turns to the door.

'I could…'

'I said I'll deal with it, Catrin,' he shouts across me and I flinch. He's never raised his voice to me before.

The phone trills out again. This time Dai marches over and grabs at it with such rage that the books next to the receiver topple to the floor.

'Stay inside, Bev, I'm telling you, don't leave the house.' Dai's shoulders are tense, and he shifts his weight from foot to foot. He listens to Bev for a second before cutting her off mid flow.

'Do you hear me? Stay in the bloody house. Don't talk to anyone.' He spells the last words out and slams the receiver down.

I've never heard him swear at Bev before. Neither my father nor I dare say a word as he dashes past us, cheeks reddened with rage. The door slams after him, shuddering in the frame.

I turn to my father but he says nothing and takes a swig from his mug, setting it back on the table.

Still, we've got enough of our own problems to sort out.

'I found her camera,' I say, leaving the words hanging in the air, checking his expression for any admission or surprise.

My father's hands stay on the mug, studying the handle as if it was the most interesting thing in the world.

'Where?' he asks.

'You tell me.' I won't let him have it that easily.

'Catrin...' It's the same heavy warning tone as always.

But I won't stand for it anymore. I swing the camera around and hold it up to him. He looks away as if even the sight of it pains him. Brings her back when he'd rather she was gone.

'Did you know he had it?'

My father stares at his hands for what feels like forever. Finally, he looks up at me and the camera, his face full of pain.

'No.' The word comes out thick like a groan. The effort of it almost too much.

I sit down at the table opposite him. His eyes have wandered to the camera, and I wonder if he remembers her hands on it, imagining it all, recalling her as well as I do. An ache in my chest. Why won't he ever share his grief with me? I needed to see it. To know it was okay to miss her.

He shifts in his seat, hand reaching almost unconsciously to the camera as if it were her. His eyes are full of love and sorrow. I can't look at him. It's too late for us to be having this conversation. Too unfair that it's happening now.

I remove the strap and place the camera case on the table between us. Her presence seems to fill the room, and with it that terrible unease. I never knew what would happen; the house wasn't a safe place to be, with arguments blowing up at any moment, doors slamming, my mother or father disappearing into the night.

He takes the camera from the box and holds it up, the tremble in his hands noticeable. Doing exactly as I did, he presses his eye to the lens, his finger over the button. But he doesn't push it down. The camera means something else to him. He sags as if the weight of it is impossible to sustain.

'She would never have given it to him. To anyone.' My voice is cold.

He nods slowly in agreement, coming back from the past to the kitchen again.

'Catrin, they were…' His voice trails off, still unable to say it. I want to put my hands over my ears to shut out the idea, but I already know the answer, have done since I saw his darkroom, her precious photos, the way he smiled at the memory of her. She must have loved him.

'Together?' I try to save him some of the pain.

He nods and looks away with something like shame.

'How long?' As if it matters but it's something to say, to keep him talking.

'Months.'

'You knew about it?'

Was he glad she'd found someone else? Someone who would get her out of his hair, make the arguments stop. I look at his face; it is etched with a deep sorrow.

'She told me.'

Silence.

If she told him, it must have been because she was leaving. The room reels.

She always acted like she wanted to get away from us, this small life, and here's the proof she was going to do it – swap us for him. This farm for that bungalow. My father for that man. And me? Would I have been so easy to forget? My father knows what question is coming next. He leans back as if to avoid it.

212

'Was she going to take me?'

He sighs.

'Catrin, it was more complicated than that...' His words trail off, trying to save me from something. 'She was more complicated...' He sighs and gives me a long look. 'When we met, she was a mess, drinking and partying, all sorts... I'd never known anyone like that, free of obligation but running from herself.' He smiles sadly at the memory of it. 'I wanted to look after her, give her what she'd never had.'

'Stability?' I say, although it feels cruel, reducing my father and everything he's worth to one word.

He nods.

'She loved it here at first. The wildness of it. The farm. You. Then it changed. She got restless. Nothing was enough.' His eyes fill up and he blinks the tears away. 'I gave her everything I could.'

'She needed something for herself,' I say, knowing it to be true. Not a mother or wife, something that led her back to herself. Only, when she got there, she didn't know what to do, couldn't find a way to manage us and her photography. Couldn't see how she could stay and settle... Then Mr Thomas must have come along. 'She would have left us both.'

My mother didn't want me. She was prepared to leave me here on the farm while she went and lived the life she'd always dreamt of; two artists together, passionate about the world, taking photos with no responsibilities to hold them back. *Without us.* That's why my father never told me. He wanted to stop me from knowing that what I've thought all along was right – we weren't enough for her. And yet, he let me worship her, watched me try so hard to get her approval, following her around, soaking up every insult she threw at this place and the people who live here. Who am I if I remove all of that?

I jump up.

'I deserved to know.'

'You deserved better than we gave you.' He sighs.

There it is – his slide back into self-pity. I can't be here to watch it. I slam my hand down on the table.

'The *truth* was the least you could have given me. Both of you.' I shout for Swift and push my body towards the door, towards air and space, some kind of release.

25

Rainwater drips off every part of my clothes and face. A storm broke as I walked and walked out on the flats, but after the conversation with my father I couldn't find any peace out there.

Not now.

Not knowing she was deceiving us the whole time.

Fat drops of rain slip into my eyes, blurring my vision for a second. What am I doing here – standing in the pounding rain hoping to see Roddy's face?

Please let him be in.

I knock at Lorna's front door.

When I told him about my mother, he listened. No judgment or false sympathy. And I want to tell him about the camera. No. *Need* to talk to him about it. To someone who cares. My body is jangling with this strange new fear. I touch Swift's head for comfort; she's soaking wet too.

The door swings open, and I see his smile first, wide with optimism as if the world will always be on his side. Everything urgent I want to say evaporates in that moment.

'Well, well, look what the tide's washed up.' He gestures us inside.

I signal to Swift to sit down in the porch, but he shrugs.

'Don't think it's possible to make Bryn angrier than he already is.' He whistles her in.

Roddy talks nonstop about Lorna as we go into the kitchen. She's upstairs. Hasn't been out of her room since PC Quinn picked her up off Mr Thomas' doorstep. News of the pregnancy has sent her over the edge. Keeps saying everything's lost and there's no way of fixing it now Bryn knows. Won't talk to anyone, not even him.

Roddy doesn't show any signs of bitterness. He just can't be still for a moment, constantly cleaning and putting things back in their place. He picks up two mugs and shines them with a tea towel, checking them then rubbing some more. A small smile of satisfaction jumps at the corner of his mouth once he decides they're clean. He starts to make tea, laying everything out on the kitchen top first then methodically making each cup. He turns back and fore to me as he does, buzzing with energy: washing the spoon, drying it, and putting it back in the drawer before bringing the tea over to the table.

'There you go. So, to what do I owe the pleasure of this visit? I know it's not the quality of my biscuits.' He offers me half a custard cream from an otherwise empty tin.

I smile. There's a strange atmosphere. The two of us alone. I shuffle in my chair. The idea of coming here and asking him for help was easier than actually doing it. I find myself saying something else instead.

'It's all gone mad down there.'

'And you've come here?' He chuckles to himself.

I look at my tea. I'm starting to understand his humour is a way of saying he's not okay. The same way defensiveness is mine.

'I found my mother's camera. You were right.'

'I'm sorry…' He looks genuinely surprised. 'Where was it?'

I pick at a nail.

'Mr Thomas had it. He doesn't know I've got it.'

He comes to sit opposite me and leans back in the chair. It seems like whatever I say to him he'll never be shocked.

'Did you tell the police?'

'No.' Trying to convince PC Quinn it actually means something would be unbearable.

'Didn't you say she never put it down?' He tries to soften the end of his question, but the idea is there – did Mr Thomas take it by force?

'They were together.'

'Oh.' He leans across the table to reach for my arm. The warmth of his hand on the top of my jumper is the only thing I can focus on for a minute.

'Sorry,' he says quietly.

I shrug. What does it matter? Now I know my mother didn't want me. Was leaving us for him.

Roddy seems distracted. He turns to glance at the door. God, he must think I'm so strange coming all the way here in the pouring rain just to tell him that. He shuffles his chair closer.

'Look, I'm on pins with Mam up in bed. But I'm listening. Tell me whatever you want.'

I look at him, the way his dark hair flops over one eye and makes me want to reach over and sweep it away. I don't know if I came here to tell him anything, or if it's the only place I want to be.

His face is open and expectant as if it should be so easy to tell him how I feel. But it's not. Never has been. I shrug his arm off gently. He pretends not to notice and reaches back for his tea.

I try a change of subject.

'They gave Mr Thomas a proper kicking. I got one too.' I hold up my jumper where the bruise is now an angry purple colour.

He sits up straight.

'She didn't tell me that.'

'It doesn't matter.'

'It does to me, who…?'

I shake my head. Some habits are hard to lose. Never tell on your own, no matter what they've done. My voice goes quiet.

'He said he deserved it.'

'Who?'

'Mr Thomas.'

'He wanted a beating?'

'He kept saying it over and over again.'

'Did he say why? Why didn't anyone tell me any of this?' Roddy's face fills with a hurt that says he's been left out for years while Lorna, Bryn and Emily have tried to play happy families. Tried and failed. He's the glue holding them together, whatever Bryn says.

'He was telling the truth. About Emily. Doesn't know where she is.' I can't tell him why I'm so sure. Dai's face confirmed it for me.

'Bryn said the same.' He shrugs sadly. 'Mam said he nearly killed him. Didn't think he'd go that far.'

His words echo with old blows – the fact he thought he knew exactly how far Bryn would go.

'I'm sorry about…' My voice trails off.

He ducks his head towards his chest and exhales.

'Not the best news. Didn't expect to be Uncle Roddy so soon.' A feeble smile, that constant attempt at humour to cover up sadness.

'Maybe that's why she's staying away?'

He shrugs again.

'It's set Mam right off and Bryn's even worse. Em's not stupid, if she wanted help she'd be here. If she's not, it's because she wants a baby.' He sighs and drops his shoulders, the weight of the world upon him. 'Enough of our mess, what about you?'

'I need to talk to Mr Thomas. Ask him about the camera. Find out what really happened.'

'So why come here?' His voice drops and he looks up at me as if he wants me to name it.

I'm suddenly irritated at him and my own body; the way it drifts towards him at every opportunity.

There's a creak from the bedroom upstairs. Roddy loses his smile. We both sit holding our breath.

Nothing.

'Will she be okay?' I nod to the ceiling.

'I don't know. There's something she's not saying. I know her guilty look. If she was half as clever as she thinks she is, we wouldn't have any problems at all.'

I want to free him of all this. But I know the only way for that to happen is if Bryn comes home and Emily appears, so Lorna can get back to whatever version of normality she's so desperate for.

'Lorna said Bryn had to stay. Get ready for when Emily needs them.' I expect him to be half pleased, instead a cloud of concern passes over his face, and he rolls his eyes.

219

'They're mad, those two. Can't live with him… same old story. How am I supposed to…' He catches himself and looks away for a moment.

'To what?' I ask.

'To make anything of myself when she keeps on dragging me back here.' He looks at me with a serious expression. 'When I was inside, I talked to someone. First time in my life, someone really listened to me, all my shit. You can't imagine how good that feels. To get rid of it, see it wasn't all your fault.'

'Sounds good.' I squeeze his arm with a smile, wishing I could tell him that's how I feel when I talk to him.

'Yeah.' He exhales slowly. 'Except in real life it's harder to shake it off. I started doing woodwork when I was in, making shelves and stuff. I'd never been good at anything before. Finally found something. They helped me make a plan, signed up for an apprenticeship. I had just two weeks on the job before all this kicked off. Lucky for me the gaffer's a decent bloke.' He shrugs in despair. 'Asking for a week off for family reasons isn't going to cut it next time.'

'What if it doesn't happen again, or if it does you let Lorna learn her lesson. Maybe that's what she needs.'

He puts his hand on top of mine. The air hangs heavily between us.

'What do *you* need, Catrin?'

Heat floods my cheeks. It would be so easy for someone else to look him in the eye, say, 'You' and let it all happen. But my body is tense, braced for the next disaster. I find it so hard to soften, as much as I want to.

'I've got an offer,' I say shyly. It's a cop out, changing the subject again, away from what I'm feeling, but I want him to know. 'To study art. Funded,' I add because it sounds so frivolous otherwise.

He opens into a wide smile.

'That's amazing. I said you were bloody good at it.'

'I'm not going to take it,' I blurt out.

'Why not?' He stares at me as if I was mad.

'I can't leave my dad... he needs me.'

He studies me for a second.

'That's not it though. What are you afraid of?'

I breathe deeply. Blink back the emotions.

'I don't want to be like her. Burdened with a dream I can't follow, taking it out on everyone else.'

'Better to be completely stuck?'

Why do I always feel like such an idiot around him? Like he can see the things about my life that are completely obvious, and I can't.

'Anyway. We've got to sort this mess out first,' I say.

He stands up, stung.

'Okay, so we've got my missing pregnant sister, Mr Thomas who's been beaten to a pulp and says he doesn't know where she is, and Mam wants Bryn back, but she's had a mini breakdown, although that's nothing new.' He grabs our mugs and starts swilling them under the tap, cleaning them again over and over.

I get up slowly and walk behind him. I reach out one hand and lay it on his shoulder. He flinches. I let my other hand rest gently on the other shoulder. His body gives way to it. He puts the cup down into the sink and lets his shoulders drop.

'I don't know what to do, Catrin. I can't fix it. Any of it. I just want my own life.' His body sags and before I know what

I'm doing, I turn him to face me and lift his chin with my finger. We stand like that for a moment. His brown eyes searching mine – a connection holding more than a thousand conversations ever could.

A large clunk from upstairs jerks both our heads up and the moment is lost. The timing feels cruel as slow and heavy steps sound out on the landing towards the stairs.

'Brace yourself.' He grimaces as we shuffle awkwardly away from each other.

Lorna opens the door, her hair plastered to her face and make-up smudged. The stale smell of her fills up the room. Roddy smiles and gestures to a chair.

'Good afternoon, sleeping beauty. Cuppa?'

She bats his hand away and makes a feeble gesture towards me, turning her head away so she doesn't have to look at me. No matter how many times I have tried, I cannot see how she is Roddy's mother.

Roddy goes about making her a cup of tea, the same drill as before. Lorna rubs her face with her hands, massaging her eyes then her cheeks.

'How long have I been out?'

'A while.' He stirs in three heaped sugars.

She groans. He puts the tea in front of her and guides her hand towards it.

'What, did you have plans?' He kisses her on the head and my heart expands with his ability to forgive so easily.

She gives him a tired smile and grabs his jaw with her hand.

'What did I do to deserve you, eh?' She looks up at me sharply.

'More good news?'

I try to ignore the nagging memory of Lorna pawing at Mr Thomas' door like a wild animal. I look to Roddy instead.

'Not about us,' he says, and I'm grateful he doesn't mention the camera.

'What, got another case on the go? You setting up as a private detective or something?' Her sarcasm needles at me.

I shuffle my feet, ready to make a quick exit. Roddy lays a hand on Lorna's shoulder.

'Be nice, Mam. Catrin came to see me.' He says the words with warning.

I wrap my arms around myself, trying to ignore the blooming happiness in my chest. Lorna drops her head sullenly.

'This Thomas bloke. He's going to have to pay up some child support.'

Roddy rolls his eyes, his constant activity wiping over the kitchen top, checking that everything is in its place, the only give away to his discomfort. Lorna ploughs on.

'I know for a fact she wasn't in the club before she went over to Dai's.' When her words are followed by silence from us both, she shrugs. 'Lisa did say an older man. Wealthy, according to her.'

'Mam, you haven't...' Roddy tries to keep his tone calm, his smile stretched tense, his question dressed up in a false playfulness.

She swats him away.

'Of course I have. My daughter pregnant! Think I'm not going to find out how to make him pay? It's either that or cut his sodding bits off with the bread knife.'

We both smile grimly, sure that Lorna is more than capable of doing that if left to her own devices.

'What did she say?' I ask as a way of calming her down.

She gives a satisfied smile and uses her hands to make sweeping shapes on the kitchen table.

'She said…' Lorna gives Roddy a long look. 'Emily was looking for love and found it in the wrong place.'

'God.' Roddy rolls his eyes. Unable to hide his exasperation he turns and finds a new part of the kitchen surface to scrub.

Lorna raises her voice. I wonder how much of this is about needing his, or anyone's, constant attention.

'An older bloke who seems respectable but isn't. Emily's been chasing him like a lost lamb.' Lorna thumps the table. 'That's what makes me mad. He hasn't even been treating her right.' She turns to me, looking for a sympathetic audience. 'These men.'

Roddy smashes the cutlery into the drawer. Lorna ignores him.

'They make you believe you're something really special. You're a silly little thing, and you think it's the best feeling in the world. Someone who says you're beautiful. Can't keep their hands off you…'

'Mam!' He slams the drawer shut and turns to face us. He's heard this story a thousand times before. His face is painted with anger and shame. This isn't Emily's story, it's Lorna's, and that means it's Roddy's too. I want to save him, but Lorna looks stubbornly into the distance and ploughs on.

'Tell you they love you, you're the best thing that ever happened to them. And for a while it's all lovely. This new thing you've discovered. Feeling desired all the time. You're on top of the world. Until the day you don't get your bloody period. Then you'll see them for who they really are. Robbing bastards who couldn't give a monkeys about you. You were just a body. A young body to enjoy and throw away. They don't want babies, these men. They want…'

'Alright, Mam, that's enough. We know how the story ends.' Roddy's voice trembles. He must have been made to feel like a mistake his whole life.

'Is there anyone else who could be the father?' I ask. Lorna snorts with laughter and takes a large slug of her tea.

'You given up on your theory about Mr Thomas, have you?'

'Mam, don't be rude. She's…'

Lorna shakes her head.

'She's what, love? Trying to help? Fat lot of good she's been so far. Or maybe that was the point?' Lorna jumps up, throwing Roddy's arm aside. 'You started pointing the finger at that old weirdo, Catrin. You said you found her jumper, which no one has actually seen. Helping out a friend, were you? Dai asked you to cover his tracks, did he?' She gasps. 'I can't believe I didn't twig before. You've all been playing me for a complete fool.'

My mouth falls open. Roddy looks at me with shock but also something else. Does he believe her? Does he think I would do something so awful?

Lorna moves closer to me, wagging her finger.

'Did he ask you to have his back? We know what your lot are like down there.' She sneers and I jerk away from her.

'Dai's got nothing to do with this,' I shout.

Lorna shakes her head and laughs.

'Of course not, salt of the earth our Dai. Everyone loves him, can't put a bloody foot wrong. What would people say, eh, if they knew the truth about him?'

'Mam, this isn't fair.' Roddy tries to take her hand gently and sit her down again.

The image of her and Dai in the stable that day comes back to me. He was so angry with Lorna, and she had the upper hand. She knows something.

'What?' I say, not sure if I really want to hear the answer. 'What is it?'

Lorna grumbles and shakes her head, folding her arms across her chest.

'What happened?' I insist.

She leans forward with a self-satisfied grin.

'The boy.'

Without wanting to, I see his freckled face and nut-brown hair. Always on top of a horse. Dai was so proud; said his son had been born right onto a cob's back.

'Rhys,' I say, my voice a whisper.

She nods viciously.

'Bev was drunk when he fell. They panicked. Worried what the law would do to a mother who knocked her own son off the horse.'

The thud of my heartbeat fills up my whole head. The room spins a little.

Rhys rode like magic, usually bareback, the kind of thing most people wouldn't let their children do, but Dai knew he could; he'd been brought up the same. Never expected his son to fall. Eight years old and his blood had seeped into the sand in the manége. But Bev hadn't been there. That's what I'd heard: she'd rushed out at the sound of Dai shouting. She used to retell the story, her voice high and quivering. *I knew it as soon as I heard Dai's voice*. She wasn't even drinking then, was she?

'Drunk?'

Lorna shrugs at me.

'I was there. Told the police the horse spooked. Dai lied and so did I. That cob was solid as a wall.'

'She didn't drink back then.' A whoosh of anger on Bev's behalf. 'She started after the funeral. Dai told me.' The last words are gospel. Anything Dai has told me, I've never questioned.

Lorna shakes her head with a defiant snort.

'Don't be daft. I cleaned their house. It was me who had to bag up all the bottles. See to Rhys if he needed anything. She was half-soaked all day. It was me she raged at if I moved one of her hidden stashes.'

'No.' But the word is lost as soon as I've said it. A final piece slipping into place. Bev's over-enthusiastic hugs. The shrill laughter that always went on for a moment too long. The way my father and Dai tiptoed around her. My mother never left me alone with her. The time Bev had screamed at me for ruining a game then cried herself to sleep on the sofa. My mother covering her with a blanket with all the care of looking after a sleeping baby. The words, *Bev's tired, she's having a nap* and all the times I'd heard them as a child.

Lorna watches my face and nods.

'She'd been at the gin. Let herself into the manége, and the boy was trotting that horse around like only he could. She'd shouted at him that morning because she'd had a sore head and she wanted to make it up. Slurring and whining about how much she loved her little boy. Wasted, she was. She stumbled and grabbed onto him. The horse kept on moving and he smacked down onto the sand. I thought he'd get up. Then we

227

saw the blood; slow it was, little streams coming from his nose and ears. Then the blood was on her hands, and she started screaming. I took her inside. I cleaned her up and gave her coffee to sober up while the ambulance was arriving. Dai told them the horse had spooked, said I was a witness. Never asked me if it was okay to lie. Expected it, he did. And I did it. She'd been awful but her little boy was gone.' Lorna fixes me with a stern look. 'I might be a lot of things, Catrin, but I know what loss feels like. Thought it would sober her up too, change her life. Fat chance. Dai kept on telling that story. He thinks she believes him. Thinks he's convinced her it was an accident. She's a drunk, not a bloody idiot.'

I open my mouth to say something, but no words come.

'Catrin, I'm sorry… I…' It's Roddy, trying to reach past Lorna to get to me.

She elbows at him, her face proud to have caused such a reaction.

I'm lost.

My father had come into the kitchen that night, a year after my mother's death, and sat down with all the heaviness of bad news. He'd loved that boy too, the way people who've experienced loss love all new life. He took off his cap, rubbed his hands over his eyes and told me, no sweetening of the words, just, 'Rhys is dead, fell from the cob today.' And what did I do? I ran away from his sadness and out onto the marsh until my chest burned and forced me to stop. Then I let out the wildest scream until my throat choked raw. It wasn't just for Rhys. It was for my mother and the unfairness of it. The hopelessness of never knowing who might be next.

I look up at Lorna. How could she enjoy telling the story?

And Dai? He chose to protect Bev. It makes sense now, the way she rattles around the house like a little lost doll.

'And you used this to bribe him?' My voice shakes with anger at all of it.

'He never even asked me, Catrin. Not a thank you, nothing. He let me go just like that.' She clicks her fingers. 'So, I'd say he owed me, wouldn't you?'

I meet Roddy's sorrowful gaze. I shake my head at him and back out of the room. I never doubted Dai's story, never even questioned it for a second, even though I knew what a good rider Rhys was. Everyone wondered why Dai hadn't got rid of Charlie-horse, why he didn't sell him on or shoot him dead. But Rhys loved that horse, and Dai knew he wasn't to blame.

I think of my mother and her accident, the way it was so quickly glossed over, packed up as a warning for everyone else never to be caught out by those estuary tides. *Accident.* Used as if it can excuse the death that came after it because it was simply something unforeseen or unfortunate.

'Catrin, wait…' Roddy calls, but I run away from him again, Swift following close behind.

I need the cool estuary wind on my face. The pressure of walking fast to take away these thoughts and this pain.

I slam the front door closed, muting the sound of Roddy calling my name.

26

I pelt down the hill with Swift panting at my side. My father knows the truth about Rhys' death. I'm sure of it, but I need to hear it from him.

The bus pulls up. I don't look at Mac as I get on.

'Penny for them?' He smiles from his cabin, head tilted thoughtfully to one side.

I don't answer.

'A pound then?' His smile widens.

'Not worth that,' I say quietly.

His face creases with concern.

'Not like you not to be up for a bit of banter. Can usually rely on you to put me in my place.' His voice is playful and a sweep of fresh shame washes over me.

Am I really that bad, so rude?

'Bad day,' I say simply, reaching into my pocket for the purse I already know is empty.

He waves his hands at me. 'On the house. Least I can do.'

'Mr Thomas is in a bad way,' I say. It's all I can manage without going into the strange mess this really is.

He nods, looking at me through his eyelashes, his voice gentler now.

'And you're feeling guilty about it?'

'Yes.' A lump choking in my throat that I quickly swallow back down.

'Not your fault, love.' He reaches out a hand and places it over mine. We stand there awkwardly for a moment.

'Do you know what would do you the world of good?'

'What?' Part of me hopes he really will have the answer.

'A night out.' He looks at me hopefully and smiles. 'A bit of a laugh.'

It's the way he wraps his mouth around the word laugh that makes me pull my hand out from under his weight. We've been here before.

'Always playing hard to get, Catrin.' He leans forward provocatively. 'Lucky for you, I don't give up easily.'

I take a long look at him, then walk up the back of the bus, remembering the feel of his hands on my waist that night, then unbuttoning my jeans, pushing me onto the back seat. The car spun and whirled with all the alcohol I'd drunk. It was the look on his face that changed things. The victorious expression of claiming what he assumed was already his. I'd shoved him then. He'd laughed, thinking it was a game, pushing me harder into the leather of the seat so my neck hurt. And that was the only thing my mother had taught me well – how to stay wild. I kicked and thrashed, watching his face change from shock to anger, before scrambling out of the car and pelting for the marsh. Shame burning through me all the way.

Mac shifts the bus into gear and is about to pull away when Jade runs towards us, waving wildly. He smacks his hand down on the release button, beaming.

'Now then, what have we got here?'

Jade jumps up the first step, giggling. She fumbles with her wallet. Mac says, *steady, steady,* setting her off into another fit of giggles. He holds out his hand and she places the coins into it.

There it is. An almost imperceptible movement as he closes his thumb over her hand, holding it there for just a second too long. Enough to send her cheeks bright red.

'Tell your mam she ought to be keeping an eye on you. Isn't that right, Catrin? Have you seen how beautiful this one is getting?'

Jade scurries up the bus and plonks herself into the seat in front of me. We smile at each other.

'He giving you trouble?' I whisper.

Her eyes widen and she shakes her head; deep pink blooms on her cheeks.

'He gets bored driving up and down all day.'

'Maybe he should bring a book,' I say.

She giggles and glances at him. When she's sure he's not listening she leans forward, resembling her mother for just a second in the most terrifying way.

'It's good you're here because he doesn't usually let me off the bus until I've answered his questions.' She dips her head.

'What kind of questions?' I nudge Swift and dutifully she jumps down and over to Jade for a cuddle. The girl's face lights up as she strokes her fur.

'Just silly things.'

'Like what?'

She picks at a knot in Swift's coat.

'If I've got myself a boyfriend yet.'

I'm not sure what I want to say. 'Don't mind him. He plays silly games,' is the best I can manage, and the words sound ridiculous as they spill out.

'He says my mam's got no sense of humour.' She grins, expecting me to join in.

I smile grimly. Maureen might be a lot of things but at least Jade has a mother who cares.

We jerk to a stop and Jade clip clops back down the aisle. I watch carefully this time, but Mac just calls out.

'Tell your mam you're starting to look like sisters, tell her I said that.' He chuckles at the idea of Maureen hearing this compliment.

Jade nods and scampers off the bus and down the lane. He watches her go then gives me a quick glance in the mirror.

'Still sulking?' he throws over his shoulder.

I look out the window, welcoming Swift back up next to me with a hug. Mac takes the hint, and we chug on to the stop above our lane. As the bus pulls in I walk towards him, waiting for the inevitable banter.

'You've said no to me so many times, I'm beginning to wonder if you've got a bloke on the side.'

The bus doors remain closed.

'You're very close to that Dai bloke, aren't you?'

'He's a family friend.'

'Yeah, they often are, aren't they?' He winks.

'You going to let me off?' I nod at the door.

'Haven't decided yet.'

'Fine,' I hiss and reach across him to the door-release.

He leans in and grabs my arm.

'You only have to ask,' he smirks, and pulls me towards him. 'I think you want me, but you don't want to admit it.'

The weight of his hand brings back the memory of me pushing him away in the car. He doesn't know how to take no for an answer.

'You know what I think is funny?' he says. 'Everyone piled

233

on that old bloke, but no one has even questioned whether your mate had anything to do with it.'

'And what about you chatting up anything in a skirt.'

He shakes his head, laughing.

'You're wearing jeans, Catrin.' He lowers his voice as if we're sharing some kind of secret. 'And I still fancy you.'

I step away from him. 'Piss. Off.'

'I will if you will.' He laughs again and opens the doors with a swoosh.

*

The rain has driven my father inside the barn. He's parked the tractor up and is giving her the once over. The metal clang of the door lifts his head. His body tenses as he sees me, and he stands up.

'Been out a while,' he says, patting his pockets for a rag to wipe his hands.

'Did you know the truth about what happened to Rhys?'

He wipes a mixture of oil and mud from his hands in a slow and deliberate motion.

'They've suffered enough.' He says it without looking up.

He knew. All this time, and he knew the truth. Why couldn't he have trusted me?

'All you do is lie.' My voice is stony.

He looks up sharply and the hurt is obvious on his face, but I won't feel sorry for him.

'When were you ever going to tell me the truth? About any of it?'

He sighs.

'What good would it have done?'

'I'd know what really happened.'

'None of us can know that, Catrin.'

I shake my head, snatching the cloth from his hands and throwing it to the floor. I won't be fobbed off.

'You could have told me the truth.'

'That's Dai's business.'

'I'm not talking about Dai,' I shout back.

He shifts his position, standing up straighter, the cost of this conversation evident in his slow movements.

'I was trying to tell you earlier. Your mother wanted to leave. I tried to stop her.'

'What?'

'I spoke to her that day.'

'No.' The word shoots out. He's never told me this. When I ran to him that night begging him to look for her he'd said she'd be back soon. But all that time he knew she wasn't coming back.

Did he try to stop her? Their arguments were always ferocious.

'On the marsh. I found her waiting for him. She'd left me a note in the kitchen. Didn't expect me to be back so soon. Thought she had time to…'

'To what?' I cry out incredulously.

'To come back and take you with her.'

Everything stalls a little as I take in his words. She was taking me with her. Not leaving me. Not going off alone with Mr Thomas.

'But I thought…' My voice is a whisper.

'She…' He chooses his words carefully. 'She changed her

mind. The note said. She wanted to go alone with you. Not with him. She'd realised she was making a mistake. Didn't want to be saved by another man. Controlled, she said. I didn't want that. Her taking you away. Didn't want any of it. She belonged here. You belong here.' His voice chokes and I can't believe that he would actually have fought for me to stay. For her.

I'd thought he was glad she was gone.

'What did you do?' I want the answer so desperately to be beautiful, but I already know how it all ends.

'I asked her to stay. For your sake.'

As simple as that. I bet he used those words too, whilst she stood there in front of him, waiting to know if she really mattered. That's all he could manage. No love, just duty. No wonder she never came home.

'When she didn't come back that night, you thought she'd gone? Without me? Changed her mind again.'

He looks at me carefully, not wanting to let on that he knows she was capable of it. That he wasn't even shocked enough by her supposed change of heart to go out there looking for her. To doubt her absence.

'You thought she'd leave us all?'

He shrugs with a heavy weight.

'She was a mystery to me, Catrin. I tried…'

'No.' I stop him. It's not fair. I don't want to hear his side, not when she's not here to defend herself. I never saw him try, he just carried on with the same old routines while she tried to be happy in a place she hated.

'You lied to me.'

His face darkens like a storm cloud passing through.

'What would you have me do?' he pleads.

I blanch at the desperation in his voice.

'You were a child, Catrin. You didn't need to know about our mess.' His voice chokes again on the last words.

There's an instinct to go to him, to hug him and tell him it's alright. But it's not. He let her stay out there. He knew she was leaving and didn't tell me. He could have told me any other time. But it was easier not to.

'I was seventeen. I found her body. I haven't been a child for a long time,' I say through gritted teeth. 'Don't you dare hide behind that.' A rage rises in me. 'And what about Dai, what else have you been keeping from me?'

My father's eyes widen at the change of tack.

'Do you know where Emily is?'

'Catrin?' he says, puzzled, but I'm loose now; all the frayed threads of anger are blowing in the wind, and I can't stop them.

'Does he know where Emily is?'

My father turns away from me.

'How can you think that?'

'Because I don't know who is telling the truth,' I shout. 'Because everyone has been lying to me since the day she died. How can I trust you, him, anyone?' My voice clogs with emotion.

'Catrin.' His voice is soothing, and he moves towards me.

It's too late. I needed him years ago. I thrash out as he comes closer.

'And where were you? The day after I found her. Why weren't you at home? I needed you...'

His mouth tightens into a grim line. There are still things he's not telling me, won't tell me, even after all this.

237

'Forget it,' I spit at him, turning my back and trudging out of the barn.

He doesn't call after me and I know if I turn around, I'll see him slowly picking up the rag to finish cleaning his hands; a man who cannot stop his routine for anyone. Not even for me.

27

The rain has lessened to a light spatter, landing so softly I hardly notice. My pace is fast; anger is always my fuel out here. Swift has come with me. I should have left her at home by the fire, all this cold weather isn't good for her.

The high tide is due today. Half of the mud flats are covered with water already. Everyone will have put their sandbags out and called their animals inside for the night. All except the marsh ponies, left to try their luck, standing belly deep until the tide goes out again. I glance around for them but they're already out on higher ground, patiently swishing their tails as if they already know how long they'll have to endure the cold creep of water.

I shiver.

It's always the thought of the water that makes me think of her. Was she cold? Did it seep into her clothes before clogging her lungs? Had she fallen, or something worse, and it was already too late? The police wouldn't tell me all the details though I'd asked. *Too young*, they said, *inappropriate*, never realising what you imagine is always far worse. I dreamt of my mother for weeks afterwards, gasping for air and grabbing at my legs. Scrambling and swishing, up to her neck in water. A dream where sometimes I would find her just in time, but most often too late.

I push my body forwards, lungs burning with the effort, to

try and expel the rage gathered in me. My father and his secrets. This place. What did it do to her, knowing he wanted her to stay for me? For duty, not love. Did it drive her to lie down, thinking I'd be better off without her, or was there something else? The only person who can answer this question is Mr Thomas.

I spot a figure further along the marsh road, wandering alone on the mud flats. Is it Emily? I squint through the drizzle but can't make them out.

What would it be like to be able to phone Roddy and tell him I've found Emily, laugh about all the things that have been going wrong and… And what? I shake the thought out of my head.

'Emily?' I shout out as I get closer, and the figure wheels around to face me. It's Bev, a look of panic etched across her face. She shakes her head at me and turns back to scanning the horizon and the flats.

'Bev? You okay?' I say gently as I take in her hunched shoulders, arms pulling a thin cardigan across her waist, skirt and shoes already sopping and covered in mud.

She puts her hands to her ears as if to wish me away. Swift slinks around her, confused too at seeing Bev anywhere but in their house. I move closer again and reach out to touch her arm. She looks up, her hair wild and sopping from the rain.

'I can't find her, Catrin.' She shakes her head, mutters the same words again under her breath. I put my arms around her; she's cold and must have been out here for ages.

'Maybe Dai's got her?' I say to reassure her. If one of the mares had got out Dai would have caught her in a few minutes and got her back to the stud.

She raises her face to me, eyes wide with disbelief.

'But it's my fault, Catrin. I scared her away. She won't come back to me.' Her voice rises.

I take in her wet clothes and muddy shoes. It has always been so easy to accept that Bev isn't alright. Everyone saying it was because of Rhys' death and no one questioning what could be done to help her get better. We've all become used to her rattling around the stud, hugging and happy one minute, teary the next. It's just Bev. When did her problems really start if she was drinking before? And how can she live with herself now? How many times have I heard, *Don't tell Bev, it'll just upset her* and nodded along with it, thinking I was helping. How many times have they said that about me, *Don't tell Catrin*. And the secrets have piled up all around us.

I wonder if she feels it too. The same creeping sensation that something in her life isn't quite right, because everyone has been trying to keep her safe from the very thing she needs to accept.

Bev shrugs me off and moves towards one of the smaller paths around the ditches. My own shoes squelch in the mud. The tide will be coursing up this way soon and we'd have to swim our way out if we get caught.

'Bev, let's go,' I shout to her, but she carries on walking.

Swift yaps a warning as the silver water spreads further across the horizon.

I run after her striding figure again.

'Bev, I know what really happened to Rhys and I'm sorry.'

She turns slowly to me, white as a cockleshell. She stares for a moment, taking in what I've said, then her body sags.

'I didn't mean to do it,' she whispers, rounding her shoulders.

'I know.' I walk over to her and take her by the arm. 'It was an accident.' And I hate myself for saying those words. Those little words that don't add up to the huge, gaping loss of someone you love. Those words that smooth over the what and the why to try and make it better for everyone else.

Her eyes meet mine; they are full of a deep sorrow and *knowing*. Knowing what she did; having to live with it.

'It's okay, Bev, let's go and find Dai.'

She shrugs me off more violently this time.

'No. Not him. He doesn't want me to be happy,' she says with such force I find myself nodding in agreement.

'Okay, but we have to go, the water's coming and it's the high tide today.' My voice is gentle, as if coaxing one of the ewes startled with fright, and she relaxes again, allowing me to steer her towards the road.

'I was on my way to get magazines and chocolates. I was trying to do the right thing,' she says.

I nod, happy to do whatever she needs just to get her out of here.

'But I can't find her.'

I feel out of my depth. Maureen will know what to do. Relief washes through me at the thought of her taking charge.

We reach the tarmac and I take Bev firmly by the arm.

'Let's go and get those things you wanted. Maureen will have something nice for us.'

The idea seems to cheer Bev and she lets me lead her along the road. We're nearing the village when she stops suddenly and turns to me.

'Don't tell anyone about it, Catrin, please.' The pleading in her voice makes me look away.

My hands reach for Swift's now wet coat, and I push my fingers in deeper to find the warm dry fur underneath.

'Of course not,' I say, and I mean it. My father was right. They have both suffered enough.

*

The bell trills out and Maureen's head snaps up from a glossy women's magazine. Jade is behind the counter helping her stack the newspapers that haven't sold.

Maureen takes one look at Bev's dripping form and her hand reaches for the phone. Before she picks it up, she arches an eyebrow at me.

'What's happened?'

Bev looks down at the floor. I can't betray her trust.

'We fancied a walk,' I say with forced cheerfulness, knowing full well that on a rainy day with a high October tide due, no one in their right mind would go walking anywhere. Maureen nods incredulously.

'That right? Forget your brolly, did you?' She nods at Bev who is sopping wet and shaking.

I pick up a magazine. 'Was this the one you wanted, Bev?' I say cheerfully, my voice too loud.

Maureen stares at us as if watching a theatre show. Bev shakes her head and points to the mother and baby magazines.

'I was going to get these.'

I pick a bunch of them and put them on the counter. I grab a few bars of chocolate.

'And these?'

Bev shakes her head.

'Has to be the one without peanuts.'

'No peanuts when pregnant,' Maureen confirms, eyeing up Bev with too much curiosity. 'How far along are you, Bev?'

Bev shakes her head.

'Oh, I don't know. It's hard to tell, isn't it.'

An awkward silence fills the space.

'Well, what did the doctor say?' Maureen pushes.

'Haven't been,' Bev mumbles.

The answer seems to satisfy something for Maureen. She nods curtly and starts running the magazines and chocolate through the till.

'You should go. At your age there are a lot of risks.'

Bev nods but says nothing.

'And you shouldn't be out in this weather in your condition,' Maureen adds. 'I'll give Dai a call and tell him to get down here and pick you up. He should be looking after you.'

Bev's head turns in panic. 'No!'

Maureen waits for an explanation but there isn't one forthcoming.

'He's a bit cross,' I chip in. 'I think one of the mares got out.'

'My silly fault,' Bev says sorrowfully. 'Dai's so angry, but I didn't mean to scare her.' A fat tear rolls down her cheek.

Maureen leans across the till and grabs Bev's arm.

'Don't go worrying about anything. You're the one having a baby. I'll tell him that myself. You need looking after.'

'Will you phone him?' I ask her.

She bites her lip and nods.

'Jade said she saw you on the bus.' The comment is loaded. I nod and pack the chocolate and magazines into a green plastic bag.

Jade looks up from her job with fearful eyes. Maureen continues.

'Apparently we look like sisters.' She gestures with her head to Jade, but her face is grim. 'Not the first time I've heard that,' she adds. She looks at me pointedly and lowers her voice. 'She's growing up so bloody fast. Luckily, she's got a mam who keeps tabs on her. Otherwise, lord knows what would happen with that pervert around.'

Bev looks up. 'They need looking after. These young girls. Always someone waiting to take advantage of them. They need their mams.'

Maureen gives her a long look.

'That's right, Bev. Mams or not. Got to look after our own, haven't we?'

The doorbell chimes again and Dai blusters in, his collar turned up against the wind and rain. He sees Bev and a mixture of anger and relief passes over his face.

'Where you been, love?'

Before she can answer Maureen jumps in.

'I could ask you the same thing, mister. Letting your wife walk about in this weather in her condition. Now take her home and give her a warm bath and a cup of ginger tea. Always worked for me when I was pregnant with Jade. Otherwise, she'll be shivering for hours.'

'I'm fine.' Bev rushes towards the door. Dai takes in her wet clothes and the bag of magazines.

'What have you been saying?' He doesn't wait for an answer. 'We'll talk about this at home.' He's more stern than I've ever heard him speak to her before.

Maureen turns to me after they've gone.

245

'Poor dab.' She shakes her head and snaps the credit book closed.

Jade jumps up from the newspapers.

'Finished,' she says in a weary voice.

'Right, well upstairs with you. Watch the soaps, then homework. Do you hear me? And no going out tonight to call for anyone.' Maureen looks at me. 'What with the high tide and that weirdo back from hospital, I've got to keep an eye on her.'

'Mr Thomas is back?' I ask, my body lurching at the news.

'Not only is he back, but he also had the cheek to phone here and ask if I did deliveries. My god, I said to him, do you think I'm going to send my girl over to you with a bag of shopping after hearing that Emily Davies is pregnant and you broke the news.' She tuts. 'Do you know what he did?'

I shake my head.

'He hung up. Bloody cheek. As if I was the one with the problem.'

'He didn't do it, get her pregnant,' I say.

'You've changed your tune.' Maureen smiles, her mouth all jagged teeth, then notices Jade listening by the door. 'Off with you then.' She shakes her head at me. 'Sisters. I ask you. Putting ideas into her head. She's going to be up there playing with her dolls as long as I have anything to do with it.'

'Thanks, then.' I turn to leave.

'Wasn't so hard, was it?' I hear Maureen chuckle as I walk through the door.

28

The rain falls in thick sheets. Swift and I plough through an onslaught of rising wind and water. The tide is moving faster than I've ever seen, covering most of the estuary like a shimmering blanket. One of those October tides of legend; one they'll mutter about in the pub, comparing who lost the most fences or animals to the water, a strange pride in their loss.

Swift slips up on the road, her back leg twisting underneath her for a split second. I dash forwards but she's already righted herself and scampered on. I take a last look at the marsh ponies and hope they all make it out.

I haul myself over the wooden slats of the fence and Swift wriggles underneath with a grunt. Walking up towards the bungalow, it's hard to believe it was just four days ago I was here for the first time. Pelting up this very field to ring the police. So much has changed since then.

The lights are on in the bungalow. He's home.

I go straight to the back door. We've gone past the need for me to knock. Both of us entwined in a story I know only half of.

I turn to Swift and ask her to stay, moving her under the overhang so she won't get as wet. I promise myself I'll find some wood, burn my sketchbook if I have to, and build a big fire tonight for her to sit in front of. We both deserve better than this.

I wipe my boots on the mat even though I'm about to drip half the marsh onto his floor.

There are voices inside.

I stand with the door ajar, listening. Mr Thomas is angry, his voice raised. I can't make out exactly what he's saying, something about his injuries and reputation. The other voice is young, pleading, and begging him to let her pass.

I tread as lightly as possible towards the lounge, water dripping off every part of me as if I'm some marsh monster the high tide has thrown up.

The voices lower in some kind of agreement as I reach the door. I want to run away. Turn, run, and forget about all of this. But I can't. I've gone too far and now I need the truth. I move from the shadows and stand fully in the doorway.

They don't see me straight away. Both of them too involved in the argument. Mr Thomas tries to hush Emily, his body blocking her exit. Hands flapping around, he tells her to stay quiet for a second and listen. Emily's face is pale, her eyes darting from him to the phone on the sideboard. She says she's not a child. Demands that he get out of her way.

They are both dressed to go out. Coats on and buttoned up as if they are about to step into the storm outside. I catch hold of the doorframe to steady myself. She's been here all along, and he's been laughing at us.

I cry out and their heads snap around like two startled owls. Emily's eyes flicker with panic and she looks to Mr Thomas for help. He walks towards me, palms up, wanting to take control.

'Catrin, I can explain.'

I push him away from me. 'No,' I say roughly and shove

past him to look at Emily. I stare at her, not sure if she is an apparition after all. But she is there, her breath fast and her eyes fixed on me.

'Where have you been?' I ask.

'She's friends with them,' Emily mumbles, eyes pleading at Mr Thomas. 'I need to go, now.'

My thoughts swing and tilt like a boat at sea. I need to tell Lorna. Roddy. For a moment my mind is filled with the image of him, the heaviness he's been carrying around. How dare she have done this to him. To me.

Mr Thomas moves towards me again, taking me firmly by the elbow.

'Catrin, I was working in the darkroom. I forgot my watch to time the development and nipped back to get it. There she was, using my phone. I'm as shocked as you are.'

I shake him off.

'You liar,' I shout at him. 'You've lied about everything.' The word hangs in the air, taking the shape of my mother in the ditch. If he is capable of this, then what else has he done?

I reach for the phone on the sideboard.

'Wait, there's no need for that.' Mr Thomas lurches to stop me. 'You'll want to hear what she has to say first.' He gestures to Emily.

'Tell her what's happened. There's been a terrible misunderstanding. Catrin, I promise you.' His voice is the schoolteacher who can fix everything.

Emily stays silent.

'For goodness' sake, you cannot be serious about him after all this?' Mr Thomas loses his temper, lashing out at a pile of books and sending them flying across the room. A sudden violence that makes both Emily and I flinch. He grips one arm around his ribs in pain.

'You had my mother's camera,' I whisper, my voice choking. 'What did you do to her?'

He turns to me in surprise.

'Catrin, this isn't the time for…'

'Tell me the truth.'

He tries to bend towards me and offer a hand, jerking with the effort, but I shrink back.

There is a flash of movement. Emily runs through the doorway and down the hall.

He staggers after her, shouts her name, then, panicked, turns back and pulls the phone cord from the wall.

'I promise you, Catrin, we do not want the police involved.'

'Why, because you stopped her from leaving you? Locked her away somewhere.' I spit with contempt.

His gaze turns to fury for a second.

'Is that what you think of me? I'm trying to help.'

'Then why haven't you rung Lorna?'

'Do you know what that woman is capable of? Making deals. Using her daughter as a bargaining chip. Capitalising on other people's misery. Trying to hide a baby. I have to stop her,' he says lurching towards the door. 'She's going to make a big mistake.'

'Why?' I say, blocking his path.

'Because I know what it's like to have someone promise you something when they have no intention of giving it to you. I thought I could spare her the pain.' He pushes his way past.

As I reach the front door Mr Thomas is gripping his side

and struggling to get down the steps. He stops, breathless, and scans the garden. The sky is grey and full with pelting rain.

'She's meeting him on the flats. Wouldn't listen about the tide.'

'The current will take her if she goes out there,' I shout at him across the wind, gesturing at the field and the marsh road. There's nothing waiting for us there but cold water.

'She's gone down there. Help her,' he shouts desperately.

We share a look full of knowing, of a history, of a body in the ditch.

'Get Dai,' I shout, then run towards the fence, Swift cantering alongside me.

Please let the sight of the water scare her. Let her stop.

I sprint as fast as I can towards the road.

Please don't let it happen again.

29

I reach the marsh road and clamber over the fence again, catching my trousers on a stray nail, dragging my arms through the brambles without any care. Swift, breathing heavily, shimmies under. God knows if Mr Thomas will be able to get down to us in time, but I can't wait for him.

This part of the road is the last to be flooded. Even so, the water laps dangerously near. I've never seen the tide so high – all the humps and tussocks that would usually poke out have disappeared. It's like the marsh has ceased to exist, turned instead into a dazzling mirror of moving water, uninterrupted from east to west and reflecting the darkening clouds back to the sky.

I scan the horizon. What idiot would promise to meet someone out here today?

Emily is already further down the road, loping slowly as if out of breath. She's heading towards the village of course. And that's the worst of it. The road looks bare from here, but the strange curve and dip of the land means the water will circle in from behind, leaving her trapped on all sides. And tonight's tide is too high to try wading through the depths.

'Emily, wait. It's not safe,' I call out. My words are carried away on the wind and rain.

She pauses and turns her head to and fro, taking in the rising water. She's not thinking straight. Desperate to get to whoever is meeting her.

I sprint after her. Swift gallops alongside me yapping with excitement, the wind and rain lashing at us. I near the last bit of the road before everything disappears into a muddy flow, just in time to see Emily struggling ahead at the water's edge. She tests her footing. Wading in a little. The distance to the village looks so short, but the tide swirls around her, strong and steady in its current, filling cracks and ditches at a speed which promises nothing and no one will stand in its way.

She turns to look at me, her eyes wide, mouth shaped into an O as if she has no idea what the water is doing there and why it is trying to stop her.

I am caught too. Boots filling with water, that familiar shock of the cold at my ankles as I dash towards her. If it stopped there, we'd be alright. But the water flows past me quickly, carrying twigs and branches with alarming speed. I wade through until it's up to my calves and glance around for Swift. It's too deep for her. The sound of her splashing comes from behind me. I can't stop.

Emily is turning around in a circle, her panic visibly rising as each way out is suddenly filled with water, and she, now up to her knees, feels the cold grip of the tide.

She didn't grow up here. Her mother didn't teach her it's better to stay still like the ponies and wait it out if you can. Once you've lost sight of the bottom, never go further. Not unless you know exactly where you are. My mother used to make me close my eyes and walk out of the marsh alone, so she could be sure I would find my way if I ever needed to. It seemed cruel at the time, but now, even though the grey current is churning between us like a dragging, insistent river, I know exactly where I am.

Emily screams out in panic as the tide tugs at her from underneath like a pair of desperate hands, hanging on to her ankles, dragging her along. She stumbles and cries out. Then she does the one thing you should never do.

She runs further out.

Emily pushes her way from the road and towards the marsh. She can see the village and will think she's running towards it, but the road was never straight. Her sense of direction is skewed, and she runs off the road and onto the flats.

'Emily! Stay still!' I scream out.

Her eyes don't even focus on me; there is nothing in her mind but fear as she sloshes further, turning one way then the other in panic.

Then it happens.

Her body tumbles into the water. For a second she is out of sight, fallen deep into one of the hidden ditches.

Suddenly, she emerges as if spat back out; mouth open, gasping, and hands tearing at unseen grass to get a grip.

I rush towards her, careful to step where I know the higher ground is. But this tide is insistent and pulls at me with a strong undercurrent. I focus on finding the solid ground underneath the water.

I know this place.

My foot slips and I right myself.

I know this place.

I move towards her, now waist deep. She is submerged, struggling, her arms flapping at her sides as she's forced to swim to stay above the water. The mud must have a hold of her foot.

Swift swims alongside me, refusing to let me go alone.

'Back, girl,' I shout, but she stays at my side, the place she has never left since Dai said she was mine.

I wade deeper, dragging my body through the water, just a few feet from Emily now and still the current pushes back at me, rising higher above my waist with each second.

The tide of stories. Of warnings.

Emily is tiring, her arms are moving less, and the rising water is up to her chin.

I finally reach her, my feet struggling to keep in contact with the slippery ground underneath the water. There is a large ditch here, she must have stumbled down one side of it. I stay far away from where the edge might be. Swift circles us, her breathing heavy with the effort.

'Take my hand,' I shout.

Her face is wild. Strands of soaking hair stuck to her face, eyes panicked and mouth wide, threatening to gulp water.

I strain towards her. Her hand, slippery and cold, grabs at mine, missing the first time, then finally finding a strong grasp. I heave her towards me. Her body lurches forward then stops, jerking back and almost unbalancing me.

'My leg!' she screams.

I pull at her again, but it won't give. I take a deep breath and plunge my face into the icy tide. Eyes open and burning, squinting through the rush of reeds and fast water, I can see her foot trapped in the mud.

'Stay still.' I turn and look for Mr Thomas. Where is he, has he called for help? Through the haze of shifting water, I see him standing helplessly at the edge of the road. Why doesn't he come? Even injured, he could help us.

I take a deep breath and plunge myself back into the brackish water.

Swimming two long strokes down towards Emily's foot, I grasp her ankle and pull at it. The mud pulls back, not willing to give up its prisoner. I push at her from behind and her body strains with the effort of trying to pull herself out, kicking forwards.

My mother flashes into my mind, struggling against the same tide.

I can't think of her now.

I grasp Emily's ankle and push it down further, then pull up with all my might – with all the hope of never having to see another dead body again. Never letting this tide take anything else that doesn't belong to it.

The mud gives and her foot comes free. I swim upwards with all my remaining strength, lungs burning as I head towards the dancing light of the surface.

I push up into cold air, spluttering and coughing. Emily grabs at me but I smack her hands away. Instead, I grab her body and turn her like a sack, pushing her towards the road where Mr Thomas is waiting.

'Swim!' I scream at her.

She doesn't wait for more instructions, splashing with all her might towards the road. She'll be alright now, there are no ditches underneath her, just reeds and marshland. Mr Thomas can pull her out.

I look around for Swift. We have to get out of the water before we get too cold, before the height of the tide breaks away from the land and the current gets stronger.

She's drifted away from me, caught by a strong gush of

water. I thrash towards her, the water rushing and pitching me sideways, pushing me further away.

'Swift!' I shout out.

Her paws frantically move in the water, but she cannot beat the strength of the tide.

'Swift, come,' I scream. Our eyes meet for a second. My beautiful friend. My protector. The one who has kept me safe for so long. She stops paddling and I scream out until my throat is raw. Throw myself towards her, arms thrashing as fast as I can. The tide throws me back, pulls me under and turns me over as if I'm nothing more than a small pebble.

I reach the surface again, gasping. Search for her black and white form. She is nowhere to be seen. I push again towards where she was swimming.

A rush of relief as I see her nose struggling to stay above the water. I launch towards her with everything I have. Grab under the water at her heavy body and haul it above the surface. She wheezes and I pull her closer. The drag of the current pulls us backwards and throws us up metres away.

'Help!' I scream with all the force left in me. The grey water laps around us. I turn in a circle, trying to get my bearings.

The water knocks me under the water. My eyes sting and mouth fills but I push myself back to the cold surface, refusing to give up my grip on Swift, gasping and spitting. I scan the top of the water.

Emily and Mr Thomas are tucked next to the fence, their faces horrified.

I use them and my rage as an anchor. Kick out towards

them, Swift under one arm, the other paddling and pulling us closer and closer to the shallow ground.

At last, mud under my feet. I slip and slide but push on with shaking legs, crawling through the last of the water towards a rise in the road.

Then, headlights on the marsh. A Land Rover speeding through deep water, sending up huge waves either side, uncaring of the circumstances. It stops and Dai and Roddy jump out.

Dai forces his way through the shallows of the tide until he reaches us. He picks me up from my half-slumped position. My body is convulsing with cold. Roddy scoops Swift away from me, nearly losing his footing. He rips off his own jacket and wraps it around her and the three of us stagger through the onslaught of wind and rain towards his car.

Roddy lays Swift in the boot, covered in his coat and spare sacks. Then he rushes over to Emily and hugs her close.

Dai looks at her and Mr Thomas in disbelief. 'Why didn't you help?' he shouts.

Mr Thomas' face is white. He rushes over and tries to wrap his coat around me. I accept his jacket but push him away.

'I… I can't swim. Catrin, I'm sorry.'

The world stops for a second. Something clicks into place.

My mother trapped with water rising around her. Was he there? I look up at him.

'You couldn't help her,' I whisper, the words carried off on the wind.

Emily is sobbing on Roddy's shoulder.

'Get in.' Dai waves at the Land Rover.

As we drive away my eyes scan the water. Almost expecting

to see my mother surface as she does in my dreams, spluttering and screaming for help, but there is nothing. The water has returned to its cold, glass-like form, hiding everything that lies underneath.

30

The Land Rover squeals into Dai's driveway.

'Right, get inside and get warm,' Dai orders.

'Swift…' I say. She hasn't moved or raised her head on the journey back. 'She needs the vet.'

'I'll take her,' Roddy says. He helps Emily out of the vehicle. 'I'll come back for you, alright?'

She shakes her head in panic.

'Don't leave me here, please.'

'Go in and get warm. I'll be back in an hour or so.' He glances at me. 'It's an emergency.'

Emily glumly follows Mr Thomas inside. Dai stalks ahead of them, shouting instructions to Bev: *hot water, a change of clothes, get the fire going.*

I shake with cold, my teeth chattering, making it hard to talk. My clothes are plastered wet against my skin. Still, I open the boot to see Swift. She lifts her head a little at the sight of me, her own body trembling and a worrying rattle with each breath.

'I'm sorry,' I whisper to her and lean down to kiss her head.

'She'll be okay.' Roddy squeezes my arm. 'You need to get dry, or you'll be the one needing the hospital.'

I put my hand out to stop him. Swift is mine.

'Catrin, please. I'll keep her safe for you, I promise.' He gently pulls the coat tighter around me.

I look up at him, at his serious face. What if he doesn't know where to go or Swift dies alone? What if she needs me with her? She's my responsibility.

'I can't pay for the vet.' I choke, my voice full of shame.

'I'll sort it. Trust me, please.' He kisses my forehead, closes the boot and jumps in the driver's seat.

'It'll be okay. Get inside.' He throws me a crooked smile.

He speeds off into the pouring rain, the headlights lighting up the road against the newly fallen night.

*

Emily and I sit across from one another in the garish space of Dai and Bev's living room. Neither of us speak. We are both wearing Bev's tracksuits, like matching twins, sitting with blankets covering us and two identical mugs of steaming tea cupped in our hands.

My body seethes with a mixture of rage and grief. Too exhausted to scream at Emily, to tell her how stupid she's been. All the time I'm willing Roddy to come back. Watching the driveway for their return. For some news of Swift.

I draw the blanket around myself and stare at my hands. Emily is looking at me. But I have nothing to give her now. She sniffs and shuffles in the chair opposite. I hope Lorna comes soon and takes her out of my sight.

Emily clears her throat. I examine my hands, turning them over again and again as if I will find the answers somewhere in the lines and cracks around my fingernails.

'I was so scared.' Her voice shakes.

I fold my arms across my chest. Dip my chin.

'I'm sorry about your dog. I hope she's okay.'

'Swift,' I snap. And I want her to take back the word *dog*, so flat, so unremarkable.

'He promised he'd come,' she whispers.

The lights flicker above us, and we both look up. The storm howls outside.

'Mr Thomas was only trying to help.' Emily tries again.

Her presence is like an irritating gnat and I long to swat her away, stop her taking small bites into my peace.

The door opens with a creak and Bev pops her head around as if she's visiting and it's not her house at all. Emily starts with shock when she sees her. Cowers back into the seat, gathering the cushions and blankets around her like a shield.

'All right in here?' Bev singsongs in a voice that says nothing of the situation. Her cheeks are pink and eyes hazy. 'All comfy?' she asks with a giggle.

Emily looks away from her and Bev pretends not to notice.

'Drink up your tea, love.' She nods at her. 'In your condition, you don't want to…'

'Get out!' Emily shouts, throwing a cushion at the door and missing Bev's head by an inch.

The door slams shut. I finally look up at Emily, but now it's her turn to stare into her lap.

There's more shouting in the hall. Dai's voice raised to Mr Thomas, and Bev stuck in the middle somewhere with a keening tone. I lean forwards at the strangeness of it.

'Don't leave me until Roddy gets back,' Emily pleads.

I stare at her, thoughts clicking into place.

Bev isn't pregnant at all. She wants Emily's baby.

Of course she does. It's Dai's and she wants to save the

situation by pretending it's hers. As if catching my thoughts, Emily starts forward and places a cold hand on my leg.

'Don't let them call my mum.'

The door swings open and Mr Thomas shuffles awkwardly into the room followed by Dai. Bev hovers in the doorway but Dai shoves a hand at her, irritated. His usual composure broken.

'The phone lines are down,' he says. 'I'll take you home. We can use the pickup, go by the top road.' He nods at Emily, expecting her to follow him.

Instead, she shrinks back into the seat again, looking first at Mr Thomas then me, as if we can save her from some invisible monster.

'It's okay,' Mr Thomas says to her. Schoolteacher voice on. 'It's *all* going to be alright. Just tell the truth.' His words are heavy with emphasis.

'What is it?' I ask, my voice still hoarse, any movement an effort.

'Just the storm,' Bev trills from the doorway. 'Nothing to be frightened of.'

'Out. Now.' Dai closes the door unceremoniously in her face.

I wait for an explanation from him. Nothing is forthcoming. Instead, he speaks directly to Emily. There is something unsaid, like the hidden undertow of the tide that was pulling and throwing us around, in his tone.

'*I said I'll run you home.* We can't ring your mam.'

'No. I'm not going until Roddy gets back.' Emily stares at Dai, defying him to disagree or force her into saying something.

Mr Thomas steps forward, the self-elected peacemaker of the group.

'Perhaps it's better if you go and get Lorna, given the circumstances?' He stares pointedly at Dai.

'Bring her here? With Bev like this? She's done enough, don't you think?'

'I'm not staying here. I want to go with Catrin. I'll wait there until Roddy brings Swift back,' Emily says, her voice hard.

'And you?' I whisper to Mr Thomas.

'I will be very glad to go home and get some peace,' he says shortly.

I smack my tea down on the table. He could have helped me and Swift. He could have waded in, but he was too much of a coward. Where was he when my mother died? Did he see her struggling through that stupid window of his and stay safe in the bungalow, too scared of the water to help?

'Something stopping your *peace*?' I spit at him.

He sighs with exasperation and opens the lounge door, nearly colliding with Bev who was lurking outside.

'Whatever you think of me, Catrin, I am not the one who caused all of this.' He gestures around him. 'Now, goodnight to you all. That's the last of it.' He gives us a sharp look and steps outside.

He'll get soaked walking home through the fields, but Dai doesn't offer him a lift. Instead, he leans out of the way as the other man passes. An unspoken disgust between them.

'Let's get you home then,' Dai says to me, his face suddenly tired.

I catch his eye, willing him to tell me, to let me show him the same friendship he's always shown us. No matter what.

He pats his trousers to find the keys.

'I'm sorry for Swift, love,' he says with a tremble in his voice. 'She's a strong 'un like you, she'll be alright.'

Dai's always been the only person who understood what I needed. It's hard to hate him whatever he's done.

Emily stands up, clearly intent on coming home with me. I don't have the energy to argue. I take down my jacket from in front of the roaring fire – it leaks a damp smell of tide around us.

Mr Thomas is standing in the porch watching the torrents of water fall all around. Dai walks past him without a second look and starts the pickup, but Emily pauses to speak to him.

'You're wrong about him. He does love me,' she says quietly.

He begins to reply but decides better. Shakes his head and watches her scamper through the rain towards the car. He fixes me with a stern look.

'He's got her exactly where he wants her. Pretending at love...' His voice is bitter.

'Why was Roddy here?' I ask.

'I don't know.' He shrugs. 'I rang Dai. He must have been here already.'

Maybe Roddy decided to follow his suspicion and have it out with Dai. I don't want to admit that I should have listened to him.

'You should have been straight from the beginning,' I say.

He shakes his head.

'I'm not supposed to speak to you, Catrin. I've never been allowed to tell the truth since the day your mother died. Ask your father where he was the day after. Then you'll understand.'

Dai beeps the horn and flashes the lights. Mr Thomas makes a dash into the night and I stumble across the drive and heave myself into the passenger seat next to Emily.

As we make a turn on the drive, I look up at the house. Bev is standing in the window upstairs, pressed nearly full against the glass. She waves as we pull away, her face a picture of grief.

I let my head loll against the car window. No one says another word. It's a relief to be on my way home. Even the constancy of my father's silence would be a comforting end to this wretched day.

Instinctively, I reach down beside me, but there is no warm body pressed against my legs, no fur to cling to, just cold air on my fingers. I fold my arms instead, hoping I was right to trust Roddy to take care of her.

31

My father raises his eyebrows at the sight of Emily walking behind me into our kitchen. Dai has driven off already in search of Lorna. I expect my father to jump up and offer to make tea: his usual way of avoiding any interaction. Instead, he folds the newspaper away and looks at us both expectantly.

'It's late,' he says. 'Was worried something had happened to you.'

Emily hovers behind me. The comfort of our kitchen makes my body heavy.

'Sorry.' I heave myself into a chair and gesture for Emily to sit. 'It's been a long day.'

'Alright?'

I meet my father's eyes and an understanding passes between us. *No, I'm not,* but we won't talk about it now. I will my father to take control for once. Be an adult. We sit in silence for a minute. Eventually, he clears his throat and gives Emily an appraising look.

'Any injuries?' he asks matter of factly.

She shakes her head.

'Right. You should call your mother. Then the police.' He nods at me.

'Phones are down,' I say. 'Dai's gone to get Lorna.'

My father tuts at the thought of the house crowding with people.

'I told him, I've got nothing to say to her.' Emily's eyes well up.

My father looks down at his paper.

'Tell her the truth,' I jab. 'You can tell us too.'

She looks from one to the other of us for a moment.

'It's complicated,' she whispers then takes a deep breath, rubbing her hands together. For a second she looks just like Lorna, concocting the right story for her audience.

'Try.'

Emily opens her mouth, but my father cuts her off before she can start.

'Tell the police you've been hiding at Dai's, in the barn. They didn't know you were there.' He looks long and hard at Emily.

She shrinks back with a nod.

I glare at my father.

'Is that the truth?' I ask.

'It'll do,' he says. 'She's here. Not harmed. Best not to stir up trouble.'

'I think it's too late for that,' I tell him.

'Your dad's right,' Emily says. 'I don't want to get anyone into trouble. I was hiding and went to the kitchen to take food when they were busy.' Her tone has all the conviction of someone telling the story for the first time.

She'll have to do better than that if she talks to Maureen. My stomach swims with disgust at my father, at Dai, this place. Good luck to her trying to hide it for nine months if she really is carrying Dai's baby.

The front door swings open and Emily jumps with fright. Dai appears in the room.

'Main road is flooded. The storm has brought down a couple of trees. Everything is blocked up. Marsh road is still covered, highest tide in years.'

'No one can get in?' Emily asks.

He shakes his head.

'The tide'll be down in a few hours, but the water won't drain straight away. And they won't clear the trees until morning. You'd do well to stay here tonight. I'll fetch Lorna first thing.'

'Trapped again.' She whispers it under her breath.

'You can have my room,' I say.

Roddy won't be able to get back with Swift either or let me know if she's okay. I can't see myself getting much sleep.

She lets me guide her up the stairs with a few extra blankets.

'You should probably see the doctor tomorrow,' I offer once she's sat quietly on my bed.

'Why?'

'The baby. Just in case. You had such a fright.'

She bites her lip and nods frantically, her face paler than when she was in the water.

The slam of the front door signals Dai has gone.

*

My father is still sitting in the kitchen when I come back downstairs. There is an emptiness around me – a space under the table that should be filled by a black and white shape.

'I don't know if Swift will be okay.' My voice chokes over the words. 'Roddy took her to the vet.'

My father nods and reaches for my hand across the table.

The gesture shocks me and I nearly pull away, but the warmth of his hand over mine is comforting.

'She's been a good friend to you,' he says.

One fat tear rolls down my face and falls on the table. We sit in silence for a minute.

'Where did you go the day after Mum died?' I ask.

My father doesn't respond.

'I deserve to know.'

He looks at me sadly.

'No. You deserved better than we gave you.'

'Did you go to see Mr Thomas?'

He pulls his hand away and fingers the newspaper, pressing on a crease as if he could force it to run smooth. His jaw clenches.

'I did.'

The hurt of everything that has been left unsaid since that day drags at my body. I lay my head on my arms; the table supporting me, wood cool on my forehead. He must have known all along about the affair and was trying to save me from it. I don't know whether to feel grateful or angry; the way he thinks it can all just be forgotten and swept away in silences.

Then his hand is on mine again, heavy and unsure.

He clears his throat.

I will him to tell me everything.

He's never once said that she's dead, not out loud. Or that he loved or misses her.

'Would you have let me go with her?' My voice muffles on my arm.

'If you'd wanted to.'

Me, at seventeen, on the cusp of everything; would I have gone with her? If she'd had the chance to tell me herself, would all this be reversed – my disgust saved for her?

My father sighs.

'She didn't want you to end up like *us*. I never knew what she meant. People here work hard and look after each other, that's all. I thought she liked it here, having somewhere to belong. But all she could see was something else to fight against.' He shakes his head.

'Why didn't you tell me all of this?'

'I didn't want you to feel like you do now. She was like a fox in a trap, lashing out at us, trying to get free. I thought it would sort itself out... Those were her sorrows, Catrin, not yours... Best left alone now. All of it.'

A silence looms over us. I can't let it be the final answer.

'What did you say to Mr Thomas when you saw him?'

My father crosses his arms over his chest as if protecting himself from the memory.

'I'm not proud of it. I was angry. Too angry. Shouldn't have gone on my own, Dai told me that and you know he's always right.' He tries to smile at his own joke.

'Did you hit him?'

He shakes his head sadly.

'I took my shotgun. I wanted to kill him.'

My stomach twists. I can't imagine my father picking up his shotgun and marching over there. I stay quiet, hoping for once he'll say more and unburden himself. He traces his finger along the newspaper, mind lost in thought.

Finally, he speaks again.

'I could have killed him, Catrin. I was so angry. He was

laughing at me. At us. Looking down his bloody nose because I didn't have any fancy dreams to offer her.' He clenches and unclenches his fists as he speaks. 'He had an answer for everything. Kept trying to explain your mother to me. As if I didn't know her. Said we were holding her back. He said she felt *understood* by him.' He spits the words out with disgust. 'I should have said my piece and left, but he was talking constantly, wouldn't stop. Telling me things I didn't want to hear. How happy they were. Her thoughts and feelings. What they'd done... He was enjoying it. Trying to hurt me with the details, things I didn't ever want you to hear. I had to make sure he wouldn't say them to anyone. Not to you.'

Is that why 'the boys' always go in a group, to stop someone from stepping over the line, losing their temper and doing real damage?

'What did you do?' I whisper, afraid of the answer.

'I made him sit down. Cocked the gun and told him to sit. Wiped the smug look off his face. Didn't have so much to say then. We sat like that for a minute and...' He stops himself from finishing the sentence in the same way he must have stopped himself from taking Mr Thomas' life.

My father shakes his head as if trying to dislodge the memories and chase them away.

'I shot his settee, right next to where he was sitting. He was scared then. Started gibbering away about how sorry he was, and he'd got your mother all wrong. Said she'd strung him along. Used him as a way out. Said she didn't want anything more to do with him.'

'What?' My voice is incredulous.

He nods.

'Said she was a selfish bitch. He said that. With her lying dead. I shot his bloody sofa again. I did it to stop myself shooting him. He started screaming then, like a child, jabbering on about how she'd cheated us both. Promised us one thing then done another. Said she was a liar. I told him I had one bullet left and if he didn't stop insulting my wife it would go in his head.' He lets out a sudden sob.

I've never seen him cry. It's a strange sound. Half stifled, half whining. I grab onto his hands with all my might.

'But you left, didn't you?'

He shakes his head, eyes half closed.

'I put the shotgun right up to his temple. Told him what a miserable bastard he was to say he loved a woman then talk about her like that. She deserved better. I said he was never to talk to you. Never to tell you anything about them or what happened. Then I counted.'

'What?' I squeeze his hand.

'I thought if I could just count to ten, I wouldn't do it. If I could just stop and think about you in the house on your own, waiting for me to come home, I wouldn't waste my life on his pathetic story. So, I counted out loud. He cried the whole time, praying and wailing, even asked your mother to forgive him at one point. Then I got to ten. And I knew I couldn't do it anymore. Couldn't leave you without two parents. But if it hadn't been for the thought of you, I would have done it. Killed a man. Right there looking him in the eye.' His eyes are full of anguish. 'What kind of father is that? You deserve better, Catrin. I'm sorry. For everything.' He looks down into our linked hands, defeated – exactly as he must have felt that day listening to Mr Thomas telling him where he'd failed as a husband.

CARYS SHANNON

I move to his side, take him into my arms and hug him tight.

He clings to me like a drowning man and every moment since that day washes through our bodies. All the blame I've held in for him, the hatred. All of it; thinking his silence was because he didn't care. His isolation because he wanted it that way – never imagining the shame he was hiding about his own inadequacy.

We stay like that for a few minutes, grasping each other tight, then my father straightens himself up and wipes his face with a sleeve. Pats me on the shoulder like one of the ewes, then slides his cap on.

'Make a cuppa, shall I?' His voice is gentle.

It's like we've both just arrived in some strange new land that neither of us know how to navigate.

I nod.

He pauses for a moment, looking at me. A tentative understanding hangs between us, delicate as a spider's web. I'm waiting to see if it will be broken again or woven into something better.

'Your drawings are good, Catrin. Better than good...' He searches for the right word. 'Excellent. Your mother, I think she was afraid of your talent. She was hard on you...'

'Dad... I...'

'She was hard on you.' His voice shakes as he looks for words and feelings he's so unused to sharing. 'So you'd have no choice but to be brilliant, get somewhere. I didn't always agree, but she was your mother. She knew about those things, and I didn't...' He trails off.

'Why are you saying this?'

'I saw your letter. You left it on the side. Thought it was another bill you were hiding.'

My face burns with shame. I'd been shielding him from those things, or so I thought. The screaming red text of unpaid bills. Selling the car because I told him I'd rather walk places with Swift. Trying not to add anything to a suffering that was already unbearable.

'If I go, I could get some money,' I mumble. 'A grant.' I scratch over something I drew on the table when I was younger, moving my fingers over the bumps in the wood.

'If you go, it should be for you,' he says. 'None of this is your mess, Catrin. You've got your own life to live.'

'You need help,' I say stubbornly.

'Then I'll get some. Learn how to do things differently.'

I breathe in and out slowly. The conversation feels too big, like an open horizon.

'Are you going to tell me the truth about Dai?'

My father's shoulders relax, relieved to be on more familiar ground.

'I don't know all of it.' He sighs. 'There's trouble, I know that. Bev wanted the baby. When Lorna cottoned on, she promised it to her, asked for time then asked for money, Dai says.'

'Bev told me she was pregnant. She said it to Maureen too.'

My father nods and looks out of the window, studying the blackness of the night.

'And Dai? Is it…?' I can't even finish the sentence.

'Didn't have a clue what was going on.'

I study his face to see if he's telling me the truth. Would he choose Dai over me? Lie to me even after everything we've been through?

275

'But… isn't he… didn't he…?' I still can't say it. Not Dai, *please*.

My father looks surprised, almost amused.

'You should know him better than that, Catrin.'

'Then who?'

He shrugs as if the world is a complete mystery to him and there's nothing he can do about it.

'We'll find out tomorrow, I suppose.' He takes the kettle off the aga and pours steaming water into one cup. 'She'll want to talk after a good sleep.' He flicks his head towards Emily upstairs.

No tea for him.

A sure sign he's going to duck out. He stirs in milk and sugar then places the mug in front of me.

'Let the girl's family sort it out. It's their business.' He moves to leave then thinks better of it. 'The letter…' he says softly. 'Tell them you'll go. I'll look after Swift. Be glad of the company.' He places a hand on my shoulder and leans down to kiss the top of my head. Something he hasn't done since I was a child.

My hand settles on top of his. We stay like that for a moment. Is it really possible that we'll be okay? I'd never even considered that.

Then my father straightens up, pats me on the head with a smile, and strides out to check all is well in his world.

32

I wake to an almost imperceptible sound — the click of our phone into the handset. The lounge lights are too bright for my bleary eyes. I prop myself up on the sofa where I slept. The electricity must have come back on during the night.

A soft footstep.

I sit up just in time to hear someone carefully closing the front door.

The mantle clock says seven, just getting light. My father would be out early to check on the farm, but I know the soft rumble of his movements.

Emily.

I haul myself out of a tangle of warm blankets. Dawn air bites at my arms as I run up the stairs.

My bedroom door is ajar. The bed empty.

I pull a thick jumper out of my wardrobe and throw it over the clothes I fell asleep in last night. As I jog back to the bottom of the stairs, my mouth purses, ready to whistle Swift into action.

Swift. Nothing from Roddy. The phone must be back on if the lights are. Has he not rung because it's bad news?

In the hallway I pull on my waterproof jacket and boots. Only an idiot would be stupid enough to go out between high tides. There'll be trees and branches everywhere, water still draining away. Hasn't she caused enough trouble?

I jog down the path, jumping over the torn branches, disfigured pieces of wood and plastic thrown up from the storm last night. Piles of reeds are strewn across the path and marsh road. I pass a bright blue plastic bucket one of the cocklers must have lost to the mud out on the flats. It sits at the side of the road as if waiting for its owner to find it.

I make my way as quickly as I can, eyes on the road ahead, striding faster and faster until a stitch jabs at my side.

I'm nearly at the spot where I first saw Emily. There's a car pulled up on the cockle track not far off. Pale blue. Muddied wheels. Emily must be meeting them. No one else in their right mind would drive out here today.

My skin prickles cold; the car doesn't belong to Dai or Mr Thomas. I reach down for Swift. Empty air meets my hand.

'You're up early. Doing a bit of scavenging or what?' a voice calls out in a jaunty tone.

'Mac?'

He chuckles.

'Your face. What are you doing out here?' He glances around.

'Same as you, I reckon,' I say.

'I doubt that.' He takes a pack of cigarettes from his pocket and lights up. 'Reckon you saw me from the road and couldn't keep away.' He smirks and lights up.

'You waiting for someone?' I ask, inching closer to have a good look at the car, check that Emily isn't inside it.

'If I said you, would you believe me?' He takes a long drag and glances around again.

'No.'

'Jesus, Catrin. Just joking. Lighten up.' He holds his hands out in surrender and laughs. I see it now, his trick. The way he makes everything you say that's true seem like an overreaction.

'So, you're not here to pick Emily up?'

There it is. That gesture. The big laugh. Head thrown back. Making you doubt yourself, saying you're an idiot.

'Christ, you still on that? Haven't you got anything better to do? Wait, don't answer that.' He chuckles and takes another drag. Mac the drive, always putting on the charm – harmless, just banter.

'Well, don't let me stop you.' He stamps out the butt.

'I'm fine here.' I shove my hands in my pockets as if I could stand here all day.

His smile drops for a second at that. Then he puffs his chest out, determined to maintain the upper hand.

'What, you come back for a second go?' He cocks his head at the car.

'No,' I say. 'Once was more than enough.'

He steps closer. Always a little too close; why didn't I see it before? His insistence. Another compliment. Another drink. Another joke. All taking you where he wants you to go.

'If you want more, you've only got to ask.' His breath is close on my face.

'I didn't want more. I told you to stop.'

He jerks back at that.

'What you talking about?'

'I had bruises on my arms.'

His face jumps in shock. He takes a step back this time.

'I don't know what you're trying to say but…'

'I'm saying I told you to stop, and you didn't. So, I pushed you off and ran.' I shake a little at the sound of it out loud. This is my place. I won't be afraid of anyone out here.

He shakes his head.

'Not my fault if you were too wrecked to control yourself.'

'Is that what you do?' I ask. 'Pick someone who's having a hard time. Who's got no one to look out for them. Lay it on thick then get them pissed. Take what you want.'

'Oh, I'm not having this.' He strides over and jabs his finger in my face. 'If you want to act like a little prick tease then cry about it later, that's up to you. I haven't done anything wrong.'

'What about Emily?' I ask, sure now of everything. 'What did you promise her?'

His face drops into a scowl.

'Nothing she didn't want. Alright?'

'She's fifteen!'

'But she didn't tell me that now, did she?' Always an explanation. Always someone asking for it or leading him on.

'She's fifteen,' I repeat.

He twists away and plonks himself down on the bonnet of the car. Pats next to him as if I would just sit and join him for a chat.

'Well, you kept turning me down.' He looks up at me with wide eyes. A ball of rage broils in my stomach.

'You're using that as an excuse?'

His mouth curls downward.

'It must be nice to be as bloody perfect as you are, Catrin. Never messing anything up. Always being in the right. Must be bloody lovely.' He thumps the bonnet. His face jumps with irritation. All the charm gone.

'You should have left her alone. What were you thinking?'

'Like I had a choice.' He laughs. 'Seen what a little madam she is? She knew exactly what she wanted and that's what she got. Fifteen going on forty.'

I lurch forward and slap his face. He grabs my arm, holding my wrist and standing up. Too close. He's always too close.

'What's the matter, you jealous?' he says in a low, thick voice, pulling me closer. 'Because you know I still hold a torch for you.'

I push him backwards. He falls onto the bonnet and springs back up as if ready for a fight.

'You weren't invited, Catrin. Why don't you just do one?'

'Where's Emily?'

'How the hell should I know,' he shouts. 'Stupid little slut keeps on disappearing.'

I stare at him in shock, but the callousness of his own words slips right past him.

'She rang me this morning to come and get her. Terrified, she was.' He softens his tone, looks at me as if to say, *I'm not the bad guy here.*

'So why isn't she here?'

'She might have got lost, not everyone knows this place as well as you. Tell me, Catrin, are you really happy?'

And that's how he does it. Always switching back to you, to avoid taking any blame himself. His words circling, so you don't know where you're looking.

'You going to support her?' I ask.

'You think I'm driving up and down on these buses all day just to give my wages to some dim girl? Jesus, Catrin, why don't you try joining us all in the real world for once. I'm here to take her to the clinic.' He spits out the last words.

Of course he is. He's probably already told Emily it was her fault. Thought she'd been careful. She should have known better. She was asking for it.

'You make me sick.'

'Where you going? To call the police? Think they'll take you seriously after all the running around you've been doing? You are tragic. Everyone is laughing at you, Catrin.'

'They won't be laughing at me when they find out about this.'

He grabs me by the collar of my jacket. His mouth twists, specks of spit landing on my cheek as he speaks.

'Don't you even think of going around telling people about this. *It's private.*'

I glare back at him.

'Nothing private down here. Should know that by now.'

He drags me close to his face.

'Not a word about this to anyone. You hear?'

'Or what?'

'Or I'll tell everyone what happened that night. The way you threw yourself at me. Begging for it. How you're so fucked up, you couldn't even enjoy it. Ran out of the car crying for your mammy.' He lets go of me and wipes his mouth with his sleeve, looking over my shoulder. 'Fuck.' He pushes past.

His car keys drop onto the mud with a soft clink. I scoop them up before he sees.

Emily is waiting next to the car.

In a second Mac changes his play. His face wiped of anger and replaced by slick charm.

'I told you she was a nutter. Can't get rid of her. Obsessed.' He gestures at me.

Emily stays silent.

'Right then, love, let's get out of here and sort this out.'

'Sort what out?' Emily asks, her voice like stone.

'You know.'

She shakes her head.

'Get you sorted with the…' He loses his place and stumbles over the words, then changes tack.

'Catrin, can you do one? This is a private conversation.'

'I want her to stay,' Emily says.

He puts his hands out, cajoling, and walks towards her.

'I'm just saying, you don't want to ruin your life with this, not now.'

'You said you loved me.' Her voice quivers and there she is, fifteen and vulnerable.

'I do, love. You know I do.' He glances at me with irritation, unable to perform for two audiences at once. 'I want the best for you. You got school and all that, can't do it with a baby.'

A tear rolls down her cheek.

'Why did you call me a slut?' Her lip quivers.

'Catrin was winding me up. Accusing me of all sorts. Got me angry. Frightened.' He widens his eyes theatrically. 'Thought she was going to call the police. You don't want to get me into trouble like that, do you? I was pretending. Didn't mean it, you know that.' He takes a step towards her but she jerks away.

'What happens after the clinic?' Her voice is flat.

'What do you mean?' He smiles, trying to keep his face light.

'I'm coming to live with you, that's what you promised.'

He puts his hands up in front of him.

'Let's not rush into anything. You've got to see your mam and sort it out with her.'

'So, you're sending me home. Clinic then back to normal? You said she was mad. Said she wasn't a fit mother.' Her voice rises.

'No, don't be like that, love. I mean, it gives us a chance to take it slowly.' He reaches out his hand and takes hers, pulling her towards him.

I want to run over and prise him off, but Emily's face is full of controlled rage, and she deserves her moment. He strokes her hair.

'It'll be just like before.'

'Chatting me up on the bus, making promises, then us in your car?'

He clears his throat.

'What, too good for me now, are you?'

She looks at him searchingly, drinking in every pore of him, trying to equate the man she once believed in with this version.

'There is no baby, so you don't have to worry.' She looks at me. 'I only said it so he'd have to come looking for me. So someone would help me. Take me in. It went too far. I told Bev the truth but she wouldn't believe me, said she'd been promised the baby. She thought I was trying to trick her, planning to keep the baby for myself. Wouldn't let me out of my room after that.'

Oh god. What did Lorna do to buy herself some time with Bryn? *Let Emily stay with you, and you can keep the little one, she'll get bored of it after a week*. Bev's heart must have been filled with so much hope – after all this time she'd get another chance. A way to make it all right.

Mac cuts in.

'That Bev woman kept you prisoner then? That's what you're saying?' He turns to me, face taunting. 'And you said I was the criminal?' He moves towards Emily. 'You should tell the police about this, love.'

Her face lights up for a second.

'Does that mean I can come home with you?'

'Why don't I drop you home first, eh? Then when all this blows over, we'll see.'

Her smile fades.

'You're lying.'

'*You* rang *me*, remember. You said, come and get me, this lot are mad. Now you're telling me you've had me stressing about a bloody baby for nothing. And *I'm* the liar?'

Emily falters.

I remember the first thing he said to me after that New Year's Eve night. He pulled the bus up alongside me the next week and leaned out. *You were wasted, kid, weren't you?* He'd chuckled. *I won't take it personally, just behave yourself next time.* Twisting things, putting himself out of blame's way.

'What did you say? When she rang this morning?' I ask.

Emily answers me. 'That he'd come and get me. He loved me. We'd go back to his and live there. Wouldn't need to tell my mam where I was once I turned sixteen. Said it was none of her business. Didn't mention the clinic.' Tears roll down her face.

'Let's go,' I say to her.

'Wait a minute, this has got nothing to do with you. Come on, love, let's go somewhere private and talk.'

'You told me I was special.' Emily turns to him. 'Beautiful. You asked me for a hug on the bus. Then a kiss. Then the rest. People should know.'

'You're the one who threw yourself at me.' He screams the words into her face. 'Asking for a free lift, batting your eyelashes. You knew exactly what you wanted.'

'I wanted you to love me!'

I push Mac away from her.

'Leave her alone. She's just a child. You've done enough.'

He shakes his head in disgust and pats his jacket for his keys, turns back to the car.

'You're real sad cases, both of you. Desperate. That's what it is. Bloody desperate. You go and tell them, see who they believe. A sad pair of prick teases spreading rumours. We'll see who looks bad in the end.' He jumps into the front seat of the car and slams the door.

I grab Emily's hand and pull her across to the causeway, jumping over a small ditch on the way. The silver-white plate of tide is already making its way back towards us. A never changing rhythm no matter the madness of this place.

'Mac,' I shout out.

His face flicks towards us. I dangle his keys from my hand.

'Don't be a prick. Give them here.' He jumps out of the car.

This is my place.

I raise my hand.

'Catch,' I shout.

I fling the keys with all my might towards the cool grey water. They make a satisfying plop as they drop in.

'Are you fucking mad or what?' he shouts and runs to the edge of the water.

I tug Emily's hand, and we run breathless and giggling across the reeds and tussocks – a path only I know.

Far enough away that he couldn't catch us even if he tried, we stop, catching our breath.

Emily looks at me wide-eyed.

'You must think I'm so stupid.'

I shake my head.

'There's only one idiot and he's going to be without a car for a while.'

I look over to where Mac is pacing the marsh. A tiny figure on my landscape. This is my place, and nothing can touch me here.

33

The smell of fresh toast wafts down our hall and I close my eyes. I want to stand here and drink it in – this strange shift to warmth in our cold and lonely space.

Emily walks slowly behind me, her eyes wide and full of fear. I take her hand in mine and push open the kitchen door.

Lorna and Dai sit at opposite sides of our kitchen table, facing off like warring cats. My father hovers by the aga, buttering thick slices of toast and staying well out of it. Lorna cradles a mug of tea. As we walk in, her face whips up, brow furrowed and ready to start something. When she sees Emily she leaps up from her seat, banging into the table and causing the three mugs to shudder and slop tea over the sides.

'Don't you ever give me such a bloody fright again. Do you hear me?' She reaches over to her daughter and grabs her by both arms. Shakes her gently as if to make her point and pretends not to notice that Emily won't look at her.

Where's Roddy? He's the only one who knows how to deal with Lorna and her moods. I was hoping he'd have come back, brought news of Swift.

Lorna slides back into her seat, glancing back up at Emily and giving daggers to Dai.

If Dai notices, he doesn't show it. He is the tensest of them all, body rigid, eyes moving between all of us.

'Right,' says Lorna through gritted teeth. 'We going to sort this shit show out, or what?'

Emily flinches at her words. Pulls a chair from beside Lorna and drags it to the other side of the table. At the same time my father places two plates of hot buttered toast onto the table like a waiter who can't see the dinner was over before it started.

'I'd like to say we're sorry.' Dai raises his eyes cautiously towards Emily. His jaw is tense, hands clasped. 'Bev got carried away.' He looks down at the table, the weight of shame on his shoulders. 'Emily, she's sorry if she scared you. Said to tell you that. Really sorry... But she's not well... and your mam.' He glances at Lorna with fire in his eyes. 'She promised her she could keep the baby. Asked Bev to keep you at ours for a while.' He shakes his head and bites down on something he'd like to say but can't.

He doesn't need to tell us what we can all guess. That the wanting in Bev's heart was too much for her. The promise of a new start. A baby to give her a second chance at the life she lost. When Emily wanted to leave, she locked the door. Even though we all know it was wrong, the silence around the table shows that none of us can blame her.

'Lorna,' Dai says after a moment, looking her straight in the eye. 'You've had your fun with us, with Bev.'

Lorna glowers back at him, opens her mouth to protest, but his words stop her.

'You need to leave us alone now. Enough.'

Lorna's hand twitches and taps on the side of her mug.

'That all the thanks I get?'

Dai lurches forward and smacks his fist on the table.

'You made your choice about Rhys. And we've done good

by you. But this has to stop.' The last words are a plea through gritted teeth. His shoulders slump, his face as washed and wrung out as a piece of driftwood after a battering from the tide.

'And my girl?' Lorna spits out, raising herself on her hands to lean across the table. 'Traumatised by your wife. Locked in a bloody room. I could call the police. I could tell them a thing or two…'

'Mam.' Emily's voice shoots across us all. 'There's nothing to tell.' Her face is stony. 'I ran away. Hid at Dai and Bev's stable. Went down to the house to take food when they weren't looking. Now I'm back. That's it.'

Lorna takes a deep breath as if she needs even more air to power the anger she's feeling.

'That's it? What about the not-so-small matter of the baby I'm going to have to look after. That old pervert saw you coming, didn't he? Thought I taught you to be cleverer than that. Didn't want you to end up like me.' She glares at Dai. 'Bev would have sorted it out. She was happy to help. Would have been good for her.'

'She's ill,' Dai snaps. 'Maybe I haven't realised how much she needs help, but she does. She didn't need you sending your mess down to us.'

'And I don't need a bloody baby in my life. I've raised two. Cut my life short for theirs. Think I want to get handed all that crap again? With no thanks and no help, because this madam wouldn't be seen for dust.'

Emily draws her knees up, feet resting on the chair, and wraps her arms around them.

'You're the one who told me to ask him for a free bus ride,' she whispers. 'Told me, if you don't ask you don't get.'

Realisation dawns on Lorna's face.

'*Him?* I told you to bat your eyelashes at him, not drop your knickers.'

Emily jumps up and runs into the lounge, slamming the door.

Lorna shakes her head.

'The bloody bus driver. Didn't think she was that stupid.'

We all sit in silence for a moment. Not wanting to spell out the inconvenient truth that it wasn't the old weirdo – Mr Thomas. The man who got a beating. It was the charming, smiling man you wouldn't think twice about. The one Maureen called a good catch. The guy with all the banter, hidden in plain sight.

The jagged sound of Emily sobbing comes through the closed door between us. Lorna glances at the wall sheepishly then straightens her shoulders. She's fought too much to give in now.

'What are we going to do about that, the driver?' Dai asks, glancing first at my father then at Lorna.

'I've already taught him a lesson,' I mumble.

My father raises his eyebrows.

'What did you do?'

'He won't find his keys again. And his car won't be much use even if he does.'

The shrill ring of the phone interrupts us. I push past the table and go into the lounge. Emily is standing by the empty fireplace, eyes red and head hung low.

I catch the phone with a quick hello.

'Catrin, it's Maureen.' As always, her timing is impeccable. 'Listen. I'm not some community service, you know that. But here I am again clearing up one of your bloody problems. Mac is here. Fuming, he is. Says his car is about to get stuck in the tide and he can't get home, says it's your fault. Asked me to call the police, but I said we don't call the coppers on our own. I'd rather call Catrin first and hear it firsthand.'

'Tell him to get the bus,' I say drily.

Maureen clicks her tongue with irritation.

'That's not the only thing he's saying.' Her tone tells me everything I need to know about what Mac has decided – get in there first, ruin Emily's reputation and mine.

'Maureen,' I say, 'he chats your Jade up every time she's on the bus. He's a…' I glance at Emily.

'He told me he loved me just to get what he wanted,' she shouts out. 'He's a liar and a bastard.'

'Who's that?' Maureen asks.

'Emily,' I tell her. 'Her mum is here too.'

'She's only fifteen, isn't she?'

'Yes. He's not fit to be around young girls.'

'So, should I call the police?' Her question is loaded. I look at Emily. It'll be her word against his. Mine too. He'll have a field day.

'No. Call the boys,' I say.

'Right you are.' Maureen puts the phone down.

Lorna appears in the doorway with an unconvincing smile fixed on her face.

'Right then, let's get you home, love.' She gestures to Emily.

'I lied about being pregnant,' Emily whispers.

'What?' Lorna's mouth falls open. 'All this trouble over a bloody lie?' Her eyes narrow. 'Now you listen here. I've done my very best with what I had, and it hasn't been easy, let me tell you. Do you want people to think you're easy, is that it? Because people talk and they don't forget; believe me, I know.'

Emily shrinks back.

'I was scared! You told Bev to keep me there. What kind of mother would do that? No wonder Dad left. I want to live with him.'

'Damn right you'll be going to live with him. I've had enough of his nonsense too. What would I want with any more of this mess? I'll drive you there myself. Better off alone.' Her voice cracks a little over the last words, but she thrusts her shoulders back and walks out of the room.

Emily looks at me desperately. 'She's never loved me.'

I rush over and wrap my arms around her.

'It's not your fault,' I say, hugging her tightly. 'Someone hurt her. She loves you but she doesn't know how to show it. It scares her.' I think of my own mother, the way my father described her as an animal caught in a trap.

Emily sniffs and wipes her eyes.

'I've made such a mess of everything. I'm sorry. I need to apologise properly to Dai and Bev. I'm the one who told her to leave the jumper out there. Asked her to hide me. Thought Mac would find me that way. Didn't count on Mam's plan… And Mr Thomas. He saw me and Mac parked up on the marsh road. He told me what kind of bloke he was, but I didn't believe him. He said people pretend to love you so they can take what they want, then they leave you. I thought he was just interfering, but he was right.' She shrugs me off, disgusted with herself.

Dai calls out from the kitchen. 'We've all been together all morning after that shock with the tide. Right?'

Glances are exchanged as we gather by the front door. The silence is taken as agreement and the three of them walk out onto the drive, metres of cold air separating them. Dai fires up the engine and they're gone. They'll take the top road. The tide is on the up again.

I should wait for Roddy, check Swift is okay, but there is something I need to do first. I take my coat from the rack and head out.

34

I knock on the door of Mr Thomas' bungalow for what I hope will be the last time – all the weight of the past pushing me forwards like an advancing tide.

The door opens slowly and he nods as if he was expecting me to come. For us to finish this strange conversation once and for all.

'I was hoping you'd come.' He says it in a flat voice that couldn't be less welcoming.

I follow him through the door and down the corridor towards the lounge, my mother with me every step of the way. How much time did she spend here? How could she love him more than us?

We perch awkwardly at opposite ends of the sofa. Mr Thomas' face is pale and washed out. He folds and unfolds his hands then starts up with a jerk.

'I'm sorry, would you like some tea?'

I shake my head.

'Of course.' He sits down again, placing a palm flat on his thigh to stop his leg from trembling. 'You can ask me anything. I owe you that, Catrin.'

His careful politeness is excruciating. I don't need to know the details. Don't want to know how my mother fell in love again and forgot about us.

'My father came to see you the day after she died.'

He shifts on the sofa as if he's in pain.

'Yes.'

'Why did you say those things to him?'

He breathes out heavily. His hands constantly move and twine around each other.

'He was very angry. I suppose I was trying to defend myself. Make him see that what we had was real and not some silly fling. I loved your mother, understood her. I thought if he could see that it would help him to understand why she was leaving. Soften the blow.' He shrugs.

'Bit late to worry about his feelings, wasn't it?'

'Yes, I suppose it was. I deserve that.'

There it is again, that word.

'What did you do?'

His eyes open so wide they look as if they could burst.

'What? No, nothing. I mean… please Catrin, you have to know that I loved her more than anything.'

'Why do you deserve to be punished?'

'I behaved badly. I hurt her that day. I said some terrible things and I…'

He's lying to me now. I know it.

'What did you do?' I say the words slowly.

'You have to know what she promised me, Catrin. A life with her. Here. A partnership of equals. I was naïve I suppose. You don't expect to fall in love again at my age. I'd resigned myself to being alone. But your mother woke me up. She saved me. That's how it felt.' He wipes his hands on his trousers. 'The way she saw things was incredible. Little details. Everyday miracles, but she'd never have been so trite as to call them that.' He smiles fondly. 'She loved you…'

'Don't,' I say.

'I'm an easy target to blame, but we were happy.'

'Did you arrange to meet her the day she died?' My voice is cold. How dare he tell me who my mother was or how much she loved me. I understand now why my father nearly shot him dead.

'She was coming here. Or so I thought.' His face flashes with anger just for a second. 'Then she rang and said she'd changed her mind. Asked me to meet her out there. Her space.' He smiles bitterly. 'I should have known from that invitation something was wrong.'

'She told you it was over,' I say.

She must have planned to let him down out there. Walk it off then go back to the house for me. Whisk us off to our new life together. I wouldn't have gone; I know that now. But a conceited man like Mr Thomas can't have taken the news very well.

'What did you do to her?' I whisper.

'I took her camera. I took it.' He starts to sob, covering his face with his hands. 'Oh, Catrin, I thought it was a game at first. I held onto her. Told her I loved her. I thought she was testing me. Then she started shouting, telling me to let go. It was over. She'd made a mistake.' He wipes his mouth with his sleeve. 'I would never hurt her. I let her go but I was so angry. I wrenched that wretched camera out of her hands instead. Said I was going to break it – smash it.' He looks at me imploringly. 'You have to understand she was about to take everything away from me. The dream of living here. All of this.' He gestures around frantically. 'And for what, those blasted photos? Her ridiculous idea of freedom?'

I picture my mother out there: her most prized possession stolen, her marriage broken. Lover angered. Her mind whirling.

'Where were you when you took the camera?' My voice is steely.

He stammers his answer between gulps of air.

'I don't know. The usual place we met. To the west of the track between the big ruts and the blue car. We used to sit there and talk.'

'That's not where I found her.'

'I know.'

'How do you know?'

'I… I went back out to look for her when she didn't follow me back to the house. She'd told me that your father begged her to stay, and she'd said no. She could never go back to the farm. I thought she'd calm down. Come to her senses. Change her mind.'

'You knew she was still out there when the tide was coming in?' My voice rises. Tightness grips my chest.

'I found her, but it was too late.'

'You laid the flowers?'

His words come out in a gabble.

'I did. I mean… I went to look for her, to apologise. I was going to beg her forgiveness and ask her to come here. But…'

'Was she dead when you found her?'

'I checked. I tried. She was so cold. Catrin, her skin was freezing and blue. I didn't know what to do.'

'You put the flowers in her hands.'

'I thought it was my fault. She wouldn't have been out there if she hadn't gone to meet me. I wasn't thinking straight. Yes,

I picked the flowers. She looked so perfect lying there; it sounds strange, you know, she would have taken a photo of it. It was a beautiful image.'

There's something else. I've seen enough to know he's hiding something else.

'How did she break her arm?'

He looks up at me in shock.

'I don't know. She must have fallen.' He stands up now, a shake in his body.

'No. The mud is soft. You're lying. You didn't go back to the bungalow. You never left her. You were holding onto her, you wouldn't let her go, would you?'

He backs away from me. 'I don't know!' he shouts. 'I wasn't thinking straight. I wasn't...' He moves closer to me. 'Catrin, you have to know I loved her very much. I only wanted...'

'You can't swim. You're afraid of the tide. You could hear it coming in, rushing in all around you.'

'Yes, yes.'

'She was screaming at you. To let her go. To give her the camera.'

He covers his ears with his hands.

'I didn't know she'd be so stubborn.'

'You lost your temper.' I can see it clearly now.

'I don't know any of this. Why are you saying these things?' His eyes are like a spooked horse. Memories he's tried to convince himself aren't true come surging back.

Now I understand.

'You were so angry. When you realised she was serious, she was never coming back to you, you pushed her as hard as you could.'

299

'I would never have hurt her.'

'She must have screamed when her arm hit the rock at the bottom of the ditch.'

'She wouldn't listen!' he explodes. 'Stubborn woman. I begged her. *Begged*. Humiliated myself. But, no, she wanted to go and start a new life.'

'She must have been screaming at you to help.'

'I don't remember.'

'But the tide was coming in and you were scared. Scared and angry. So you left her there.'

'I thought she'd get out!'

'You coward!' I lunge at him. 'You left her to die.'

'No. No. I didn't, Catrin.' He pushes me away. 'I didn't know that would happen; please believe me.'

I shove him hard in the stomach. 'You hurt her, and you walked away.'

'She broke my heart, Catrin. I think about her every day. I can't leave here; I want to be close to where she was happy. Sometimes I see you out walking, so like her it's uncanny, and it's as if it never happened.' He squeezes his eyes closed.

'You should have told me,' I whisper. 'I have suffered for so long and you could have told me.'

'No.' His voice rises. 'Your father made me promise not to tell you. That's why he came. He didn't care about me, about her. He told me never to speak of it to anyone. He told me exactly what he'd do to me if I did. I've never had a shotgun in my face before, Catrin. Do you know what that does to you? What it did to me! But I've kept my word, I've carried this on my own. I lost my job. I should never have...' He stops himself abruptly.

He will never tell me the whole truth. Whether he stayed at the side of the ditch watching her struggle or not.

I stand close to him, my face inches from his.

'You deserve to suffer. If she'd known what a coward you were, she wouldn't have given you a second look. She was brave. She would have done better than this.'

He nods.

'You're right. And there's not a day that I don't regret walking away from her. But you have no idea how it feels when you've loved someone with all your heart and they throw you away as if you were nothing. It was finished, just like that.' He claps his hands together. 'This love I'd waited my whole life for – the stuff of sonnets and poems – was ripped away from me.'

'This is not about you!' I turn on him. 'She had a life, a family. You could have told me the truth.'

She loved me. It wasn't my fault.

'Call the police and tell them what really happened.' I lurch for the phone and shove it towards him.

'It was an accident, Catrin. I told you.'

I jab the receiver at him.

'Tell them the truth.'

He shakes his head.

'There is nothing to tell.' His voice changes then, back to the teacher's tone. 'You tell them, Catrin, if you feel so strongly about it.'

He knows I can't. They won't listen to me. I'm standing so close to him I can feel his breath on my face.

'You will move away from here,' I tell him. 'Do you hear me? The police might not believe me, but my father will, and

Dai. Sell your land to Simon and go.' I choke up. 'I thought she'd killed herself. I've spent the last three years scared of myself, of being like her. You could have explained it in a second!' I push him backwards, run towards his office and that big picture window.

All this time he's watched me out there. Walking Swift, sketching, herding the ewes. He's been sitting here in comfort while I've been out there in misery. He could have given me her camera, explained what happened. But he chose to stay silent. To save himself.

I pick up the wooden chair in front of the desk and hurl it at the window, watch as the estuary shatters into a thousand tiny pieces in front of me. The chair lands with a thud on the grass outside.

'She would have wanted me to know she was coming back for me.' I walk out, jump down the porch steps.

'Catrin!'

I turn and see him cast in shadow in the doorway.

'She didn't want you to end up like her. To be stuck here.'

'*I belong here*,' I shout back.

*

I run and run back to the estuary. Sloshing through the rising tide. Stopping only when I reach the spot where I found her body. I drop my hands to my knees and scream for her and for me.

'I forgive you,' I shout out to her and the horizon until my throat burns raw. 'I'm sorry and I forgive you.' Then I stand breathless watching the light break over the water – a glint of yellow in a world of green and grey.

I close my eyes, and my mother is there, caught up in a moment of looking, crouching to find some curiosity, watching the clouds and waiting for the shadows to fall perfectly. She is fully present in every movement of her body. She turns and catches sight of me, and a smile fills her face. She raises her camera up, everything else forgotten, and I hear that familiar click and whirr. I raise my hand to wave at her for the last time.

My eyes flicker open to an empty estuary.

The wind blows through the tussocks of grass, bending them with the promise of another storm; ponies pick their way to higher ground with three new foals in tow. Light falls, turning mud to gold, and the silver half-moon of tide moves soundlessly towards me.

For the first time, there is no anger to expel, no rage to walk off, only the growing warmth of knowing – I *was* loved.

Home then.

35

A movement catches my eye out on the flats. Someone is walking straight towards me. I ignore the fast beating of my heart as I make out the two shapes – one ambling along, the other trotting alongside.

When they get close, Swift spots me and bounds over, tail wagging.

I breathe out. Run towards them both.

Roddy stops a little way in front of me and shrugs.

'There you are,' he says with a crooked smile.

Swift careers around me and I cry out in happiness, bend down as she shifts and shuffles around my legs, licking and nipping my fingers. I laugh and bury my face in her fur.

Roddy is watching us, a huge smile on his face.

'Thank you,' I say, my voice choked.

'She's had the all clear. The cold got to her, but there's nothing to worry about. Spent a night under some lamp like a sunbed. Reckon she must feel like she's had a holiday to Greece or something.' He laughs.

Swift bombs off into the reeds following a scent. We stand and watch her go. There's a new carefulness now we're alone.

'I hope Mam behaved herself. Apologised to everyone…' He studies my face and laughs at my expression.

'Yeah, that's no surprise. Sorry.' He takes another step towards me, but something holds him back.

'How's Emily?' I ask.

Then I see his discomfort. The older brother who couldn't protect his little sister from the world. His failure weighing heavy on already overburdened shoulders.

'I stopped in to see Dai and Bev first, to get things straight. Nice people,' he adds. 'I'm mortified to be honest.' He laughs sheepishly.

I lean over and hug him.

He freezes for a moment then wraps his arms around me and squeezes me tight. Without words we're both saying maybe it's alright and we've done the best we can.

We smile at each other. He takes my hand.

'Do you know what I like about this place?'

I shake my head, shy at the warmth of his palm over my fingers.

'Every time the water comes in, it covers everything, then it goes away and takes all the crap with it. It's like there's a chance to get clean every day. Have a fresh start. I like that.' He looks around at the windblown grass.

I expect to feel a hardness in me, the way I think of this place as belonging only to my mother and I – to our memory. But instead, there is something as soft as moss that wants to spill out into the world. Where I had built tight walls, I want to let that tide drag them all away and leave me glistening, washed clean of grief and other people's stories.

'Yeah, I like that too,' I say.

He squeezes my hand.

'I left Bryn with Mam and Emily. Thought they could sort themselves out for a change.' He looks at me side-on. 'Wondered if you fancied going for a walk? You know, just for fun. I'm back to work tomorrow.'

I glance down at the muddy grass under my boots, then up at him. There's a lightness like the first rays of sunlight after a storm; the heat of his hand, the warm sense of him being so close. I reach up and kiss him. For the first time I want to feel everything.

Neither of us can hide the wide smiles taking over our faces. The estuary feels small, even though we're the only two people for miles around.

'I need to go to the village,' I say. 'I've got a letter to post.'

Swift comes bounding back and runs in between us. I reach a hand down to smooth her coat before she hurtles off again.

'Want some company?'

'Yeah.' I smile. 'I do.'

ACKNOWLEDGEMENTS

Thank you to the team at Parthian Books, for bringing *Truth Like Water* into the world. It could not have found a better home. Huge gratitude for getting this novel into the hands of readers, and for all you do in supporting and promoting Welsh writing and writers.

Sincere thanks to Carly Holmes, my editor at Parthian. Working with you has been a delight, and the novel is stronger, leaner and more balanced thanks to your thoughtful edits, insights and questions.

The earliest draft of this novel was written as part of my MPhil in Writing at the University of South Wales. This was my first experience of being part of a writing community. It's where I learnt that writers are not 'other', rather they are writing. Thank you to my tutor Christopher Meredith for encouraging me to write a 'North Gower novel', and to Philip Gross and my writing cohort for the vital feedback and encouragement at that critical, embryonic stage.

Thanks to Literature Wales for all you do, and for supporting me in taking time out to write some very early chapters of this novel.

Truth Like Water was shortlisted for the 2021 Caledonia Novel Award which led to some pivotal feedback from judge Laura Williams. Thanks to Laura and award founder, Wendy Bough, for this experience.

In 2020, I was delighted to win the Jericho Writers Friday Night Live award. Thank you to the Jericho Writers team for making it an unforgettable event and to Debi Alper for her editorial notes.

A moment that changed my writing life forever was joining London Writers' Salon. My eternal gratitude and admiration to Matt Trinetti and Parul Bavishi for creating this generous-spirited, open and inclusive writing community. I would not be writing these acknowledgements if it weren't for everything I learnt, and the incredible community support

I enjoyed, in this space. Much love to Eimear, Niamh, Lindsey, KK, and all members of the Gold group and wider LWS community.

To my writing buddy Sandra Marslund – I owe you so much. This book might be in a drawer were it not for your insistent encouragement and support. I'm so proud of how much we've grown as writers, and value our friendship immensely.

To Helen Siddall-Butchers, thank you for the safe, therapeutic space you provided that helped me find my way back to myself and my writing.

To Sarah Longfield, thank you for the question that made me stop procrastinating and press send on my submission to Parthian.

To my parents for an extraordinary early childhood of travel and adventure, for bringing us back to our roots in North Gower, and for building a life on that unique estuary landscape – thank you.

To my sister, Harry, for being you. And to Mum, for everything.

For the friends who've seen me through life, and never stopped asking, 'How's the book going?' Laura and Rhiannon, I love you both. Ac Bran – caru ti.

To my biggest champion, Manuel, there are not enough words to thank you for the unstinting support you've always shown me. For the many desks you've built, the cups of tea you've made, the monologues you've listened to, and the choices we've made together. I'm lucky to walk through life with you. *Te quiero.*

To the best non-human company anyone could wish for. Tail up: Crocky, PequiRey and Borre. *Os quiero.*

Thanks to all the libraries, librarians, bookshops and booksellers who help *Truth Like Water* to find readers, and who keep us all reading – humanity needs books.

A book is an object until it meets the reader. So, finally, to you, lovely Reader, thank you for choosing this novel – for lending your imagination to my words – I hope you love the characters as much as I do.

PARTHIAN   Fiction

Untethered
PHILIPPA HOLLOWAY
ISBN 978-1-914595-85-1
£10 • Paperback

'A mood of ancient magic flits
like birds through these eerie
and delicate modern folk tales.'
– Samira Ahmed

Stepsisters:
Stories from the Irish
EDITED BY
BRIAN Ó CONCHUBHAIR &
TARA MACLEOD
ISBN 978-1-917140-91-1
£10 • Paperback

Showcases the depth and
power of contemporary Irish
women's writing.

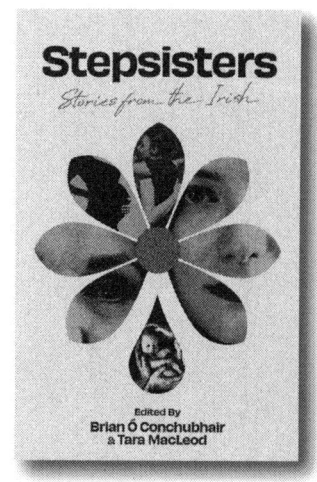

PARTHIAN   Fiction

The Colonel Comes By
BRYONY RHEAM
ISBN 978-1-917140-80-5
£10 • Paperback

'Skilled, perfectly formed,
and compelling ... a deeply
satisfying collection.'
– Karen Jennings

Boundary Waters
TRISTAN HUGHES
ISBN 978-1-914595-84-4
£12 • Paperback

'A gripping yarn ...
this epic tale of fortune-seeking
and ill-starred love.'
– Kate Pullinger

Unspeakable Beauty
GEORGIA CARYS WILLIAMS
ISBN 978-1-913830-46-5
£11 • Paperback

'A truly impressive achievement
from a rising star of
Welsh literature.'
– Gosia Buzzanca,
Buzz Magazine